HOPE'S GAME

MICK WILLIAMS

ISBN: 978-1-937979-89-8

First printing 2020

Hydra Publications

Goshen, Kentucky 40026

www.hydrapublications.com

For Craig Ostrouchow: thank you for trusting me with your baby.

Dedicated to

Arthur Melvyn Williams
November 9th 1941 - May 30th 2019
and
Ann Elizabeth Meadowcroft
August 2nd 1941 - June 5th 2019

Chapter 1

Nothing is as fragile as the innocence in a child's eyes.

Charlie stared into Amelia's twin pools of coffee brown, which drew him in and hypnotized him. Two blended sets of DNA; his deep brown, with tiny flecks of Kate's blue shooting out into perfect, pure, innocent white.

Despite his hatred towards the donor of the second set of genes, Charlie felt himself drawn to his daughter, with a father's instinct, and an overwhelming urge to love and protect.

Amelia giggled and balanced an ice cream cone in one hand, and a ragged-looking teddy bear named Mr Fluffy in the other. "Daddy, your ice cream is melting. Look, it's running all over your fingers."

Molten ice cream and red syrup ran between his knuckles, broken with random colours of sugar drops. Charlie laughed as he licked the back of his hands.

"I know you were tired, but can you push me higher than last time?" she said. Her tiny feet swayed and dangled beneath the seat of a swing, each wrapped in a pink Barbie sneaker. A wayward lace snaked down towards the protective, shredded, rubber playground.

"Of course, I can, but let me take care of this lace first. Knowing you, you'll step on it and go flying. No injuries allowed at the park, okay?"

"Okay," said Amelia's tiny voice. "Tie my lace, then, Daddy."

Charlie knelt and looped the string around his fingers until he could pull it tight.

"How high do you want to go?" he asked as he stepped behind her and gripped one side of the swing.

"High enough to touch the sky," said Amelia with a giggle. "I want to poke the sun and burst it, like a balloon, with my finger."

"Ice cream first. Eat that, so you can hold on with both hands. I can hold Mr Fluffy."

He leaned in to place a kiss on her forehead and dabbed the tip of her nose with his cone.

"Look at you. Now, who's a messy monkey?" he said over her squeal. "I'd better eat mine, too, before it covers your face."

Moments later, Charlie pulled back the swing while Amelia held onto the chains at either side of her seat.

"Let's not burst the sun," he said. "Not today. We might want to sunbathe later."

"Just push me high, then, Daddy. All the way to the top."

Five punishing minutes later, Charlie felt the exercise burn in his shoulders. "Okay, how about we go and see the ducks, now? Give Daddy's arms a rest."

"By the lake? Can we get duck food? Ellie says we shouldn't feed them bread, like mummy said. It 'spands in their stomachs and makes them feel poorly. There's proper duck food at the lake shop. She said it looks like rabbit poo."

Charlie stifled a laugh and lifted Amelia from the swing. "And how does Ellie know what rabbit poo looks like?"

"They had some at school, in her classroom."

"What, they had rabbit poo in her classroom?"

Amelia giggled again and then burst into a run.

Charlie watched as her little legs pumped with nine years of experience and sped her across the playground towards the treeline that surrounded the area. Her lace tugged loose again and flapped like a spare limb as she ducked into an opening in the bushes.

"Come on, Daddy. Keep up, or else we'll have to play hide and seek."

Charlie jogged across to the opening as the white of Amelia's t-shirt disappeared into the foliage. Another giggle mixed into the rustle of leaves.

"Do I have to count to ten?" asked Charlie.

A car drove by the park. The noise from its damaged exhaust bounced off the sides of adjacent buildings and drowned out any other sound. As the sound faded, Charlie stared into the bushes and searched for traces of white.

Nothing but green and brown stared back.

"Amelia? I didn't count to ten yet, so can we start again?"

Nothing.

"Amelia?"

His heartbeat quickened as the sounds of families on the other side of the bushes broke the silence.

"Amelia. We've not started the game yet. Where are you?"

Nothing. And then.

"Over here, Daddy. Don't be such a slow coach."

Charlie relaxed, followed the sound and pushed through

the bushes. Leaves and litter crackled beneath his feet while his eyes strained to find his daughter.

"Are you in the bushes? I can't see you."

"Yes, I'm right…"

Amelia squealed, a high-pitched note that sent bolts of pain through Charlie's stomach. It tumbled and rolled in response.

"Are you okay? Did you fall over?"

Nothing.

"Amelia! Answer Daddy."

Charlie burst through the other side of the bushes. A circular lake shimmered in the sunlight, with couples walking dogs, or pushing pushchairs. An elderly couple glanced at him in disapproval. Their eyes telegraphed their thoughts; a father who'd lost sight of his child. This wouldn't have happened in their day.

A second before panic set in, Charlie glanced a flash of pink to his right. He turned, relieved, but only to find an ice cream wrapper.

His heartbeat rose further as he stumbled back into the bushes.

"Amelia! Amelia! Answer me. No games, now!"

Nothing.

And then, through the trees, something caught his eye. A shade of brown, different to the others. He raced towards it, then stopped and swallowed to keep down rising bile.

Mr Fluffy lay, face down, in the dirt.

A wash of heat flooded his face as Charlie dusted it down and turned in circles, helpless and hopeless. Tears welled and stung his eyes as he blundered back towards the lake before he stopped and fell to his knees.

At the far side of the bushes, where the sunlight poked

through and offered an entrance to the beauty of the lake, Amelia's sneaker lay on its side. Its tiny treads held pieces of dirt and bark, but Barbie still smiled and pointed to the lace that threaded its way across the soil, towards the safety of the path.

Chapter 2

Three years later

The heavy green door that led from reception to the shop floor always felt like a challenge to Charlie. Management bitched about productivity and efficiency, then installed a barrier that made it almost impossible to get into the workplace.

Something about fire risk and the dampening of sound.

The damned thing weighed so much that it took both hands to pull it open. As soon as the door peeled away from the frame, a barrage of electronic noise bled through. Row upon row of conveyors lined up on a smooth concrete floor like sentences on a page. They stretched from the door all the way to the far wall, hundreds of yards away. A mechanical arm hovered over each belt. Sparks of solder, or blinding shots of weld, lit up each one to create a robotic light show.

Charlie counted five people wandering between the belts,

maybe one per fifty belts. Watching machines programmed to do nothing more than what they were told to do.

Greg's office sat in the far corner. Past the line that delivered resistors to the relentless robot fingers that placed them onto green, fiberglass boards. Another mechanical arm secured them with a wisp of hot solder.

A corrugated metal staircase climbed the wall to a door that didn't seem too different to the one Charlie had already fought with. He headed towards it and its huge window of thick glass and unfolded the page one more time.

An invitation to the office, 4.30 pm sharp, to meet with Greg Watson and Angela Hilderstone, head of human resources.

Charlie knew that his time was up. Too many early finishes and late starts. Too many days where his blurred eyes betrayed his ability to concentrate. Too many days where his human failings were beaten and surpassed by machines that didn't turn up for work, still drunk from the night before.

Because the machines didn't have missing daughters.

Or a borderline drink problem.

Charlie smirked at the cheek and nerve of the letter. Typical management crap. No summons at 9.00 am, or even at 11.00 am, after breakfast, but one at 4.00 pm., just before he punched his card to head home to his empty house, and his empty life. Might as well get one more full day from the man before we punch his card for good.

Greg wasn't a bad man. Years ago, he'd meet the boys for a pint, and he almost seemed to fit in and enjoy the jokes and banter. Then, when the company went public, and shareholders ran the show, he shrunk into himself. Wore sharper clothes. Listened to the bean-counters and followed their lead. Became a company man.

Hilderstone was an enigma. No one, in the history of the

business, knew her marital status, what she did in her spare time, or even if she had a heartbeat. There were so many machines here, there was a possibility that an android had already replaced HR.

The protective soles of Charlie's work boots clanked against the metal stairs as he climbed them, his eyes on the office door, while his ears ignored the cracks and roars of technology below him.

This was it. Enough chances. No more leeway.

Greg had run out of patience.

No allowance for loyalty. Or that your life fell apart while you were searching for your abducted daughter. Just cold, hard facts.

Machines did a better job, and they were cheaper in the long run. And sober.

He thumped his knuckles against the glass panel in the door and entered the office. Hilderstone's mouth hung open, as if she'd started to say, "come in". A summons by letter was enough. He didn't need an invitation to his own dismissal.

The long, solid wall to his right showed the epitome of a successful company; rows of certificates and bar graphs stamped in gold, surrounded by corny motivational posters. To his left, the glass wall looked out onto the shop floor. Up against it, Greg sat behind his lavish desk, Hilderstone at his side, with his laptop open and pen poised and ready to go. He gestured to an empty chair.

"Charlie. Please, take a seat."

Charlie wondered what they'd do if he picked up the chair and literally took it but, instead, pulled it out and slumped into it.

Greg cleared his throat while Hilderstone plastered a sickly smile across her pinched face. When Greg paused for a moment too long, she spoke to fill the awkward void.

"Charlie, thanks for coming. I imagine you've heard the rumours?"

He glanced over her shoulder at the shop floor. Five years ago, the room had buzzed with life, and conversation. The sounds of a busy and committed workforce. Replaced, one by one, by machinery.

Hard to hear the rumours coming from a row of robots, he thought. He nodded, and Greg cleared his throat once more.

"You know, I've been your biggest supporter for the past three years," he said. "Since, you know, the disappearance…"

"Abduction," interrupted Charlie.

Greg squirmed in his seat. "Yes. Well, that. Ah, since then, I've done everything I can to make your life here as comfortable as possible, even when you've not made it easy on yourself."

Charlie nodded again as Greg tapped a few keys on the laptop.

"In the past two months, you've called in sick five times. Personnel has also sent you home twice, due to intoxication." Greg sighed and looked at him like a naughty schoolboy, but Charlie could see the strain in Greg's eyes. He found this tough. "We've been patient, Charlie, and we've followed the disciplinary process to the letter, but I'm afraid we've reached the end of the road."

"You mean I've reached the end of the road," said Charlie. He eased back into the chair. "Greg, let me make it easy for you because you're right, you have looked after me. I can't thank you enough, and I know I've overstayed my welcome by about two years. I know what's coming, so why don't you hand over the paperwork, and I'll be on my way."

Greg sat, motionless and wide-eyed, as Hilderstone's smile faded and she pushed forward a piece of letterheaded paper and a sealed envelope.

"I appreciate your being candid, Charlie," she said. "I'm sorry that we have to let you go, but we think it's in everyone's best interest. Your safety at work is of paramount importance, and we don't think your condition affords you that safety amongst the machinery here."

Charlie blinked quickly. "My condition? Now I have a condition?"

Greg sat forward. "Charlie, please. Use this day to kick start your life. It's time to move on. Clean up. There's a severance cheque in the envelope. I hope you find it useful to get you by for a while, but you should go home and maybe consider getting some professional help."

Charlie pushed back the envelope and worked to keep his tone of voice steady. "I don't want your pity money, Greg. No one knows what I've been through this past three years. No one. You think I can leave here and go back to my nice, comfortable home?

"Kate left me six months after someone took Amelia. We sold the house six months after that, with zero equity. I've gone from having a nice, comfortable home and a loving family to a crappy flat and microwave meals. You have no idea. No one does, but I certainly don't need professional frigging help."

"I'm sorry," stammered Greg. "And you're right, I really can't imagine. I wish I could do, or say, something."

The chair screeched as Charlie pushed it back and stood. "Do I need to sign anything?"

"No," said Hilderstone, who snapped to attention with relief, "but you should take these." She pushed back the paper and the envelope.

Charlie grabbed them and turned to the door. He thought about slamming it in a final fit of anger, then decided against it.

"Thanks for everything, Greg," he said. "And, don't worry, I won't bother asking for a reference."

———

"HERE YOU GO. I suspect you're ready for this." Lucee, the barmaid, slid a pint towards Charlie. Condensation already ran down its side and left a wet trail along the varnished top.

"Saw you park up and walk by the window and figured, with that look on your face, you'd be in here. So I poured your regular."

Charlie emptied a third of the glass before he placed it on the bar and fished out some money.

"Thanks, Lucee. That's the second thing I've had pushed towards me in an hour, but I don't mind this one."

"Oh? Bad day at the office? Wife doesn't understand you?"

Charlie looked up and glared.

"Sorry," said Lucee. "Barmaid habit. Meant nothing by it."

"No, that's okay. Bad day at the office. Well, last day at the office, actually."

"Oh. No more work?"

"Nope."

"Sorry to hear that." Lucee beamed her best smile. "Still, there's plenty out there."

Charlie lifted the pint. "I'm sure there is. Cheers, Luce. Going to find a quiet corner."

A small alcove at the side of the bar sat empty. Charlie dropped into a corner booth, took another drink, and then slid his finger under the envelope's seal and pulled out the cheque.

Fair play to Greg. Given that he'd effectively been fired, he wasn't entitled to any severance under the company's employment policy, but the cheque would cover two months' rent, with money spare for food and bills.

And beer.

Might have to cut back on the beer if things didn't improve.

Charlie took another drink and sighed. Or maybe he would give up the food instead.

How had he got to this point? Amelia's abduction wrenched the heart from his life, and the fact that the police, and countless search parties, found nothing, only prolonged the emptiness and pain. Kate's refusal to accept it as anything less than negligence on his part drove the pain even deeper. The weight of guilt kept him awake night after night and ate away at his core like a cancer. Whenever he slept, nightmares jarred him awake a few times a week.

She always slept like a baby, and never stirred.

Along with her relentless shopping sprees, her attitude and temper grew worse by the day until neither of them could stand it any longer. Their circle of manipulated friends sided with Kate, which left Charlie with his lifelong friend Nick as the last remaining shoulder to cry on. Only Nick had seen the scratches and bruising that came from Kate's attacks.

Did he miss her? Of course, at first. Despite her increasing paranoia and violence, Kate had a huge personality that filled the house. Once Charlie retreated into himself and a bottle, it took over until it buried their marriage. He still saw her from time to time, sitting in her favourite coffee shop on the high street. She normally nursed a steaming mug and appeared as lonely and single as him. A few months ago, he caught her eye through the window and considered sitting and talking to her, but her gaze narrowed into a glare that he knew only too well. He took the hint and left her alone.

Charlie drained the rest of the beer and searched his

pockets again. When he pulled out a bundle of small change, he left the empty glass on the bar and stepped out into the street.

The car's wipers smeared a greasy film across the screen as he pulled out of the pub car park and onto the road. A light drizzle of misty rain dampened everything; the road, the light, and Charlie's spirits.

Despite the dull light, the small clock on the car's dashboard read 4:45. The bank was a five-minute drive away. Thanks to the shortest termination interview in history, and his lack of funds for another pint, he still had time to deposit the cheque he knew that he didn't deserve.

Charlie managed a grim smile and tried to remain positive.

Everything happened for a reason.

Chapter 3

Something about Charlie's part of town reminded Nick of the opening credits of old American cop shows; where a police car skidded around a corner in a dizzy whirl of blue and red light, sending paper and litter flying into the air, until the camera settled on a random homeless guy, huddled inside a doorway, with a blanket and a brown paper bag.

Charlie's flat was in a converted house in the middle of a terraced run, on a street so narrow Nick had to weave around wheelie bins and lampposts to reach his front door. The rear was off limits, due to an infestation of triffids and weeds in the tiny yard. Cars lined the kerb for the entire length of the street, so Nick left his Audi at home and jogged here once a week.

Since the divorce, someone had to make sure that Charlie was still alive.

He knocked on the door and watched it rattle in its frame. Since he had the ground-floor flat, Charlie answered in seconds. Convenient for the entrance but, then, he also got to hear the knocks for the flat above.

A dark ring curled beneath each eye, and he looked like he hadn't slept in a week. He ran a hand through his knotted hair and stepped back onto a pile of fast food menus.

"Nick. Come in, mate."

"Cheers, fella." Nick stepped over the litter and into the living room. Even in the dull light afforded by a tiny crack in the curtains, it was a pitiful sight.

"Jesus, Charlie, when are you going to get some decent furniture?"

In one corner, an old school television sat on the largest of a nest of tables. Its plastic rear was so deep, only a miracle of physics stopped it from either collapsing the table, or toppling backwards onto the floor.

A faux-wood cabinet filled the main wall. Pictures littered the open shelves, each one a different image of Charlie with Amelia. Dust covered the shelving behind the stained-glass doors.

A threadbare sofa leaned against the back wall, with foam showing through in tufts on each arm. Nick often thought to ask where the varied stains came from, but decided ignorance was bliss. The smaller-sized table from the nest set stood beside it, while the middle-sized one served as a coffee table.

Crumpled beer cans covered both.

"It'll be a while, now," said Charlie. "Last night, I officially joined the ranks of the unemployed."

"Seriously? You lost your job?"

Charlie nodded.

"Turned up for work drunk again?"

"No, Nick," said Charlie. His voice raised an octave. "I was stone cold sober. It turns out I'm not as efficient as a robot. The damn things have taken over everything. I think there might be a dozen people left there now, not counting the management. And half of them are pen-pushers, and the other half make sure the machines do as they're told. And, if you'd seen them, you'd know they always do as they're told because they're programmed."

Nick switched from one foot to the other, unsure of what to say.

"Sorry," said Charlie. "Meant nothing by the pen-pusher thing. No offence."

"None taken," said Nick. He kicked a beer can from beside the sofa until it rolled beneath the TV. "You know, if you spent half as much money on furniture as you do on beer, you'd live in a frigging palace."

Charlie dropped onto the sofa. The frame sagged and moaned a protest. "Go ahead, make fun. You know I couldn't care less about material crap." He pointed to the cabinet. "It's her, Amelia. Until she's back, I'm nothing."

Nick knelt before him, hesitant to sit on the sofa. "Mate, if Amelia came back now, she wouldn't recognise you. You need to snap out of this. If you're depressed, get yourself to the doctor, and get a referral for treatment. If you've got an illness, get yourself…"

"I'm okay," said Charlie. "Really."

"No, you're not. Really," said Nick. He stood and used his foot to group together a mound of empty cans. "Look at this place. Don't get me wrong, I love you like a brother but, for God's sake, you live in a shit tip. I don't remember what colour your carpet is. You *do* have carpet, right? We've got to do something. Something that'll motivate you and get you to kick start your life."

Charlie laughed, but it sounded empty, and lacked any humour. "Not the first time I've heard that."

"Exercise," said Nick.

"What?"

"Exercise. It's not only good for the body. A healthy body leads to a healthy mind."

"Are you having a laugh? I exercise."

"I don't think pulling ring tabs off beer cans counts as exercise, mate. I can't even see you breaking into a quick walk, unless it was five minutes to closing time and you were six minutes from the pub."

"That's funny," said Charlie. "The bloke who lost his job gets witty comments from his so-called mate. Did you come here to encourage me, or have me jump out the window?"

Nick glanced around the room and grinned. "You're on the ground floor, mate. I doubt that would accomplish much. Plus, looking at the state of the frames, the glass might fall out in one piece before you even got to it."

Charlie couldn't help but smile and shake his head. "You're hilarious, you muppet."

"I'd try to get you a job at my place, but…"

"Yeah, I can't do that desk thing. I can picture you, sitting there with your typewriter…"

"It's been a while since I had a typewriter, okay? No, I can't help you with the job, but I can help you get back into shape. I'm off tomorrow. Promise me, no booze tonight, okay? I'll call in the morning, and we'll go for a run."

"Seriously?"

"Yeah. Nothing too strenuous, just a steady jog. Start slow and build up."

Charlie considered the offer. "Okay, I'll give it a go. Like you said, when Amelia comes back, she'll need me in good shape."

"Hey, if that's your motivation, use it. Tomorrow, right?"

"Right."

"And no booze."

Charlie hesitated, and then, "Right. No booze."

Nick moved towards the door. "Sorted. See you in the morning, Flash."

AT A STEADY PACE, the run back home from Charlie's flat took Nick twenty minutes. The smell of fresh-baked bread greeted him as he walked through the entrance hall into the living room. He sat on the sofa and kicked off his running shoes.

"I'm back."

Pots and pans rattled in the kitchen, before a door clicked shut.

"Just loading the dishwasher. Have a good run?"

"Yeah. Usual. I did call in to see Charlie, though."

The sink drain gurgled as the dishwasher sucked in water. "Oh? And how's he doing? I'm going to make a coffee; do you want one?"

"No. I'm fine, babe, but, thanks. Honestly, I'm worried about him. He lost his job today."

"I'm not surprised, from what you've told me. It's a shame. Did you mention the project?"

Nick sat on the carpet, legs outstretched, and pulled at his toes to stretch his hamstrings. "No, not yet. It didn't seem like the right time."

A cute laugh came from the kitchen. "You overthink things. He just lost his job, so now would be the perfect time."

"I'm taking him out for a run in the morning."

Another laugh. "Sounds like you're taking him for a test drive when you put it like that."

"I suppose I am, in a way. The project's a big thing, with possible complications. Not something anyone should jump right into. I'll sound him out first. Ten grand is a lot of money, but it's no good to someone who can't spend it."

A head peered around the kitchen doorway. "Is it that dangerous? He is your best friend. Don't turn your best friend into a vegetable."

"Now, who's putting things in an unusual way," laughed Nick. He stood and wrapped his arms around her waist. " 'Dangerous' might not be the right word. Yes, there are risks, but we've taken every precaution possible. Initial testing is positive, but we can't go live until we know exactly how it works on its intended audience. And we can't do that, unless we hook it up to human subjects."

"God, Nick, you sound like a salesman. Or one of those vile animal lab testers."

He kissed the top of her head. "And we both know I'm neither of those."

She nuzzled her head beneath his chin. "No, you're not. You're a good man who works too hard. And when are you going to invite Charlie over here? You see him every week. We've been here almost twelve months, and you've not mentioned it once. I know it'll be a shock for him, especially based on what you've said about his place, but you deserve all of this, Nick.

"And, regardless of what I think, he is your best friend. He should see what you've accomplished. And you don't need to feel guilty about anything. Well," she said as she reached around and squeezed his rear, "other than this."

Nick smiled. "I know. I will, one day. And, I might need a shower, but you can keep doing that."

He looked through the window at the gravel driveway and manicured lawns that lined it. And beyond the drive, to the small building at the side that housed his gleaming black Audi. Compared to Charlie's grimy flat, this house was the palace he'd mentioned. All earned through hard work and commitment, something Charlie had lost since Amelia's disappearance.

There had to be a way to help his friend get back on his feet, or to, at least, help him recapture some of the spark and humour he missed.

Soft hands left his rear and slid up through the sweat on the inside of his tee-shirt.

Nick scooped her up with ease and made his way to the bathroom.

Tomorrow.

Tomorrow, he'd tell Charlie about the project.

Chapter 4

Despite the insistent pull of habit, not addiction, Charlie made it through the evening and resisted the urge to grab a beer. He stretched on the sofa and glanced at the clock, again. After an almost sleepless night, where he'd seen the time change at least once an hour, it now read 8.30.

A barrage of sleep-robbing dreams plagued him, the most common one being the day Amelia vanished. He relived the blind panic, and scramble, around a park that Charlie knew like his own home. Only now, darkness and danger covered it. Previously innocent bushes took on a sinister tone as the entrance to another world Amelia had taken.

An entrance Charlie couldn't find, however hard he tried.

Kate's reaction sat at number two on the nightmare chart, after the stomach-churning moment he'd opened the door to the family home, knowing his daughter was still outside somewhere. Lost and alone, or snatched by someone with evil intentions. A home that should have been filled with the expectation of warmth. Consolation. The shared burden of worry.

He touched his face and shuddered as the image flashed again. Kate's eyes, feral and livid, and her teeth bared, as sharp nails raked through his skin. And the pierced shriek that vibrated his ears and, then, the push, the rejection.

The blame.

A splash of cold water shocked away the nightmares. At least for now. Charlie clutched the edges of the basin, glanced into the bathroom mirror through blurry eyes and spoke to himself.

"You need to sleep, mate. Seriously, you look like crap."

His reflection stared back with no argument, and Charlie lined up another insult before a knock at the door startled him.

Nick? As early as this?

Andy's beaming smile greeted him as he pulled open the door.

His brother hoisted up two bulging carrier bags. "Supplies!"

"Hiya, Bro."

"See what I did there? Supplies? Surprise?"

"What are you doing here?"

"I brought supplies. You didn't get it. Never mind. You going to invite me in, or leave me standing out here, like a delivery guy?"

A wave of embarrassment washed over Charlie. Andy hadn't been to the flat in weeks and Charlie wished he'd at least picked up the litter from the floor.

He stepped aside. "Sorry, Bro. Come in."

Andy edged in sideways and manoeuvred the bags through the entrance. "I'll put these in the kitchen. It's a food shop, off Mum and Dad."

"They didn't need to…"

"Bloody hell, Charlie," said Andy as he stepped into the living room. "Is it the cleaning maid's year off? What a frigging mess. How do you live like this? And, most important of all, how do you find the TV remote under all this shit?"

Charlie stepped behind him into the room and scuffed him around the back of the head. "It's not that bad."

"Yeah, Bro. It is."

"I've been meaning to get to it, I've just been busy."

Andy shook his head and dropped the bags in the kitchen. "I can see that. Looks like you've been working overtime at being the beer can recycling champion of England. To be fair, you might have it in the bag. And runner-up in the glass bottle competition, too. Gold and silver. Congrats, Bro."

"Okay, funny man. Now, both you and Nick have had a go. I get the message."

"Yeah, it's okay getting the message," said Andy as he tapped the side of his head, "but does it compute? And how's Nick? Haven't seen him in months."

"Doing good. The usual Nick; trim, lean, sharp haircut, still doing his office thing, looks good in jogging gear or a suit."

"Is this a man crush in the making?" asked Andy.

"You're a proper comedian, aren't you? We're going running this morning. I thought you might have been him, to be honest. He didn't give me a time."

Andy smirked. "You? Running? Without a nasty case of diarrhoea? I'll believe it when I see it. Anyway, you need to call Mum and Dad. They miss you, and it's been too long."

"I will."

"No, I mean this year. Call them. They worry about you. We all do."

Charlie sifted through the bags. "They shouldn't waste their money on me, I'm okay."

"Ah, so you have food?" said Andy. He opened the fridge door and surveyed the shelves, then reached inside and took out a bottle. "Half a bottle of milk..." He twisted off the lid and recoiled at the smell. "…which is borderline yoghurt. A potato that has better legs than me, and…" he counted, "…eight bottles of beer. Heck of a diet plan, Bro. What do they call this one, the Hops Diet?"

"I'm okay," said Charlie again, as a feeling of being cornered crept in. "I just haven't been to the shops yet."

"Of course, you were going that way after you tidied up, right?"

Charlie pushed the fridge door closed. "Look, if you wanted a bitching session, you should have called and saved the walk."

"Not that you can park anywhere near here, but I drove."

"Whatever."

"Mum and Dad wanted me to check on you," said Andy. He pushed aside a stack of unopened letters and sat on the armchair. "The shopping was an excuse."

"Tell them I'm all right. When I get back from running, I'll start looking for another job."

"They won't believe either of those statements. How about I tell them you emigrated? That's more believable."

Charlie slumped onto the sofa. "Wow, you're on form today, aren't you?

Andy's face grew serious. "Charlie, we worry about you. All of us."

"I told you, I…"

"I know what you told me, but you need to get help. You've lost a lot, we know that, but so have we. And, now, it's like we've lost you as well. And I hate to state the obvious, bro, but life goes on. It has to. You should step back on the train before it leaves the station for good."

"What train?"

"Sorry, I was going for deep and profound. You should stop drinking your life away and get back into it. Who knows?

You hated that job so, perhaps, this is the kick up the arse you've needed."

"Seems every man and his dog think that," said Charlie. He took in a deep breath, held it, and then let it escape slowly. "I will. Promise."

"You will what?"

"Get myself sorted."

"That's quite a broad statement. You think one thing will come along and everything will fall into place?"

"No, but I'm starting this morning with the jogging. Maybe I'll enjoy it and make it a habit."

"Okay, that's a start. What else?"

"I'll get a job. One I enjoy."

"Okay. What else?"

"Bloody hell, Andy, do you want a list?"

"Call Mum and Dad."

"I already said I would."

"Good, but do it soon, not after your next life-changing event. They're not getting any younger, you know? And neither are you, looking at the state of you."

"Thanks for the pep-talk, Bro. Really appreciated. I already feel like a new man."

Andy didn't flinch at the sarcasm, but put his hands on his knees and hoisted himself upright. "Okay, one of us has to get to work. Promise me something."

Charlie followed his brother and wrenched open the door. "I'll do my best. What is it?"

"Leave the beer alone, at least for a while. And tidy up. The place looks like a tornado blew through it."

"I'll do my best."

"Do your *very* best."

Andy reached up and wrapped his arms around Charlie. The closeness and the warmth surprised him and took his breath away. He struggled to remember when he last felt that way.

"I love you, Bro," said Andy. "Come back to us."

Before Charlie could reply, Andy stepped into the street and walked away.

AT EXACTLY TEN O'CLOCK, Nick hammered on the front door.

Charlie didn't give him the satisfaction of stepping inside for another round of abuse and joined him in the street. He looked Nick up and down and laughed.

"We look like Laurel and Hardy."

Charlie's assessment of Nick to Andy was perfect. Nick jogged on the spot. Bright colour splashed across the brilliant white of his running shoes and clashed with the jet black of leg-hugging trousers, while a plain white t-shirt formed itself to his torso. By contrast, Charlie sported a pair of bargain store tennis shoes, and a mismatched t-shirt and shorts ensemble that wouldn't have looked out of place on a charity store mannequin. He knelt and tugged his laces tighter to buy some time and avoid any awkward conversation about the flat.

"So where are we running?" he asked.

"Like I said, let's start slow and build up. How about we just run to the park and do a lap of the lake? Then, we can have a steady jog back to warm down."

"Warm down? I don't think you've got that right, mate," said Charlie. "We're supposed to warm up."

Nick smiled and shook his head.

Charlie frowned. "What? And how far of a run is that? It must be about five miles to the park."

"It's half a mile to the park," said Nick. "A lap of the lake is another mile, and then another steady half back here."

"Two miles? Are you having a laugh? You said start light, not run a tenth of a bloody marathon."

"Stop whining and warm up, otherwise you'll pull a muscle and blame me for that too."

"Thought we were supposed to warm down. Make up your mind."

Twenty minutes later, they reached the park.

While Nick barely broke a sweat, Charlie paused every few minutes to catch his breath. He bent double with his hands rested on his knees while his lungs gulped in desperate gasps of air.

He pointed to a bench that faced the lake. "Let's sit there for a bit. I'm knackered."

Nick sat at one end and brushed dirt off his shoes while Charlie collapsed at the other and leaned back against the bench. "I used to be fitter than you."

"Yes," said Nick. "You did. And not so red faced. Now, you can't get to the end of your street without looking like an asthmatic pensioner."

"Cheers, mate. Between you and my brother, I'll be ready for an arsenic sandwich by lunchtime. He was bitching about me making a change."

"Well, on that note, maybe I can help. As I remember, you used to be pretty broad-minded. Are you still up for trying different things?"

Charlie inched a little farther to the edge of the bench. "I told you a while ago, Nick, I don't go with men."

"You can be such an idiot sometimes. I'm talking about work."

"Oh." Charlie slid forward. "Go on."

"Well, when I say work, it's more of a trial, but it pays well."

"How well?"

"To the tune of ten grand," said Nick.

Charlie barked out a laugh. "I can earn more than that at a fast food place, mate. Give me a break."

"Not ten grand for one year. Ten grand for one day."

Charlie felt the blood drain from his face as he sank back into the bench. "Did you just say ten grand for one day's work?"

"Yes, I did. And when I say work…"

"I'm not being a sex slave," said Charlie. "Not for anyone. It's humiliating, and undermining. Well, unless it's for a smoking-hot girl, and all she wants is…"

"You're not that lucky, mate. It's trialling some new tech. Can you stop being a whiny little bitch for a minute and give me an open mind?"

Sweat pricked at Charlie's palms as a mix of excitement and anxiety swept through him, and he wiped them across his sweaty joggers before he shuffled into a comfortable position. "Go on. I'm all ears"

Nick turned and crossed one leg over the other. "Okay, imagine a world that doesn't exist. Heck, a world that couldn't exist, and yet it could in your mind."

"Nick?" said Charlie.

"Yes?"

"You sound like the bloke at the start of a film trailer. Stop the sales bullshit and sci-fi spiel and just tell me."

"Sorry. Okay, where I work, they need people to take part in a new type of game. Well, when I say game, it's not actually a game, yet. It's a program running across multiple servers that needs individuals with something specific in their genes or mind to test it.

"I'm not a hundred percent on what it does, it all very hush hush, but you'd need to do a psychiatric evaluation and get through the interview stage. If you're selected, they'll hook you up to some shit-hot new tech that you get to try years before Joe Public. And they'll pay you ten grand for the privilege."

Charlie paused and thought for a moment. "So it's a computer game."

"More like social networking, but taken to the next level. You know how there's VR and AR? Well, it's the next big thing, a massive leap forward from those. Basically, you go Under…"

"Under?" said Charlie. "Like Australia? And what are all these 'R's you're talking about?"

"They'll explain the 'R's at the interview," said Nick, with a wave of the hand. "Under's the name of the place you go. They do something where you go into a different reality, like a world you create yourself."

"Like hypnosis?"

"Not sure, mate." Nick rapped his knuckles against the bench. "But it feels as real as this. You create your own world, or at least that's the idea. If it takes off, they're looking at giving you the option of choosing abilities to become whoever you want to be. Obviously, in your own, make-believe world, but still… it sounds unbelievable."

"Sounds impossible," said Charlie.

Nick smiled. "It does, doesn't it? But I've seen it. They need different personalities, different characters, to push the servers. To really test them. I heard they've only used employees so far so, now, they have to branch out."

"So, why the ten grand? That's a lot of money."

"Yes, it is. It's unchartered territory. This thing hooks up to your mind, so who knows what goes on in there? All I've noticed from the employees is that Alma, the cleaning lady, does a much better job now she's been Under. We should put the Government Under, it might solve everything."

"Ten grand?" said Charlie.

"Yes. For one day. But you have to pass the assessments first. What do you think? Could be the start of a new chapter."

"Or a kick up the arse."

Nick fished a business card from his pocket and handed it to Charlie. "Here, take this. There's a presentation to get things started and, then, they'll get the assessments underway. Get there for nine thirty tomorrow, and check in at reception. The address is on the back."

Charlie took the card. The words, *'Ellen Wakefield – Project Manager'* were written across the front while, while the address and the company name filled the reverse.

"ASP?" said Charlie. "What kind of name is that?"

"Algorithm Server Programs. Don't ask what they do. I could tell you, but..."

"What? Then you'd have to kill me?"

"Something like that. Well, not me, obviously. But we do know a guy."

"Obviously." Charlie stood and stretched his legs. "Okay, what do I have to lose? I'm in. New chapter and all that. Ready for a race back to the flat?"

"Always," said Nick as he sprang to his feet. "Are you?"

"Hell, no," laughed Charlie. "I'll call us a taxi."

Chapter 5

Charlie rolled upright off the sofa and clutched his head as the shrill screech of his alarm snapped him awake from the latest nightmare.

Last night's reward for his run with Nick lay scattered around the living room floor. He weaved around the obstacle course of empty bottles and cans into the kitchen and flipped the switch on the kettle.

"Why do you do this?" he asked himself as he lifted the milk bottle from the fridge. When its contents slushed against the sides, like yoghurt, he put it back, turned off the kettle, and went to the bathroom.

Images from the last dream flashed through his mind. Not Amelia this time. He didn't remember dreaming about his daughter last night. This time, Kate took centre stage. Memories of her jealousy, and terrifying fits of rage. Just like flipping the kettle's switch, a similar hairline trigger held back her temper, ready to be tripped by the slightest thing.

In the nightmare, they watched television. A reality dating show, where strangers were stranded on an island, every one of them a model with a perfect body, and a brilliant, white smile. One by one, they were whittled down, until two remained, fated to be together forever.

Or at least until the cameras stopped rolling and they entered the real world.

Kate turned towards him. 'She's attractive, don't you think?'

A familiar feeling of nausea rolled in Charlie's stomach as he fought for the vaguest and safest answer. 'She's not bad. She's not you, though, is she?'

Another stomach tumble and a rise in body temperature as the temper terrors circled like vultures, riding on the thermals of a calm voice. 'What do you like about her?'

'Well, none of it's realistic, is it?' would be the defence. 'None of it. They find a gorgeous setting and then audition thousands of people, until they find the best looking, and most dramatic. I'd bet every one of them is a drama queen.'

And, then, paranoia breaks through the calm, and the voice takes on an edgier tone. 'You still would, though, wouldn't you?'

'Would what?'

'Sleep with them. I bet you'd sleep with every one of them. Probably the men, too.'

And that was it. Cornered and defenceless. Whatever words came next didn't matter. Wouldn't even be heard. No argument worked against someone with no opinion but their own.

The switch flipped, and jealousy poured out in waves of aggression. Waves that left marks on his body, but always in places that no one else would see.

Back in the present reality, he ran cold water and splashed it over his face, then dried off, and glanced into the shaving mirror.

"Got an hour to make you look presentable," he said to his ragged reflection. "Big day today. Ten grand. Ten frigging grand. That's a new start."

Nick's business card was tucked into the corner of the mirror. He tugged it free and studied it again.

Ellen Wakefield. What a cool name. And she was a project manager. Charlie pictured her in his imagination. Tall, with slender curves, and a waterfall of luxurious blonde hair cascading down the back of her stylish business suit. Men watched her every move while she only had eyes for Charlie.

How do like that, Kate?

At nine o'clock, Charlie pulled the door closed behind him and walked into the next street to find his car.

Despite the easy drive out of town, he glanced at his phone's GPS. The screen glared in the sunlight and flashed from its magnetic grip on the dashboard. Google Maps said the address for the ASP facility was a twenty-minute drive away; not because of distance, it was four miles from A to B, but because roadworks had traffic backed up on the main road.

He found the gridlock in no time and rolled to a stop behind a white Mini. The girl in the Mini stared into the rear-view mirror while she applied bright red lipstick. Charlie noticed her blonde hair and wondered if it was Ellen Wakefield. She put away the makeup and gently slapped her cheeks to generate colour. Charlie smiled and did the same. As blood rushed to his face, a memory of Amelia played in his mind. Her cute laugh echoed around the park as he pushed her on a swing.

"Higher, Daddy. I want to poke the sun and burst it like a balloon with my finger."

"I don't think I can get you much higher than this," he said.

"Of course, you can," came the confident reply. "You can do anything."

The image vanished as quickly as it came, but the message remained. As the Mini pulled away, Charlie put the car in gear and followed. While tears pushed behind his eyes, he forced a smile.

Positive thoughts.

This assessment was nothing more than a job interview, but for the shortest, best-paid job in Charlie's life.

The start of a new chapter, and a much-needed kick up the arse.

They wouldn't want to see a moping, miserable and negative candidate, but someone filled with zest, fun, and a desire to try new things and live life to the full.

Charlie stretched every inch of his five-foot-ten frame and leaned forward towards the rear-view mirror. "This is your day," he said. "No more crap. You've paid your dues, and it's time to move on. Remember, you can do anything." His beaming grin filled the mirror. "Thank you, baby."

He glanced at his phone in time to see it light up before a ringtone chirped. He touched the screen to receive the call.

"Morning, Bro," said Andy's cheerful voice. "I might be able to get the afternoon off, if you fancy a game of snooker?"

"Would love to," said Charlie as the traffic inched forward, "but I've got an interview, and I'm not sure how long it will take."

"About time. Is this for that call-girl job you've been after?"

"Funny. No, it's some kind of research at the company Nick works for. He's not told me much, hush hush and all that, but it's something to do with trialling a new type of game. They'll connect me to some servers, or whatever, and I can imagine different worlds."

"So they're going to tap into your brain?"

"I think so."

"They'd better be powerful servers. I've been trying for years, and still haven't managed it."

Charlie laughed and felt his spirit rise another notch. "That's because I won't let you. Privileged information. Listen, I'm driving. Is it okay if I call you later?"

"No problem. Why don't you call me after you call Mum and Dad?"

"I promise, I'll call them. Talk to you later. Love you, Bro."

The Google Maps screen returned as the GPS lady directed him to turn right off the road. Charlie brimmed with confidence. He glanced through the side window and searched for a business sign. Neat lawns bordered tall, red brick walls that ran left and right until they turned into the English countryside. An opening sat in the middle, but gave no indication of what lay inside. No gate. No barrier. No entry booth. Just a tree-lined, gravel drive that wound into the property and out of sight.

If this was the ASP facility, it looked more like the entrance to a grand country house, not a location carrying out super-secret research.

With no other options, he turned the wheel and guided his car along the drive. Gravel popped beneath his tyres as he followed the tree-line and emerged into a large courtyard. Arched, Perspex canopies offered protection from the weather in front of tinted glass entrance doors. Again, Charlie looked for a sign or an indication he had the right place, but nothing, not even the doors, gave a clue.

He followed the drive around the side of the building and, finally, saw other signs of life. A tidy row of parked cars lined up along the edge of another well-manicured lawn that separated the car park from the building. In the distance another building, much bigger than the entrance structure, stood back connected by a glass corridor. Through the cloudy glass, Charlie could make out the silhouette of yet another building on the other side of the grounds.

How big was this place?

He counted twenty-five cars, none of them Nick's, before he pulled into a vacant space, locked the car, and walked back to the entrance.

Neither glass door moved as Charlie edged closer to them. He paused and looked for a handle, or a panel or intercom, then jumped as something squawked from above and behind him. He turned to see the glassy eye of a camera, and a tiny speaker mounted into a post that supported the canopy. His confidence took a tiny dip before he squared his shoulders and smiled.

"Can I help you?" asked a female voice.

"Hi. Yes, I'm here to see Ellen Wakefield."

"Name?"

"Charlie Green."

Silence, and then the doors parted with a whisper. "Please, come to reception to sign in, Mr. Green."

Charlie walked through the doors, over an odd entrance mat, and into a foyer tiled in gleaming granite. Every wall was featureless, and painted a plain washed beige, except the far wall that had an elaborate desk set into it. A closed door book-ended either side of the desk, each with a wire-meshed window, and a small red panel.

A head peered over the top of the desk's counter.

Charlie headed towards it.

As he reached the desk, the girl smiled and handed him a plastic bowl. "Good morning, Mr. Green. I'm Ashleigh. Before you enter the facility, I'll need to store your keys, phone, and wallet. Don't worry, they'll be quite safe with me, but this is as far as they can go."

"How do you know what I'm carrying?" asked Charlie.

"The mat at the entrance scanned you as you stepped over it." Ashleigh smiled again. "Don't worry about that, either, it only shows us what we need to see."

Charlie smirked at the innuendo and remembered his newfound confidence as he emptied the contents of his pockets into the bowl. "I wouldn't be worried about that, Ashleigh." He gave her a sly wink. "Far from it."

Ashleigh didn't bat an eyelid. "Good for you, Mr. Green," She swung around a small tablet mounted on a holder. "If you could place your left hand on here, we'll get you signed in."

Charlie laid his palm flat on the tablet's surface and watched it glow green. Ashleigh stared at a monitor, nodded, and replaced the bowl with a plastic fob on a purple lanyard. Behind her, a printer whirred into life.

"Okay, that's good. Give me a second, and I'll get your access pass. This will grant you entry into the first building over my right shoulder. Don't bother trying any other doors with it, it'll just signal security in the far annexe. You don't want to annoy security."

Charlie couldn't help but smile at the friendly tone in Ashleigh's voice while she warned him of unknown repercussions, should he venture off path. She reached back to the printer, grabbed a piece of plastic, and attached it to the fob. "There you go, you're all set. Head through the doors and follow the corridor. The presentation is in the first room you'll come to. Best of luck."

"Thank you," said Charlie before he slid the lanyard over his head and held the card up to the panel. The panel turned from red to green, and the door opened into the glass corridor.

The view from inside the corridor looking out was crystal clear compared to the cloudy view from the outside looking in. Charlie could see a second corridor, identical to this, that stretched away, presumably, from the other door. It led to another red brick building with no visible windows or other doors.

The thump of his footfalls echoed off the glass walls and seemed to chase one another up and down the corridor, and he tip-toed until he reached another door. With another card swipe, this one opened onto a large room.

An overhead projector hugged the ceiling and hovered over twenty chairs arranged in four rows of five. A manila folder lay on the floor beneath each one.

Tables lined the rear wall, covered with biscuits and coffee urns while, to the front, hung a huge white screen behind a raised platform. Three chairs waited on the platform. Just as in the entrance foyer, one door was set into the wall on each side.

These folks like their symmetry, thought Charlie.

A heavy chair sat alone on the far wall, a few feet from anything else.

At the back of the room, a few people milled around and made small talk while they sipped coffee and crunched biscuits. Charlie saw a man sitting alone in the centre of the second row, took another deep breath of confidence, and sat beside him.

He offered a hand. "Hi. I'm Charlie."

A glance at the lanyard around the man's neck said his name was Simon.

Simon slid to the opposite side of his seat and almost fell from it and onto the floor. He re-balanced, glanced around the room, and offered a shaky hand in return. "Simon. You're here for the tests, too, huh?"

"Tests?" said Charlie. "I thought we were here for assessments? To see if we're suitable for whatever comes next."

"Assessments. Tests. It's all the same. Don't let them take you away, brother. You've seen the other corridor, right?"

"I have. It goes to the building next door."

"Exactly," said Simon, as if that explained everything.

"Oh. So you know what's in there?"

"No idea. My card won't allow me through."

"But you tried?" asked Charlie.

Simon slid back to the edge of his seat. "Are you crazy? Do you know what security will do if you try to swipe against a door you're not supposed to?"

"No idea. Is it that bad?"

"Damned if I know, but the girl at reception seemed pretty mean about it. Not worth the risk." He gestured to the side wall. "And what's with that chair? Looks like one of those electric chairs from prison."

"Still no idea," said Charlie as he took another deep breath and placed his hands between his knees. Based on the chatter behind him, and the behaviour of people like Simon, ASP's search for personalities spanned from one end of the mental spectrum to the other.

Simon slid forward, looked at Charlie's hands, and wrung his own. "I have to say, I'm excited about this."

"Oh?" said Charlie. "You seem a little nervous, to be honest."

"I can trust you, right?"

"I think we're in this together," replied Charlie.

"Cool. Truth is, I can't wait for the aliens."

Charlie raised his eyebrows. "I'm sorry? Aliens?"

Simon spun around in his seat and grasped Charlie's hands. "The aliens. I read there's a world here where we get to communicate with them. You know, talk them out of invading us. I want to be an ambassador for Earth."

"Where did you read that?" Charlie pulled back and tried to stop the smile that tugged at his lips. His forced confidence took a huge leap forward.

"On the Internet. It's something to do with this program we're testing for. I research everything, brother. And I mean everything."

"Clearly," said Charlie. "And the Internet never lies. Winston Churchill said so."

"He did?"

"Yes," said Charlie, ready to have some fun, "and you don't have to worry about aliens. They're no threat."

"No, you're wrong. And, anyway, how could you know that? Did you research them, too?"

"Didn't need to, because you can bet the aliens researched us."

The guy stared blankly. "I'm not following."

"I'm not surprised," said Charlie. "Think about it. If an alien race made the effort to fly light years to invade our planet, they'd research us first, right?"

Simon frowned. "Okay, makes sense."

"Have you seen daytime TV? The reality chat shows?"

"Eh?"

"It's all about the mind rays."

Simon grew animated again. "Of course. See, I knew you'd understand."

"Yes, but for the mind rays to work, we have to have minds. The aliens would tune into one of those shows, you know, Jerry Springer, or Jeremy Kyle. They'd see the specimens onscreen and plot an escape route to the other side of the galaxy. They'd run faster than the speed of light. Wouldn't touch us with a barge pole." Charlie nodded with intelligence. "Our stupidity is our best defence."

"You've lost me again."

"Yep, thought I might," said Charlie. "And, anyway, it's not the aliens that should concern you. It's the ants."

"Ants?"

"Yeah. They're everywhere. In the walls. Under the streets. Beneath the soil. Millions upon millions of them."

Simon scratched up and down his arms.

"Ants that dig. March. Fly," said Charlie, "Come the day they all collaborate and rise as one force, we won't stand a chance."

"You're making me itch, man. Stop it."

"You've heard of death by a thousand cuts?"

Simon nodded.

"Imagine death by a million ant bites. And the scariest thing of all?"

Simon cowered away but had to ask, "Go on."

"They're already here," whispered Charlie. "Been here the whole time. Waiting."

"Jesus, you're sick." Simon stood and moved back a few rows, muttering under his breath. "Frigging weirdos."

One down, thought Charlie, before someone else slumped into Simon's empty seat.

The aroma of musky aftershave took his breath away. He turned to find a good-looking man with a mop of curly blonde hair.

"What's up, dude? Welcome to the circus. I'm Jack, as in Jack the Lad. Parents must have known what was coming when they named me."

Jack flashed a perfect white smile and thrust out a hand. Charlie shook it and introduced himself, but Jack had already turned to face the back wall. "What a bunch of losers. Looks like it's you and me, then. If there's only one spot, I apologise in advance. No hard feelings."

Charlie wished for Simon's return. "None taken, although, I think they're after different personalities, so you'll be fine."

"Yeah, I'm made for this stuff," said Jack as he spun back. "Never failed at anything I've... hang on, do I know you?"

Jack studied Charlie's face and smiled. "You're famous, aren't you? Are you in a band?"

"No, I'm just…"

"No, hang on. I'll get it. Always do."

Charlie waited while Jack stared.

"Got it! You're off the telly; the bloke who had his kid abducted. Wow, that was…?"

"Three years ago. I'm okay now, thanks for asking. New chapter."

Jack slapped his shoulder. "I was going to say, 'some bad shit', but yeah. So, anyway, where's all the women? I always score at these sessions, then have a session of my own, if you know what I mean."

Charlie ignored the obscene wink while Jack bounced in his seat. "This is going to be sick, dude. I hope they've got the ability option sorted."

Charlie nodded and reached beneath his seat for the folder, hoping that Jack would go away.

"Wait 'til you go under. If they've got the abilities option running, you can be anything you want."

Jack's relentless bouncing grated on Charlie's nerves. "Under? Under what? What are you talking about? Have you been here before?"

"No, but I'm a tech geek. I've been following this on the dark web. They've done one test already, only with women."

"Maybe that's why there are no women here," said Charlie.

Jack punched his arm. "Genius. Never thought of that. Yeah, they want different kinds of people…"

"Personalities."

"Yeah, that. I'm going through. Sorry, again."

"You seem very confident about that."

"Are you kidding?" Jack spun to face Charlie. "Dude, look at me. I'm perfect. Good looking, intelligent. The real deal."

As Charlie prepared to move seats to follow Simon, the rear door slammed open. Two burly men dragged in a huge figure in an orange jumpsuit, wrestled him into the heavy chair, and strapped him into it.

The room bustled with hushed murmurs.

"Bloody hell," whispered Charlie. "Who's that?"

Jack smiled. "Like you said, different personalities. Messed up, or what? Not too good looking, is he? He's no threat to us."

"Maybe he's part of the assessment, to see how we'll react when…"

The right-side door at the front of the room opened, and an attractive woman with high cheekbones, and a head of dark hair, stepped onto the platform.

In seconds, every seat was filled.

When the hush died to silence, she spoke. "Hello, everyone. Thanks for coming. I'm Ellen Wakefield, lead project manager. Welcome to Project MindSpace."

Chapter 6

"I thought she'd be blonde," said Charlie.

Jack smiled and shook his mop of curls. "Like me? Look at her, though. You still would, wouldn't you? She's so tidy I'm having trouble concentrating. Did she say 'minefield'? That can't be good."

Charlie shook his head. "MindSpace. That's probably a play on words."

"I'd like to play on…"

Ellen Wakefield's amplified voice drowned out Jack's annoying lechery, and Charlie focussed on the platform.

"I'm sure you've all done your research before your visit here," she said. "Ten thousand pounds for a day's work is enough to pique the curiosity of the most sceptical person, but I won't stand here and bore you with the details right now. Let's get the assessments underway, and those of you that are accepted will get full disclosure before you go any further."

A few groans sounded around the gripped spectators.

"I know," she said, "I'm sorry, but we don't want to waste any time, ours or yours. However, before I assign your assessment rooms, I would like to introduce two of my colleagues who'll help me oversee this. The three of us will each take a large interest in you over the next few hours, so I think it prudent that you know who you'll be spending your valuable time with."

On cue, the door to the right opened and a tall guy in a well-fitted suit marched into the room and stood beside her.

"Gentlemen, this is David Collins. David is our graphic designer and project manager. Some of the things you'll see today came from his vivid imagination."

Collins took a bow as everyone clapped.

The door opened again, and a young girl with a beaming smile joined the others.

"And this is Joanna May. In short, Joanna came up with the idea behind Project MindSpace. She's the brains behind the project, and she created what you're about to experience. However, don't let that young appearance and charming smile fool you, she's sharp as a tack, and twice as dangerous."

Joanna smiled, blushed and raised a hand in an embarrassed wave.

The clapping started again until Ellen Wakefield held up her hands. "Okay, as I said, I will explain everything in good time. For now, if you would reach beneath your seats, you'll find a folder. To proceed, we'll need your signature to say you accept everything that's written in there. That includes the non-disclosure agreements, and the waving of any rights to the data and information we gather.

"We also need your assurance that there will be no legal activity of any kind concerning the outcome of any assessment, or future testing, carried out here at ASP. In a moment, I'll stop talking and give you thirty minutes to let you read through the pages and sign your lives away. Or at least your minds. Please, be sure to read everything. And, while we don't anticipate any issues, for ten grand, you may need to be more than a little flexible with us."

A cautious ripple of laughter washed over Charlie as he gripped the folder.

"Finally, from all of us, our thanks and gratitude for your time and participation. To those of you that pass the assessments, we'll see you on the other side. To those of you that don't, we wish you all the best. You can rest assured that, somewhere down the line, you'll have the opportunity to try the immersive experience of Project MindSpace for yourselves in a more relaxed environment. Again, thank you for coming. We'll be back for you in half an hour."

The three filed from the podium to a chorus of claps and stepped towards the door to the left.

Charlie flipped open his folder and pulled out a sheaf of papers and a pen as Jack leaned into him.

"I'm going to smash this," he said, and then pointed to Ellen Wakefield as she left the room. "And, when I've done that, I'm going to smash her, too."

FORTY MINUTES LATER, Charlie sat in a room barely larger than his bathroom. Foam insulation covered each wall. A single, circular dome light hung over a white laminate table and two chairs. Technology covered the table. Charlie glanced nervously at the computers. A bundle of wires snaked from them, disappeared under his shirt, and were glued to his chest and back, while a clip monitored his pulse rate from a fingertip. Two more pads pulled his face tight at the temples.

Joanna May sat in a chair opposite, while David Collins stood behind her with a clipboard.

"Sorry," said Joanna, "but I'm afraid you're stuck with the

brains of the operation. I can ramble a bit so, if I go on, just tell me to get to the point and get on with it."

Charlie nodded, unsure of what to say.

"First things first, let's get the boring stuff out of the way. Obviously, I'm Joanna May. If you continue through the process, I'll be the one assessing you. We'll try to keep things consistent. Please ignore the computers, they're completely harmless, and are here to simply track your reactions to the questions I'm about to ask. David is here to take notes that we can compare with the readings. Is that okay?"

Charlie nodded again.

Joanna smiled. "Okay, man of many words, you don't need to be quite so nervous. How about we start with something easy? What's your full name?"

"Charlie Green."

"And your date of birth?"

Charlie answered a list of simple questions before Joanna leaned forward. "Okay, that's the base questions out of the way. Charlie, are you, or have you ever been, in love?"

For a moment, Charlie froze. He imagined the readings on the computer peaking and dipping while he searched for an honest answer. The first awkward question immediately put him on edge.

"I, er, I have been. Yes."

"Good. Given the choice between material wealth and no relationship, or a happy relationship and no wealth, which would you choose?"

Every rib of the carpeted floor stood out as Charlie stared at it and considered the question. "I just want to be happy."

Joanna May glanced at the screen and continued. "Have you ever been in an overly stressful situation?"

"Other than this one, yes," said Charlie as a darkness crept over him. "Very overly."

He couldn't see the readings, but Joanna frowned before she leaned back in her seat. "Okay, something a little lighter. Would you prefer to travel the world, or go into space?"

The questions continued until sweat soaked Charlie's underarms, before Joanna pulled out a pack of random pictures. After guessing what each image portrayed, she took off the pads and the finger clip. "Okay, final test. We need to find out if you're susceptible to hypnosis."

Charlie sat upright as the thought of losing control set off alarms in every one of his senses. "Why do you need to do that? I've answered all your questions. In fact, I think I'd like to…"

"Relax, Charlie," said David Collins. "To enter the world of Project MindSpace, your mind needs to accept the program. If you have no ability to let it in, as some people do, it won't work. I promise, we won't make you do a naked table dance, or anything embarrassing." He pointed to the corner of the room where a small device with a blinking red light stared down at them. "Everything in this room is recorded. You're well within your rights to view the tape when we're done if you have any concerns."

"And," said Joanna, "we mentioned that you may have to be a little flexible with us. This isn't exactly a test for acne cream, is it?"

Charlie barked out a laugh and nodded. "Sorry. A few of your questions caught me off guard."

"That was the idea," said Joanna, "but all applicants answer the same questions. Like I said, we're trying to be consistent. So are you ready?"

Not for the first time Charlie's stomach churned, but he eased back into the chair and nodded.

"Okay. First, you need to be comfortable, and relaxed.

Difficult, I know, but think of your happy place, somewhere you feel at ease. Now, raise both your arms before you."

Charlie lifted his arms. After the time spent sitting in the assessment chair, each limb felt heavy, and lethargic.

"We need your arms to be about eight inches apart."

Charlie spread his arms until Joanna leaned forward and closed them to half the distance. "I can tell you're a man, no test needed there," she smiled. "Now, close your eyes and mouth, and don't acknowledge me until this is over."

Silence filled the room until Joanna spoke again. "Imagine your left arm has a balloon tied to it. The balloon is filled with helium and is lighter than air. Now, imagine your right arm is holding a stack of heavy books. Trust your imagination and believe these things are on your arms."

Charlie blanked out everything and imagined the weights.

"Each time I snap my fingers," said Joanna, "your left arm will get lighter, and your right arm will grow heavier."

The silence in the room overwhelmed Charlie's senses until he heard the click of Joanna's fingers. He peeked through a crack in his eyelids to find that his arms hadn't moved.

After half a dozen snaps, he felt a nudge on his shoulder. David Collins stood behind him.

"Okay, I think that's everything we need," he said.

A haze filled Charlie's head, and he shook it and rubbed his face. "Cool. So, what? You'll be in touch?"

"Won't need to," said Joanna. "Charlie, we'd like you to be part of the test."

"Really? How is that possible? I was so boring, I depressed myself. And I don't think the hypnosis thing worked, either."

Joanna tapped her temples. "It's all about what's going on in here. You're level-headed, with a good combination of experiences. It's not all about flamboyance, since we hope everyone will have access to MindSpace. So, congratulations. If you'd like to grab a coffee and take a seat in the conference room, you can join the other successful candidates, and we'll give you more of an explanation of what we have in store for you."

***

DAVID COLLINS ESCORTED Charlie back to the conference room and held the door for him. "Look forward to working with you, Charlie."

"Thanks," said Charlie. "Me, too. I mean, I look forward to working with you, too."

Collins smiled. "Got you the first time. See you later."

Charlie stepped into the large room. The tables at the back had been cleared, leaving a single table holding a coffee urn. The huge projector screen still hung on the near wall and wafted like a sail in the breeze from the closing door.

Simon sat on his hands in the far corner, surrounded by empty seats. The guy in the orange jumpsuit was chained to the heavy chair with a guard on either side. Two people Charlie hadn't noticed before took up random seats in the middle, while Jack sat front and centre. He bounced like a child and waved when he spotted Charlie and patted the seat to his side.

"Charlie! My man. God knows how, but you made it through. Come and sit next to the star candidate. Who knows, some of my charm might rub off on you."

Charlie eyed the remaining fifteen empty chairs, then trudged over and took the seat next to Jack.

"Congratulations, Jack. I didn't think you'd have any problem getting through."

"Piece of cake, dude. And that Wakefield chick is already

warming to me. Done the ground work, if you know what I mean?"

"I probably do," muttered Charlie under his breath.

"They can't help themselves, mate. Feel sorry for them sometimes, but..." laughed Jack, "...who am I kidding. They love it."

Charlie cringed inside. "I'm sure they do. I'm going to get a coffee. Want one?"

"Nah, I'm good, mate. Ready to get stuck in."

Charlie excused himself and escaped to the back of the room. Simon didn't make eye contact, and Charlie hoped he wasn't too traumatised by the questioning. Ten thousand pounds was a huge motivation.

Hours old coffee poured from the urn like sludge. Charlie filled a mug and wandered around to kill time, until a door opened, and Ellen Wakefield led the same procession onto the podium.

She smiled as Charlie took his seat, before she addressed the room. "Congratulations to you all. The six of you who passed the assessment stage and are now ready to test the MindSpace program."

Simon's words flooded Charlie's mind. *Assessments. Tests. It's all the same. Don't let them take you away, brother'.*

No surprise, he looked a nervous wreck.

"Before we get into it, I'd like to introduce one more person; someone who should be able to explain the concept of the project in layman's terms. Once he's finished, you'll have one opportunity to back out and go home. As soon as we take you into the facility, there's no going back until testing is complete. Are we all clear on that?"

Charlie nodded and was certain he heard Simon squeak, while Jack fist-pumped the air and shouted a, 'Hell, yeah'!

"Okay, then, prepare to be dazzled by the man we call John Warburton."

The door opened once more, and a man in a razor-sharp suit almost jogged into the room and mounted the platform. He stood for a moment, stroked his tidy goatee, and surveyed the room. A gold chain glistened behind an open collar before Warburton tugged at his lapels and clasped his hands before him.

"Gentlemen, congratulations, and welcome to Algorithm Server Programs. I'm John, and my role here is primarily inside sales. If you need to know anything about the features, and benefits, of Project MindSpace, I'm your man."

He pulled a laser pointer from his pocket and nodded. As if by magic, the projector screen behind him lit up and displayed an old gaming arcade. Charlie recognised large *Space Invaders* and *Galaxian* consoles from old nineties films.

Warburton smiled. "Ah, I see recognition in some of your faces. Gaming. I don't care what anyone says, we all love it in one form, or another. People that don't play video games and find it too nerdy will find another way to challenge themselves, or escape from the real world. It's what we all do, right? It's what we all need."

Charlie nodded.

"That's right. Because we must all escape reality from time to time. We need to exercise our brains in a different way. We used to be able to wander down to the arcade with a pocket full of ten pence pieces and spend the afternoon shooting aliens, or centipedes. Then, thanks to advances in technology, we could do that from the comfort of our own bedrooms with consoles."

"That's not all we did in our bedrooms," whispered Jack with a snigger.

Warburton didn't skip a beat. "The latest technology takes

us out of this world by using more of our senses, not just our hand to eye co-ordination. Speaking of hands, put 'em up if you're aware of VR?"

Charlie raised his hand while Jack tried to touch the ceiling.

"Good," said Warburton. "Virtual Reality. You've all seen the films, right? How about AR?"

Again, Jack's hand shot up. Charlie remained stationary.

"Ah, not so many. Okay, let me explain the distinction between the two. With VR, you'd wear an HMD…"

"A head mounted display," said Ellen Wakefield.

"Yes. Sorry, guys, I get a little acronym happy sometimes. With VR, you'd wear a headset of some kind and then, through an input device, the VR will immerse the user in a created environment. Let's say you want to swim with dolphins. The VR will block out the real world and put you in the water. It feeds the sounds and sights into your headset and, without getting wet, you can swim in the ocean with dolphins."

Charlie shook his head as Jack sniggered again, probably at the thought of getting wet in VR.

"With AR, or Augmented Reality," said Warburton, "you'll still see the world you're in, but the AR will overlay images onto it. Like overdubbing extra sounds onto a basic music track. In this instance, you could still swim with dolphins, but in your house. It'll still be your wallpaper, but the AR will add the dolphins to swim across it. Not as realistic, but great for games like *Pokémon Go*, right?"

Warburton nodded, and the screen behind him changed. A circular image appeared onscreen, a black ring with slashes of purple cut through it.

"All reality programs need an input device. With VR, it would be a headset, and an input, to relay the images. With AR, it could be something as easily available as your smartphone. You guys went through those assessments to try what I call PM."

He waited for a response and, when none came, Warburton coughed and continued.

"Okay, tough room. They have VR and AR, we have PM. Project MindSpace. There are servers at another location that store the means for you to access your own worlds, but to do that you'll need an input device. That's where this bad boy comes in."

He dazzled the screen with his laser pointer. "I've tried to come up with a cool name for it, The Relayer, Echo, but that takes us back to dolphins, Boomer. I even tried Precious," he laughed, "but someone stole it. We settled on The Chip. I campaigned for Common Holographic Interface Piece, but we call it The Chip because, well, that's what it is. It's the chip that communicates what goes on in your mind with our servers. It's your hub, or your router. Your connection from reality to the make-believe world you create with your mind."

He paused for a moment. "Okay, that's the complicated part out of the way. Are you all still with me?"

Charlie nodded and added to the murmurs from behind him. Jack had settled back into his seat, his eyes glazed over by technology.

"All right, so how does it work? It's deceptively small, about the size of a mini donut, but not as tasty. It sticks to the back of your neck and accesses your thoughts and brainwaves through your spinal column. You know how your phone will pick up signals anywhere near a tower? Same with The Chip. We're working on Wi-Fi applications and satellite usage but, for now, it will link with our servers anywhere within a fifty-mile radius. That distance is growing, and we expect coverage on a par with mobile phones within months. Now, down to the nitty gritty. The million-dollar question. How does it do what it does?"

Warburton nodded again and a huge, leather chair appeared on the screen. It looked to Charlie like a black dentist's chair, but with a hole in the centre of the headrest.

"We'll get you comfortable in one of our chairs. We don't have a cool name for those yet. The Chip will go onto your neck, and you lie back and relax. The Chip will sync with the servers while we monitor your reactions and vital signs. Once you close your eyes, your mind will register darkness. Once this happens, The Chip signals the servers and, as they say in America, it's on. It sends messages back and forth, from your mind to the servers and back again. Whatever you envision, the servers will create that world in your mind. Now, I'm sure you're thinking you can do that with your imagination."

Another screen change, this time to a field of tulips.

"Flowers, right? But when you go Under, and that's what we call the state when your mind is synced to the servers; they're no longer just flowers. They'll sway in the breeze, and you can run through them, or pick one and smell it. You can imagine a windmill at the other side of the field and then walk through it and go inside the windmill. You can swing off the windmill's blades, if you want to. To all intents and purposes, this field will exist in your mind. For real. That's a real field of flowers until we bring you out."

Warburton surveyed the candidates. "I can see some of you are a little overwhelmed by this. Perhaps it's time for me to shut up and let you ask any questions."

Someone behind Charlie spoke first. "So, despite your spin, we basically see environments?"

Ellen Wakefield stood and walked to the front of the platform. "John, may I?"

Warburton gestured to the edge and stepped back.

"Yes, you will see environments. But you will also be able to interact with them and be whoever you want to be. Imagine, as John mentioned, you were playing *Pokémon Go*. Imagine you found whichever creature you were searching for. Don't forget, your mind is always working subconsciously.

"It will flesh out the part for you. So, in your Pokémon game, you can be an actual hunter, in a hunter's clothing, able to reach out and grab the creature. Feel it squirm in your hands and hear its protests. Or maybe you'd throw a net over it and then take it to your own cabin you picture, somewhere in a remote forest. Maybe there's a horse tethered to a tree you pass on the way. You could mount the horse and ride it to your cabin.

"That's what Project MindSpace does. If you can imagine it, it can happen. Your subconscious, and our servers, will combine to create it. You experience it completely. Touch, sound, taste, smell, and sight. All senses."

"Will we see each other," said Charlie, "if we're using the same servers?"

"Great question," replied Wakefield. "Yes, if you are close, then you may bump into one another but, and here's the complicated part, you'll only see that person in your terrain. For instance, let's say you are riding your horse through the forest. You might see the man next to you, but he'll be reacting with his own world, not yours.

"We're trying to iron this out, so it might seem a little strange at first, but he might be on a flight to Mars, for example. In his world, he's strapped into a cockpit, flicking switches, and checking in with Mission Control. In his mind, he's there, ready for lift off.

"In your world, he looks like a loony, lying on the floor, playing with thin air. It's a complex program, not perfect yet, but it's getting there. We hope that, with your help, we can make it available to the public sooner rather than later. And we have also added characters and items to the program which you may meet or interact with. Whether you choose to do so is entirely up to you."

"What about abilities?" asked Jack.

Charlie jumped, and had almost forgotten that Jack sat beside him.

David Collins stood and walked to the front of the podium. "Don't believe everything you read on the Internet," he said.

Charlie craned his head to see Simon, but his head was bowed.

"The abilities program is still in testing," said Collins.

"And what about him?"

Charlie turned as someone behind him pointed to the guy in the orange jumpsuit. Throughout the entire presentation, he hadn't made a sound, and he stared with pure hatred at the man pointing the finger. As Charlie took him in properly for the first time, he noticed a name patch stitched to the front of his overalls that said, *'Lucas'*.

"Does he get ten grand? What's he doing here? Is he part of the program, or part of the assessment?"

Ellen Wakefield showed a glimmer of annoyance that disappeared as quickly as it came.

"I'm not at liberty to discuss individual cases," she said, "but everyone in this room has undertaken the same assessment."

"What about risks? How safe is this?" said the same guy.

"Preliminary testing showed minimal risk, but that is something we're monitoring. Hence the big payday and the papers you signed."

It seemed as if the room held its breath.

"Okay," she said, "if there are no more questions, shall we get started?"

Charlie jumped again as mild panic quickened his pulse. "What, now? We go into the other world now?"

"Time is money," said Warburton, "and we don't like to waste either."

"This is it," said Ellen Wakefield as she clapped her hands together. "Those of you that wish to continue, please join us on the podium. You will not leave the facility until testing is complete, but you will leave with a cheque for ten thousand pounds. Those of you that don't, please make your way back to reception, where you can hand in your access pass with our thanks. We appreciate your time and thank you, again, for coming."

Charlie was almost knocked over when Jack leaped from his chair and jumped onto the podium. He swallowed heavily. "We're doing this now?"

Ellen Wakefield nodded. "No time like the present."

The chairs behind him scuffed across the floor as the two guys in the centre of the room rose and left through the main exit without looking back.

Simon stood, gave Lucas a wide berth and ambled towards the podium.

Joanna May smiled at Charlie and gestured towards him. 'Come on', she mouthed. 'There's nothing to be afraid of'.

Charlie took a deep breath and climbed the stairs onto the podium.

"Sweet," said Jack. "The Three Musketeers. I'm D'Artagnan."

"Four, actually," said John Warburton as he pointed to Lucas. The guards unshackled the huge man.

"He's coming, too."

Chapter 7

The group followed Ellen Wakefield off the podium, through the door to the left, past the assessment rooms, and through another door at the end of that corridor.

She carded them into a hallway flanked with more doors on either side.

The guards dragged Lucas through the first one and closed it.

Wakefield continued as if nothing had happened. "Okay, guys, for obvious reasons, we'll split you up again into separate rooms. In here, we'll hook you up to The Chip and monitor what goes on in your heads. Our systems will translate what you're thinking into code we can then analyse. It goes without saying, there is so much the mind can conjure, we won't be able to understand all of it off the bat, but that's part of the reason you're here. And, even though we can read the code, we won't be able to visually see what you can see."

"You're missing out there, girl," muttered Jack.

"Once you're done, we may ask you to explain what you

saw, what you imagined, and if you came across any glitches. Don't forget, this isn't the final version of Project MindSpace, but it's close. Once we iron out all the glitches, we'll be able to release it globally, and you'll all get a lifetime's access to it. By then, to answer your question, Jack, we should also have abilities enabled."

"Result!" said Jack. "So it wasn't just a rumour."

"What are abilities?" asked Charlie.

"Anything you can imagine," said David Collins. "The ability to fly, superhuman strength, telekinesis. You name it; if you can think it, you can do it. It is your world, after all."

"Isn't that dangerous? I'm no expert, but I'd say that's definitely open to abuse."

"Which is why the public version will be an enclosed environment," said Warburton. "If there's no one but you in there, how much damage to living things could you do?"

"The public version?" asked Charlie.

Ellen Wakefield pushed open a door. "Here we are. Best of luck, guys. Have as much fun as you can once you go Under, and remember as much as you can for when we bring you out. I can't wait to hear what you create." She pushed open a door. "Simon, you're in here, with David."

Simon brushed past everyone and entered the room. Before anyone else could see inside, David closed the door with a quiet click.

"Jack, this one is yours. You're with me."

Jack smiled as she continued. "And, Charlie, if you'll follow Joanna, she'll get you hooked up."

CHARLIE JUMPED as the chair reclined.

"I'm sorry," said Joanna with a giggle. "I should have

warned you. It's a bit like going to the dentist, I suppose; except, this visit will be fun."

"That's good," said Charlie. He placed his arms against the soft leather and let his head sink into an opening in the headrest.

"Try to relax. Applying The Chip is painless. In fact, the worst part is removing it; you might itch for a few minutes, like you do when you take off a plaster. The Chip is very sticky, but not in a way to pull out any hair, like a plaster would."

She leaned behind the chair and Charlie flinched as he felt a cool pressure against his neck.

"Nothing to worry about. I'm applying it now. It uses non-contact technology to access readings from your spinal column, so it's totally non-invasive. In a moment, I'll ask you to close your eyes. Once you do, you'll find yourself in which-ever world you've imagined.

"As they said in the presentation, it'll be made up of your direct thoughts, and information pulled from your subconscious. Whatever happens, it's your world. You have full control. There are other forms in there, some you can interact with, and some you can't, but none of them can harm you. When it's time, I'll pull you out. Try to remember as much as you can."

Charlie raised a hand and gave her a thumbs up.

"Nervous?" she asked.

"A little."

"Don't be. Once it goes public, people will do this for entertainment. You're getting paid for it. Ready?"

"I think so."

"Okay. Charlie, close your eyes."

COOL.

Everything was cool to the touch.

Charlie propped himself up on his elbows and looked around. A swathe of luscious green grass met a clear sky on the horizon, and he realised he lay, on his back, in the middle of a huge field.

Each blade of grass felt alive against his palms, each point of contact distinct against his skin. The blades around him swayed in a soft breeze. Leaves rustled to his left, and the scent of freshly mown lawns reminded him of warm summers from his youth.

In one fluid motion, Charlie got to his feet.

"Wow," he laughed, "it's been a while since I could do that. My knees didn't even crack."

He glanced down at a pristine pair of shining black dress shoes, then up past the razor-sharp pleats of midnight blue suit trousers, to a trim-fitted white shirt.

I wonder if I have a six-pack inside that, *he thought.* Hell, it's my world, I could have a twelve-pack!

The volume of the breeze dipped a little and, then, a voice spoke.

"Welcome, Charlie Green."

Charlie spun on the spot and searched the trees for signs of life.

"Hello?" he said. "I don't see you, where are you?"

"I am everywhere, Charlie Green."

Something about the voice sounded familiar.

"Yes, very cryptic," said Charlie. "If this is my world, I command that you show yourself."

"There is no call for any commands here, Charlie Green. I am your guide as you begin to understand and explore this world. You need only to ask."

"Okay, I ask that you show yourself."

"Sorry, I can't. You should think of me as a voice... voice... voice over..."

"Is everything okay?" asked Charlie. "Any more voices, and you'll be a conversation."

"The Guide is a work in progress. There are glitches. We are working on them but, for now, I am here… here… here to help. Do you like the way you are dressed?"

"Of course. I've always wanted to rock a suit."

"Subconsciously, this is how you would like to appear."

"And I feel fitter. Healthier."

"In Under, there is no illness, Charlie Green."

"Please, call me Charlie."

"I can do that, Me Charlie. This world is yours to interact with as you wish."

"No, not Me Charlie, just Charlie."

"Very well, Just Charlie. If you need my help, shout my name twice… twice…"

"Funny. I don't know your name."

"Yes, you do. John Warburton."

Charlie laughed. "Typical. They used the sales guy for the voiceover."

"Thank you for trying Project Mine… MindSpace …MindSpace … work in progress…"

The breeze returned, and Charlie did a slow pirouette to take in his surroundings.

"Since there's no one else here, I guess I can talk to myself," he said. "This place is awesome, Just Charlie."

He laughed and took off at a sprint into the treeline.

"I could run for hours," he shouted. His voice bounced back off the trees as he ran. Wind buffeted his hair while he considered the possibilities.

Amelia, *he thought.* I could imagine Amelia, and she would appear. I could be with her again.

A counterargument formed immediately.

Yes, you could. But only once. This one time. Could you cope with waking and there being no Amelia in the real world?

As the argument raged, a deep rumble and clattering came from the other side of the treeline. Charlie jogged through the maze of trees and skidded to a stop when he broke through the other side.

The ground dropped away and changed from vibrant green grass to a darker, muddier brown. At the base of the drop, bricks swirled in a whirlwind of dust. One by one, they crashed together until the beginnings of a wall formed.

"Am I doing this? Trying to block my own thoughts?"

The bricks blurred into a flurry of activity, and the wall grew upwards. Stained glass windows appeared, as well as a huge, arched doorway. The base of a roof formed, which tapered inwards until it reached a summit. Then, the last brick clunked into place, cement filled the cracks, and everything went quiet. Charlie stared at the building while a bell tower shimmered into shape at the peak of the roof.

He sat and dangled his legs over the edge of the drop. "Bloody hell. It's the church where I got married. Where did that come from?"

The bell chimed and vibrated rocks thirty feet beneath Charlie's feet.

"Am I supposed to go in there? John? Can you hear me?"

When no response came, Charlie peered over his knees at the ground below.

"Okay. This is my world. And even though it seems real, it isn't. It's all in my head. So, in theory…"

Wind took his breath as he pushed off the edge and plummeted to the ground. He landed with a soft thump, with his knees flexed, and his arms wide for balance. Small puffs of dust wrapped around each foot as Charlie strolled towards the building. Shapes moved behind the coloured glass and, as he grew closer, the buzz of conversation filtered through the door.

"That's weird. I don't remember that at my wedding," he said to himself. "To be honest, I don't remember that many people at my wedding. Kate didn't have that many friends."

He pushed open the door.

A narrow red carpet sat on a polished tile floor and crept up three steps before it disappeared into the distance. The entrance hall seemed endless. The same door was set into the left wall at intervals for the entire length of the hall until they, too, blurred out of sight.

Charlie stepped outside and jogged around to the side of the building. Front to back, it was about the same length as a dozen houses in the street at home. Back inside the entrance, the hall stretched to a fine tip and ended at a point in the distance that seemed miles away.

Dusty footprints followed him up the three steps and then faded until Charlie reached the first door. The handle felt warm to the touch. He turned it and stepped into a huge ballroom.

The buzz of conversation grew to a murmur and, now, he could hear the strains of soft orchestral music in the background. Crystal chandeliers hung from oak beams above a crowd of people that milled around, chatting and laughing. The tiled floor from the hallway continued into this room but changed to a chessboard of black and white squares. Each man wore a black tuxedo with a frilled white shirt, while the ladies swished and swayed in blinding white ballroom gowns. Charlie stepped closer to the clink of glasses, and the smell of fresh, toasted canapes.

A voice stopped him in his tracks.

"Hey, dude, check this out!"

Jack stood in the corner and gazed at the wall.

"Cool, isn't it? Damn, I wish I had abilities."

"They said we might bump into each other. Hello, Jack. What do you make of this building? And these people? Why are they dressed like this?"

Jack frowned and pointed to the wall. "Building? Dude, I'm on a beach. There's a mirror leaning against a palm tree here, and I look sick."

"You mentioned sick before. So, you're ill? I thought there was no illness here?"

"Ill? No, sick. Excellent."

"Sick means excellent? What kind of world is this? So, you don't see these people around us?"

"Dude, I'm surrounded by babes," said Jack. "and I'm so hot right now I'm creating my own humidity. My hair's frizzier than ever and, of course, the chicks dig it." He turned and faced the room. "I know, I know.

Form an orderly line, ladies, I'll get to you all in a moment. You can't rush perfection. Charlie, I'll have to get back to you, man. Heaven awaits."

Jack turned back towards the wall as the bell chimed again. Everyone in the room carried on as if nothing had happened but, in the far wall, another door appeared and swung slowly open.

Curious, Charlie threaded through the crowd, until he reached the door. A strange smell came from the room ahead and he jumped as something clanged.

"What the hell? Am I still doing this?"

He palmed open the door and gagged. The clanging sound came again as Lucas raised his arm and slammed a machete into the remains of a mangled corpse. Blood spatter and flecks of bone and tile flew into the air as the metal scythed through flesh and bounced back off the hard floor. He lifted his arm again, then paused and turned his head.

A chill swept through Charlie as Lucas looked him in the eyes and grinned a black toothed smile. A blood-soaked butcher's apron replaced his orange jumpsuit. He raised the machete, until its tip pointed at Charlie.

Charlie retreated into the ballroom and slammed the door closed. In the corner by the entrance, Jack still gestured to the wall.

Charlie joined him and tried to control his shaking hands.

"I don't know how, but I just saw into Lucas's world."

"They said there'd be glitches," said Jack. "Back off, man, I'm busy."

The crowd continued to mill around, oblivious to anything going on around them.

Charlie spotted Simon across the room as he raised an arm and pointed to the ceiling. His other arm wrapped around the shoulder of an attractive, dark haired woman dressed in a black cocktail dress. She followed his pointing finger, no doubt observing a UFO, or some other conspiracy.

Then, her image shimmered. Parts of her face faded and then reappeared. Simon continued explaining whatever they saw, and then smiled as the woman moved towards the door in the far wall. Charlie shuddered as he followed her through the door, and it closed behind them.

The bell chimed again.

Jack continued to gesture but, as the bell chime faded, the room fell silent. Charlie watched as the crowd slowed and then froze. Smiles paused in open mouths and cocktail glasses hovered with beads of condensation waiting on their sides to drip to the ground.

At the back of the room, the door opened again. Charlie braced himself to see Lucas and his bloodied machete, or Simon and his conquest. Instead, a stunning woman pulled the door closed behind her and sensually weaved her way through the crowd towards him.

Long, brown hair disappeared over the shoulder of an open-necked, red dress. Her legs formed perfect shapes through the fabric, and glistening blue eyes pierced his as she grew closer. Charlie's knees weakened when she smiled.

He turned to Jack. "Jack. Jack! Look!"

Jack ran his fingers through his hair and smiled at the wall.

When Charlie turned back, the woman was gone.

"Oh, come on, karma Gods," said Charlie. "After the shit I've been through, I deserve this."

The room moved again, as if invisible hands were winding it up. The sound returned, and Charlie stepped into the crowd and searched for the woman. In a room of black and white, a stunning woman in a red dress should be easy to find, but the room resembled an Othello convention, a world of positives and negatives with no hint of colour.

A young girl smiled at him before someone caught his arm. Excited, Charlie spun to come face to face with Lucas. Back in his orange overalls, he looked dangerous, but blood-free. His lips parted to show a row of rotted teeth, and the stench of decay made Charlie gag before Lucas gripped his arms. He lifted them as if he was about to hand over a baby.

"Got something for you."

Charlie's arms sagged as Lucas dropped something into them. The 'gift' weighed the same as a baby, but one end was a blooded stump. The other had five fingers, curled into a dying grip. Charlie recoiled and dropped the stolen limb to the ground.

"What the…"

As he fought the urge to scream, the bell chimed again and, in the blink of an eye, the room emptied. The black and white people shimmered out of existence to leave a chessboard of black and white that looked stark without its inhabitants. Charlie stared until Simon popped his head out from behind the door at the far end of the room and smiled before he disappeared again with a wink.

Charlie felt a breeze as something brushed across the back of his neck. His peripheral vision sensed red before a seductive voice whispered in his ear.

"That's enough. Wake up, Charlie."

____

Chapter 8

____

Joanna May jumped when Charlie moved in the chair. When she looked up from her monitor, his eyes snapped open and searched the room in confusion.

"Charlie, it's okay. You're back with us."

After a pause, he took a breath. "Wow. Talk about intense."

She tried to stay calm. "No kidding. Your readings were off the chart. What happened? And how come you're back so soon?"

"So soon? I must have been Under for an hour."

"Nowhere near. Ten minutes, to be precise."

"Ten minutes?" said Charlie. "How is that possible?"

"We're not sure, to be honest. It's something we're still researching, but we think it's something to do with the way your mind processes signals. In the real world, your senses will, well, sense something. They'll send a message to your brain, which will then process that message and interpret it.

"When you go Under, you're already in your mind which, basically, cuts out the middleman. All those signals are instantaneous since you're creating that world, so you can process information much quicker. Hence, you're able to experience as much, in your case in ten minutes, in Under as you would in an hour in the real world. A four-hour session would seem like a day."

"It was so realistic."

"That's the idea," said Joanna, "but it's also the idea we pull you out when your time's up. You shouldn't be able to do it yourself. Can you explain what happened?"

She took notes as Charlie recited his time in Under. Everything seemed comparable to what the previous test subjects had said, until he came to the girl.

"She was stunning," he said. "I've no idea who she was, but she was my ideal woman. Tall, slim, dark hair, red dress. I think she told me to wake up."

"She brought you out? Could it have been someone from your past?" said Joanna. "Or someone you may have seen somewhere?"

"No chance. I couldn't have imagined anyone as perfect. She told me to wake up, and here I am."

"She interacted with you? You didn't initiate the talking?"

"No. She looked me in the eyes from the other side of the room and came towards me. I turned to tell Jack but, when I turned back, she'd gone. Then, she reappeared right behind me, touched my neck, and told me to wake up. At least I think so, it all happened so quickly."

Joanna glanced at David Collins, who shrugged his shoulders. "Programming said the artificial intelligence would learn more from each visit."

"I'm aware of that, David, but they won't interact until approached. They don't initiate contact. Plus, no one in programming has mentioned a woman in a red dress. And certainly not one that could cause the subject to come out from Under. We control that. The way the coding spiked just before he woke suggests the AI is stronger than we…"

"Did I do something wrong?" said Charlie.

"No," she said. "I'm sorry, Charlie. We programmed the added characters to learn from each visitor to Under. It's impossible to code emotion, so the AI will develop that side of the project as it goes. And we're learning alongside it. That's the purpose of the test sessions; to assess the strengths and iron out the glitches."

"I saw a few glitches. The voiceover sounds as if he has a stammer, and some people don't seem solid, like they fade in and out. And, I hope it didn't learn much from Lucas. After what I saw in his world, I'd demand a refund if I'd paid for that session."

"Yes, I'm sorry you had to see that. Mr. Lucas has… issues, shall we say? Again, the crossover is something we're working on."

"So is that it?" said Charlie. "I'd love to try it again."

Disappointment lined his face and Joanna wished she could put him back Under. Instead, she leaned in and peeled The Chip away from his neck. "I'm sorry you were short-changed, but we need to collate the information from all four of you and compare it to our readings. As we said before, we're not sure of the long-term effects of this, so we didn't plan on multiple visits for the testers. The last thing we want to do is cause you any mental harm."

"I get ten grand for ten minutes' work?" said Charlie as he rubbed the back of his neck.

"Don't forget, you also went through the assessments," she said. "Perhaps you should consider it compensation for having to see into Lucas's world."

Charlie laughed. "It'll take over ten grand to make that go away."

He eased up and swung his legs out of the chair. Joanna took his hand and pulled him to his feet.

"If you sign out at reception, Ashleigh has a cheque waiting for you. Would you mind if we hung on to your contact details, just in case we need to get in touch? Data protection covers that part, so we'd have to shred them once you were done, otherwise."

"You get to keep the inner workings of my mind, but you can't keep my phone number?" smiled Charlie. "Of course. I'd give anything to meet that woman again."

"How about ten grand?" said Collins. Joanna turned to admonish him, but he smiled and shook Charlie's hand. "Just kidding. That's yours. Thanks for coming today."

Charlie turned at the door. "No, thank you," he said, "it's been entertaining." He pulled the door closed behind him.

As soon as it clicked shut, Joanna slammed her hand against the desk. Pins and needles shot up her arms, but her anger washed the sensation away. "Damn it, David, what are you trying to do? The servers still don't have complete security, and you're inviting back someone that almost crashed our equipment? Did you see those readings?"

"Of course, I did, I was sitting right beside you. I was joking, okay? After that, someone needed to lighten the mood. Jesus, I'm surprised the polygraph's needle isn't smoking. What the hell just happened?"

Joanna shook her head and gathered the ribbons of paper that had streamed from one of the machines. "I have no idea. We need to check with the others and find out if anyone else had a similar experience."

"And if they did?"

"Then, we need to do more testing, regardless of the dangers, security, or mental."

"Hey, don't fry the kid's brain. That'll be one hell of a lawsuit."

"Let's examine the readings first. The way his brain reacted, the program could have been written for him. No other subject meshed like that. I need to know why."

"Okay," said Collins. "Once the others finish, we can compare notes and then have a brainstorming session."

Joanna barely heard him. "The thing that concerns me most of all is the woman. Who the hell is she, and how was she able to bring our subject out from Under?"

Collins shrugged again. "Damned if I know. Like you said, let's check the readings and see."

"Hurry the others," she said. "Bring the subjects out early, if need be. I hate to admit it, but this scares the crap out of me."

CHARLIE SLID the cheque into his pocket and placed a hand over it for extra security.

Ten thousand pounds was a life-changing amount of money. The kind that could pay for a new car, or act as a deposit on a nicer place with proper parking and no garbage outside the front door.

He pulled it from his pocket and stared at it in silence, this time without the embarrassment of Ashleigh's giggle at his shaking hands. What Ashleigh didn't realise was that his hands shook from his experience in Under, not from the excitement of a large cheque.

The woman in the red dress was stunning and, since Jack hadn't seen her, she must have been meant for him. Charlie racked his brain and tried to pull anything from his subconscious that might have created her. Was she an actress from a film he'd seen, or a model from one of the reality shows on TV?

He drew a blank and smiled. Perhaps he should bank the cheque and leave the cash there for when Project MindSpace went live. Then, he could revisit his world and search for her. Based on what Joanna May had said, he could spend an entire day in there and let his imagination run riot.

He switched on his phone and slid it into his pocket, then pulled it out again when it chimed. A missed call message showed from Andy.

Charlie called him. "Hi, Bro. Everything okay?"

"Yep, how'd you get on? Did they inject any fresh brain cells?"

"Hilarious. It was amazing, and scary, at the same time. I met an incredible woman…"

"Listen," interrupted Andy. "I'm off for the afternoon, and out on a run. Want to meet, and you can tell me all about it? I can be at the bench in about five minutes if you fancy a chat?"

"Sure, but run slower. I can get there in about ten."

"Done."

Charlie climbed into his car, drove out of the ASP property, and headed into town.

Ten minutes later, he pulled into the park and rolled to a stop by the children's play area. A cloud settled over his mood as he walked up the hill and slumped onto a wooden bench. Andy appeared on the opposite side of the park and jogged to him, then sat and took a few breaths.

Charlie determined to cheer up. "It's no good for you."

Andy rested his arms against his knees until his breathing slowed. "What?"

"Exercise. Do you know how many people suffer heart attacks while exercising?"

"No clue."

"Me, neither, but I'm sure it's a lot. I do know how many people have heart attacks while they're in the pub, though. Not many. You should stop running and have a pint instead. It's safer."

"You can be such a prat." Andy shook his head and gestured towards the play area. "Still come here a lot, then?"

Charlie looked across the park at the winding concrete path, bordered by the bushes Amelia vanished into.

"I'm down to once a week, now. Trying to ween myself off. Every time I come here, I still hope I had a bad dream and she'll come running up the path. Or she'll stick her head through the bushes and tell me we were playing hide and seek, and I lost. But it's real, Bro, and I definitely lost."

"I wish there were answers. Or even a clue who took her. Just some kind of closure."

"The only closure I want is to have my little girl back. It's the not knowing that kills me. I keep asking, *Why me? What did I do to deserve this?* I've spent my entire life trying to do the right thing and, in return, life takes a huge dump on me from a great height."

Andy wrapped an arm around him. "Give it time, Bro."

"I've given it three frigging years, Andy, and it still feels as raw now as it did on day one."

"Don't forget, I'm always here for you. So are Mum and Dad. Did you ring them, by the way?"

"Not yet. Haven't had time since we last spoke, with taking part in the research program." Charlie mentally shook himself. "Speaking of which, a new start. Positive thoughts."

"Yeah, whatever. So what's this research about, then?"

"I can't say too much. Signed a confidentiality clause, but it's something Nick's place is working on, a kind of virtual world where anything you imagine appears in your head, but it's like you're there, living it. They connect you to servers that work with your brain…"

"So much for your clause. And they found your brain? I didn't think Nick was such a high-flyer. Having said that, it's been so long since I've seen him, I doubt I'd recognise him."

Charlie smiled and landed a playful punch. "I met someone while I was Under."

"Under what? And who'd you meet? Like a scientist person?"

"Under is what they call the place you're in once you're connected. And, no, not a scientist person. I don't know who she was, but stunning doesn't come close to describing her. She appeared in my imagination and singled me out from across a room. I'd love to take her to dinner and get to know her."

"Ah, so not real, then."

"Well…" said Charlie.

"So when you say met, you mean fantasised about."

"Well…"

"Why don't you fantasise about a clean flat and see if that comes true?"

"Bloody hell, will you give me a break? I haven't felt this positive in ages. And check this out."

Charlie leaned to one side and pulled the cheque from his pocket.

Andy whistled. "Wow! I'm getting dizzy. Am I counting the correct number of zeroes on that thing?"

"I know. For half a day's work."

"Any jobs going at your place?" said Andy. "I struggle to make about double that in a year."

"They said there might be risks with having the servers communicate with your brain; that's why it's a lot of money but, to be honest, I feel better than ever. I'd go back in a heartbeat. For free."

"Because you might find a hot scientist chick? Your motives are strong, Bro. So, what's next? Spoon bending? Teleportation?"

Charlie ignored his brother's sarcasm. "A visit to the bank is next. I'm terrified I might lose this cheque."

"I'm terrified I might jump you and steal it," said Andy. "Don't forget, I can forge your signature."

"Funny. I'll bank this, then go home and start looking for a job. I've got a bit of a buffer now, and I'm more confident about the future. She ignored Jack…"

"Who? And who's Jack?"

"Oh, the girl in the project. Jack's a dick, one of the other candidates. She ignored him and came straight to me."

"Of course, she did, because you look like Brad Pitt. Meanwhile, back on planet Earth…" said Andy.

Charlie stood and clapped his brother on the back. "Come on, give your brother a hug. Then, I'm off to the bank."

Andy wrapped his arms around Charlie. "I worry about you, you know? Look after yourself. You going home after the bank?"

"Probably," said Charlie, before he smiled. "Unless I go for a quick pint first."

Chapter 9

"Charlie completed the assessments."

"He did? Damn, what were the other candidates like?"

Nick kicked his work shoes beneath the coffee table and laid back into the plush sofa.

"Come on, now, no need to be like that. I don't know too much, but he's a good guy, and he seems to be made for what they want."

She reclined and sank into the other sofa with a mug of steaming coffee. "And what do they want? Mindless monkeys that will do their bidding?"

"You're mean," said Nick. "I don't know the intricacies of the research, but it takes a certain type of person to accept the program. Someone not too hung up on themselves. There's a lot of peripheral activity that goes with MindSpace that some people don't seem able to connect with."

"Those are some long, complicated words, darling," she smiled. "I like it. So come on. How did he do?"

"His readings were off the chart. To be fair, it's still early in the testing, but his reactions to the program were the strongest they've seen so far. The other candidates connected, but not in the way Charlie did."

"And what makes him so different? I don't understand how it all works and, since you'll only tell me half the story…"

"You know, I'm sworn to secrecy, babe. Need to know, and all that."

"I know, and I don't want you to have to kill someone…"

"Not today."

"No, not today. But, since I don't know all the details, I'm having to fill in the blanks for myself. Why would Charlie connect any better than the others?"

"Open-mindedness, I guess," said Nick. "Some people are too full of themselves. I don't have full access to the research, I'll just tweak the program when suggestions are raised and make sure it operates to its full capability before we move it to the next stage."

She smiled again. It had taken months for her to allow it to happen, and it still didn't happen often enough. When it did, he worked to make it last as long as possible. "Peripheral activity. Capability. I love it when you talk dirty," she said. "Those long words get my motor running."

Nick smiled back at her, stood, and crossed the room before he knelt on the floor before her. He pushed his body between her knees. "Do they, now? And what happens when the motor's running?"

"Oh, you know," she said. "Things tend to move quickly from one thing to the next. And it's a motor, so things could get messy. Without a good mechanic, things could get really out of hand."

He leaned back and stroked her leg, starting at her calf before he worked his hand up to between her thighs. "Messy and out of hand, huh? And what happens when things get messy, or out of hand?"

She giggled and pushed her foot against his chest. He fell backwards onto the thick rug that lay in front of the gas fire, before she slid his car keys to one side and put her mug on a coaster, left the sofa, and straddled him. "When things get messy, someone has to clean up. Are you man enough to clean up?"

When she pressed her lips to his, the taste still seemed forbidden, but its sweetness lifted him above the world.

"Oh, so now I'm your house bitch?" he said.

She bit his lower lip and pressed her body harder against his. "You're my bitch. Let's leave it at that."

Nick laid his arms back in surrender. "Coming from a place where you can be anything you like, I can cope with that."

"And this Charlie fella. Who's he?"

"Charlie?" said Nick. "Charlie who?"

"That's what I'm talking about. Why don't you take me upstairs, programmer boy, and do some coding of your own?"

"How complicated would you like it to be?" he said. "Code comes in many ways."

He shuddered with excitement when she leaned in and the tip of her nose touched his.

"I couldn't care less. So do I."

Chapter 10

Charlie woke the next morning to the annoying chirp of his phone. He rolled over and fumbled for it before squinting to make out the number. The time read 7:30, and the words, *Unknown Number* stretched beneath it. At the second attempt, he answered the call.

"Hello?"

"Charlie Green?"

The cheery voice sounded familiar.

"Yes, who's this? It's really early."

"I'm sorry about that," said the voice. "This is Ashleigh, from ASP, calling on behalf of Joanna May."

Charlie snapped awake, slid a pillow up the headboard and followed it until he rested upright. "Morning, Ashleigh. It's no problem, I woke a while ago."

A smile sounded in her voice at the obvious lie. "That's good. Joanna got the impression you enjoyed your time during the research and wanted to ask if you'd like to come back?"

Goosebumps rushed up and down his arms as his stomach

tumbled. He swung his legs over the edge of the bed. "Really?"

"There's no more funding, so we can't pay anything extra. And you'd have to sign another agreement to waive any additional risks, but The Chip is yours to try again, if you'd like to."

"I'd love to. What time would I need to get there?"

"Well, as you might have gathered, we don't hang around, so come along whenever you like. The team is here all day. The sooner you get here, the longer you can stay."

Charlie swung his legs out of bed, then leaned against the wall when he stood too quickly. The previous night's beer sat like a weight in his stomach. "Cool. I'll be right there."

"Great. Sign in at reception, just like before. Look forward to seeing you."

The phone went silent as Ashleigh disconnected the call.

Charlie yelled out a, 'Yes!' and padded to the bathroom.

———

WITH THE ABSENCE of rush-hour traffic, he reached the facility in no time.

He pulled into the same parking space and strode through the entrance to reception. Ashleigh slid a folder of papers across the counter.

"You just need to sign these. Feel free to read them. They explain the additional risks, since you'll be the first person to use the technology twice. Joanna says it's kind of unchartered territory."

Charlie whipped out the pages and scribbled a signature without reading the notes. "You guys run a well-oiled machine. I trust you."

Ashleigh smiled at his confident wink and handed over a

key card. "Here you go, then. I guess you know the drill. Have fun."

"Thanks, Ashleigh. I intend to."

He swiped through the door and breezed past the interview rooms to the second door. The panel buzzed like an angry wasp when he held the card to it. He tried again, but it still glared a solid red.

Through the small window, a door in the next corridor opened. David Collins leaned out, smiled, and mouthed, "Be right there."

Collins opened the door and held it for Charlie. "Sorry about that. We trained Ashleigh to be security conscious. I doubt she considered your entry past the first door."

"No problem, I'm grateful to be asked back."

"Believe me, it's our pleasure. Please, follow me."

Charlie followed Collins along the corridor. The door to the room he left was ajar, and Charlie glanced inside. Two technicians in white coats hunched over a console, their backs to the door. The dusty odour of warm machinery seeped through the doorway, and a bank of monitors beeped and flashed, *'Upload Complete'* in unison.

Collins pushed open the final door into the room Charlie had used before. "Might as well have you in a familiar chair," he said. "Please, step inside."

He stood aside, and Charlie entered the room to find Joanna May sitting behind the chair. Ellen Wakefield sat beside her. She stood and offered a hand.

"Charlie, thanks for coming back."

"It's my pleasure," he said, "but I thought the trial was a one-off?"

"We thought so, too, but the program seems to have taken a liking to you. None of the other candidates connected the way you did and, even though we think we know why, we'd still like you to go Under again so we can continue to assess your readings. We got more information than expected in the initial session so, as long as you're okay with it, we don't want to waste the opportunity to take a few leaps forward."

"Of course not, I'm fine. But what do you mean about the other candidates? How come they didn't make the same connection? They looked as involved as me when I saw them."

"They connected in their own worlds, that was bound to happen. But they were too self-absorbed, and so weren't as susceptible to the outside programming as you were. Being so focussed on what they wanted, rather than exploring the program, they missed so much."

"You mean, like the woman in red? What if my subconscious created her?"

"We're convinced it didn't. While we can't physically see what you see, the whole event was out of place and very distinctive. We recognised the code. You found the Hope program."

"Hope?"

"Yes, that's the character's name. Hope seems to have singled you out. The artificial intelligence is programmed to learn from each visitor since there are attributes we can't create purely from code. Hope is our special character, one we can focus on and monitor. Her code is specific to the system, and it leaped out when you met her. She has privileges the other characters don't. We'd like you to interact with her again, so we can assess her development."

"Believe me," said Charlie, "to say it would be a pleasure would be the understatement of the century."

"Great. Would you like to get started right away?"

"Send me Under," grinned Charlie.

"And you're okay with having the three of us in the room?" said Joanna May.

"I don't mind at all. Anything I can do to help."

"Okay, let's hook you up."

Charlie unbuttoned his shirt and lay back in the chair while Joanna stuck pads to his chest and temples. Their wires led from him into the back of equipment that looked like a small mixing desk. A thick cable led from that and branched out into various monitors.

She followed his gaze. "If you ever did any old-school sound mixing, you'd have called that cable a multicore."

"The only old school sounds I know are my Oasis CDs," laughed Charlie.

"This might be a little more developed. And I owe you an apology. I didn't explain any of this to you on your first visit." Joanna tapped the thick cable. "Inside this sheathing is the means to relay all of your vital signs to our equipment. Where we used to have a network of cables, we now only need one."

"If that covers my vitals, how can you see what happens in my mind?" asked Charlie.

"For as close as we are here, a combination of good old-fashioned Bluetooth and Wi-Fi does the job. The Chip interacts with our servers and works as a two-way channel. It sends information into your mind, based on what you send out of it. By the time MindSpace is complete, and goes global, we'll have the capability to use satellites, just like your phone. The Chip will be portable, and something you could apply from anywhere. Through subscriptions, we'll still be able to monitor access and allocate blocks of time per user."

"I never thought of it like that," said Charlie. "When you say global, you really mean global."

"Absolutely. The applications are endless. Which is why we value your data. There's much to learn, but the readings coming from your mind surpass everything we expected."

"It's been a while since I felt useful to anyone. Glad to be of assistance"

Charlie felt Joanna's hand rest on his shoulder. "You're sure you want to go Under again?"

"Certain," said Charlie.

Joanna reached back and picked up The Chip. "Very well. Let's get to it."

ANOTHER FIELD.

No, the same field, with the same freshly mown smell and rustle of leaves broken by trilling birdsong.

But a different time.

Charlie rested his arms on a heavy oak table and looked around at a luscious green expanse and the thick treeline to his left. Beyond the trees lay the church where he first saw Hope.

This time, the field wasn't empty.

He sat at a wooden dining table. A silver candelabra filled its centre and glistened in the sunlight. More silver sparkled on each side of it; place settings rested on red napkins, with tall-stemmed wine glasses waiting to be filled.

A table set for two.

Charlie smiled and thanked his subconscious, then slid back his chair. Somehow, it moved across the grass and he stood, ready to go to the church to find Hope. Then, they could return for a romantic dinner.

Then, he remembered Lucas and his machete and dropped back into his seat.

If his subconscious had set up this potential meeting with Hope, what if Lucas's subconscious had set up something similar in his world? And, since his world had collided with Charlie's on the first visit, what if Lucas had plans for Charlie?

No. Hope was worth the risk.

He turned left and studied the trees, checking between the thick trunks for signs of life. When nothing appeared, he turned back.

Hope stood beside him.

Cutlery clinked as he jumped and nudged the table. "Damn. I'm sorry. You startled me."

Hope smiled as Charlie's heart hammered a staccato rhythm against his chest. Her hair hung over her shoulder in a ponytail which left her face full, and exposed. Slight dimples bookended a stunning smile while twin suns reflected in her eyes. Golden orange blazed in the centre of swirling blue pools that drew him in. She wore a white apron over a black, frilled blouse, while perfect legs filled out a tight black skirt that finished just above her knees.

She reached into a pocket. "Greetings, Charlie. Would you like to see the wine menu?"

Hope's voice purred like the cutest kitten. Each word raised familiar goose bumps that coursed up and down Charlie's arms. In an instant, he forgot the entire English language. His tongue stuck to the roof of his mouth and he managed nothing more than a confused mumble, followed by, "You know my name."

"Of course, and it's okay," she said, "you don't need to speak. I know exactly what you want."

She placed the menu on the table and walked behind him, trailing a finger across his shoulder. Charlie tried to turn to follow her, then stopped and shuddered as her touch brushed his neck. When he turned back to the table, she had taken the seat in front of him.

"Do you like what you see?"

The ponytail had gone, replaced with loose hair that framed her face. A strapless red top replaced the waitress uniform. Charlie had no idea what lay beneath the table, but his heart threatened to burst from his chest at the thought.

Hope rested her chin against her clasped hands and grinned before she gestured at the landscape. "Here, I mean. Our surroundings."

"I do," he said. "It's beautiful. Peaceful and clean, not like home."

"Do you not like your home?"

"No. It's dirty, and there are too many people and cars."

"Here can be whatever you want it to be. We can work together, if you like. To make this world perfect for you. Am I dressed to your liking?"

"You are," said Charlie. "Hope, you're beautiful."

"Thank you, Charlie. And do you like my name?"

Charlie stared at her smile, and her full lips that glowed a brilliant red. "I do. It suits you. Am I making you look like that?"

"What do you think? This is your world but, then, I am also me."

"I don't understand. And how come no one else can see you? You seem so real. Human. Your voice is perfect."

"I am real," said Hope. She sat back and put her hands between her thighs. Charlie glimpsed a black skirt over bare legs. "And you can see me because I trust you."

"How can you trust me? We've just met. You know nothing about me."

"My dear Charlie, I know more than you can imagine."

A hint of worry gnawed at Charlie's stomach. "How is that possible? I thought I saw projections of my thoughts, and my subconscious. How can you be real, and how can you know me?"

Hope leaned forward and placed her elbows on the table. "Close your eyes, Charlie, count to three, and then open them."

Charlie closed his eyes while his nerves settled. When he opened them, a full plate of food lay before him. Steak and chips, his favourite meal. A bottle of uncorked wine sat, wedged at a tilt, in a silver decanter. A single drop of condensation ran down its side and vanished into the ice.

Hope picked up her fork. "What you see is real. Go ahead, cut into your steak."

Charlie sliced through the meat and put the steak on his tongue. His mouth flooded with saliva as the flavour hit his senses. "Oh, my God."

Hope giggled. "No, Charlie. Not yet. I'm still Hope."

Charlie chewed and swallowed. "No, that's a saying we use to express delight at something. In the real world."

Hope reached across the table. "This should be your real world. Take my hand, Charlie."

He reached across, and Hope entwined her fingers with his. Sweat pricked his palms as her touch stroked his skin.

"Do I not feel real?"

Charlie studied her slender fingers, each tipped with a manicured red nail. Then, he glanced up into her eyes. She held a fierce gaze that seemed to penetrate his core as if she could read his thoughts.

"You do. All of this is so real, it's scary."

"Don't be scared, Charlie, you have nothing to fear," said Hope.

"No, that's another phrase we…never mind. Hope, what do you want from me? I mean, there must be something if you're showing yourself to me like this." He tried to shake the confusion from his head. "God, I don't even know what I'm saying."

"I like you, Charlie. You are genuine, not like others that have been here."

"Others? Oh, like Jack and Lucas?"

"I want full honesty between us," said Hope, "and I believe you are honest. I will never hurt you."

Charlie frowned. "Hurt me?"

"Yes. Like your wife hurt you."

It took a moment for the words to register before Charlie's stomach took a full tumble. "I… How do you….?"

Hope squeezed his hand. "Don't worry, Charlie. Or be scared. You are full of kindness, a good person. Do you like games, Charlie?"

Confusion returned as Charlie tried to process Hope's words. "What? What kind of games?"

"Good games. I ask questions, you answer them and, at the end, if you're really good, I'll reward you."

Hope batted her eyelashes and stroked the back of his hand. The confusion settled as Charlie wondered what the reward could be. He considered her question. "Like an interrogation?"

"Yes, that could be one game. And pretending. Next time we meet, let's pretend we are a real couple."

"I could definitely play that game," said Charlie.

Hope clapped her hands with excitement and stood. Her red top finished six inches above the waistband of her skirt. A flash of tanned, toned skin took Charlie's breath away, before he noticed that she wore no shoes. Her bare feet sank into the grass as she walked around the table towards him.

"No, forget that." Her voice buzzed with excitement. "Let's pretend that we've just met. We want each other so much that the rest of the world doesn't exist, so it's just us. Oh, I don't know. Okay, let's make it up as we go along. That's what you need to figure out; what kind of game we are playing."

"Hope, I don't understand."

"You need to work it out." She walked behind him and leaned into him. He could feel her warm breath on his neck. "And, then, you must come back to me. Now, wake up, Charlie."

Chapter 11

"How can those readings be so erratic and yet there be no sign of cardiac arrest? How is that possible?"

Joanna glanced at the monitor that displayed Charlie's vital signs. The pulse of his heartbeat raced up and down like the rhythm of a rave party. She patted David Collins on the shoulder and sat beside him.

"Calm down, David. Only dogs can hear you when you speak like that."

Collins pointed to another screen. "But look at the code. There is no way it can move at that speed and still process accurately. I can see the Hope program at work, and I can see where he's projecting, but it still seems like too much information. How are the servers handling that amount of traffic without melting down?"

Ellen Wakefield leaned into the conversation. "Because we designed them to handle this and more. David, imagine how the code will appear when MindSpace goes global. And this is a small part of the program. It's exactly what I hoped for, if you'll pardon the pun. I suspect the AI is learning from Charlie's mind at a quicker rate than any of us anticipated. It really is quite fascinating. Joanna, did Charlie sign the papers?"

Joanna nodded.

"Good. It may be worth keeping him Under for as long as possible. There's so much valuable data here, we could advance the other program to completion ahead of time. Then, we can apply for full funding and launch ahead of schedule."

David Collins sat between the two women, looked back and forth between them, and gestured towards the chair. "Ellen, we have no idea of the risks. His eyelids are dancing like he's the bionic man switching between sleep cycles."

Charlie's body rested in the chair, every muscle relaxed, except his eyelids. His eyes flicked from side to side beneath them. His eyelashes bounced and fluttered, as if they were sending rapid Morse-code signals, opening at random to expose orbs of pure white.

"We both know he's not asleep," said Ellen. "Mentally, he's not even in the room. This is nothing more than a natural reaction to the activity in his mind."

"Well, then, look at his heart rate," said Collins. "If it elevates any further, I'm bringing him out. This can't be safe."

Joanna shrunk into her chair as Ellen turned and fixed Collins with a glare that silenced him. "You'll do no such thing. I respect your work, David, but there's much more at risk than what happens in this room. If you don't wish to be a part of this, the door is right behind you. I suggest you use it."

Collins ground his teeth. "Very well. But I'd like my objections noted."

"We have more than enough notes in here already," said Ellen, "but I've heard you, okay?"

Before Collins could answer, they jumped as Charlie's legs stiffened, and the heels of his shoes squeaked against the chair.

Joanna thanked the interruption, grateful for the break in arguments. The tension between the lead project manager and the man a step beneath her had gone from acute to palpable.

Charlie's eyes snapped open.

"Well, I'll be damned," said Ellen. "It's happened again. I read about the first occurrence in your report and thought, perhaps, an outside influence had woken him. But, unless he's tuned in to raised voices and bad attitude…"

"No, it's identical to last time. He came from Under without our help."

Charlie twisted in the chair and raised an arm. "Hello? I'm right here."

Joanna stood and moved to the rear of the chair. "Sorry, Charlie. Hold tight a sec, and I'll remove The Chip."

Ellen wouldn't wait. "Charlie, we saw some extreme readings I'd like to ask you about but, first, tell us how you woke? The program is written so we have to bring you out. You're not supposed to do it for yourself."

"I didn't," said Charlie. "Hope woke me."

Ellen glanced at Joanna, who shrugged her shoulders.

"You're telling me that an AI, with limited interactive skills, overrode our core program?"

Charlie smiled. "I'm not sure about limited interactive skills. I'd say her skills are spot on."

"Explain," said Ellen after she frowned. "What happened in there?"

Charlie waited until Joanna had removed The Chip before he spoke. "From the beginning?"

"It's a very good place to start," smiled Collins.

"Okay. When I opened my eyes, I stood in a huge field, the same one I woke in the first time I went Under. I recognised the trees and remembered that I met Hope in a building on the other side of them."

"That's good," said Joanna. "Your mind retained the information, and the setting, from your first visit and allowed you to begin where you left off."

"But, then, I remembered I met Lucas there, too."

"You needn't worry about Lucas," said Ellen. "You won't be seeing him again."

"At last," said Joanna, "you finally sent him back. The man scared the life out of me."

Ellen paused for a moment and glanced away before she spoke. "Another department took care of Mr. Lucas. Charlie, please continue. I assume you were happy to pick up where you left off?"

"Of course. And, it gets better," said Charlie with a smile. "I mentioned to my brother I'd like to take Hope to dinner…"

"You know she's not real, right?" said Collins. "We programmed her, and you're embellishing her with thoughts from your subconscious."

"Maybe, but that bit's weird because, when I was Under, she insinuated she was real. I can dream but, at least, this time, when I woke, there was a dining table with place settings for two."

"So your subconscious set up a date for you," said Joanna.

"Yes. And I didn't need to search for Hope, either. As I looked around, she appeared beside me, dressed as a waitress."

"Odd choice, to have your date as a waitress," said Collins.

"Just to begin with. She walked behind me and brushed against me and, then, when I turned back to the table, she sat opposite me. A bottle of wine appeared, and we started talking."

"Did she initiate the conversation?" asked Ellen.

Charlie thought for a moment. "No, I think I started it, but she asked me if I liked what I saw."

"Based on your readings," said Collins, "it's safe to say you said, 'Yes.' "

"Of course. She looked stunning."

Joanna smiled as Ellen fidgeted with impatience. "Go on, Charlie," she said. "What happened next?"

"She said she wanted to play games."

Joanna glanced at Collins and then at Ellen. They both wore the same expression of surprise. "Hope asked you to play games? Are you sure you didn't ask her? This is your world, after all."

"Unless that's what Charlie wanted," said Ellen.

"It caught me off guard, to be honest. And she knew things about my life I've not mentioned to many people, and definitely to no one since I've been here."

"Don't forget, your mind is linked to the program once you're in Under," said Joanna. "It seems the AI is more inquisitive than we suspected, and a lot stronger. Are you comfortable to discuss what type of games she suggested?"

Joanna smiled again as Charlie blushed. "Nothing like that, at least, not yet."

"Not yet?"

"She wants me to figure out what game we're playing and then go back Under."

Joanna's smile vanished. "Hold on a second. The AI asked you to go back?"

Charlie nodded. "Is that a bad thing?"

"That would depend on whether your subconscious wanted her to ask you back, or she did it independently. The code was too fast for us to follow clearly, and there's so much of it that it'll take a while to get through. The idea of the AI making requests that go further than a single session is intriguing, though. That opens up all kinds of possibilities."

"And would you like to go back?" asked Ellen.

"Of course, I would. I'd like to spend a whole day in there."

Collins leaned forward in his seat and clasped his hands between his knees. "Charlie, don't forget that we haven't tested the program this far before. We don't know what risks that may hold."

Ellen glared at Collins. "If any," she said. "You signed the release papers, right?"

Charlie nodded.

"Then it's up to you. If you'd like to go back Under, say the word."

"The word," said Charlie.

Joanna grimaced and reached for The Chip.

NICK SPUN on his chair until he faced a whiteboard that took up a third of the office's rear wall.

Its surface looked like the interior of an abattoir, with splashes of colour raked across the clinical white. Every small square indicated a day that had an important event noted within it, hastily scribbled in blood red pen.

"Busy weeks ahead," he said to himself as his phone chirped an annoying sound. He spun back and pressed a flashing button.

"Yes?"

A stressed voice spat out a clipped message. "Sorry to bother you, sir, but David Healey from the Ministry of Defence is on line one."

Nick reclined in his chair. "Thank you, Julie. I'll take it in here."

"I'll pass him through."

He waited until a faint click signalled a connected call. "This is Nick Cumberland. Can I help you?"

Nick smiled to himself. After many cabinet meetings, he knew David Healey to be a beast of a man. At over six feet tall, with the shoulders of a lumberjack and the ruddy face of someone who drank way too much whiskey, he liked to think he could bully his way through every conversation and encounter.

"Don't give me that self-important crap, Cumberland," said Healey. "I know damned well that bimbo of a receptionist told you I was holding. The powers that be are chomping at the bit, and pushing for updates. So, update me."

Nick's smile grew into a full grin. After months of having to pander to Healey's bullying tactics while MindSpace got up and running, he now had the politician begging for information that would further his career. "David? Great to hear from you. We're all doing well, thanks for asking. How about you? How's life behind the big desk?"

"No one gives a shit about how I'm doing," said Healey, "not even my bloody wife. Your project, however, is keeping me awake at night. What kind of progress have you made? The damned Russians are hacking every bugger's computer while we're sitting around, sipping Earl Grey tea. Tell me you've got something important I can take back to the board room."

"Earl Grey tastes like perfume," said Nick as he bit his knuckles to contain a laugh that burst to escape. "We're not drinking that." He slid papers aside to reveal the results of Charlie's latest tests. "To calm your quaking nerves, David, we've had a major breakthrough in testing."

"You're going to make me ask, aren't you? I'm sure you loathe politicians; I can tell by the way you patronise me."

"Yes, I do," said Nick, "but I'll put you out of my misery.

Our AI has already taken a form of sentience. Asking questions, leading conversations, and pushing thoughts."

"That's the bit that intrigued me during your presentation," said Healey. "Pushing thoughts. So has your AI had your test subjects doing things against their will?"

Annoyance raised Nick's body temperature a few degrees. "That's not the idea, David, and you know it. She's started to take the lead on encounters, and we're monitoring the code to see how she adapts to different situations. She is becoming more proficient at reading her subject, and presenting herself in a way that puts her in control."

Healey paused for a moment, and Nick checked to see the light still flashed on his phone. Finally, the politician spoke.

"That's all well and good, Nick, I'm sure it's all sparkles and roses. The important question, however, is how are you getting along with adapting the damned thing to military applications?"

Chapter 12

Mum and Dad stared back from one of those pictures where the eyes followed every movement.

Charlie turned away from the framed photograph, kicked himself for not calling them, and checked out the room.

Of all the places I would have brought me, he thought, this isn't one.

But it still seemed familiar.

He sat on an uncomfortable plastic chair that faced a large desk. An identical, but empty chair waited beside him. The back of an old computer monitor perched on the nearest edge of the faux-wood desk, while a much more appealing seat nestled behind it. Certificates hung in a laser-perfect line on the back wall. Charlie craned his neck to read them.

Mike Zeferino. Mortgage Adviser of the Year.

The dates on each covered a five-year period. The oldest gave Charlie the clue that jolted his memory.

Two years before their marriage, he and Kate had sat in this room to arrange their first mortgage.

Behind him, a matching shelved cabinet with glass doors filled the wall. Volumes of thick books and plastic binders covered each shelf.

When Charlie turned back, Hope sat behind the desk.

"Greetings, Charlie."

Her hair was teased up high into a bun while brown-rimmed glasses accentuated her eyes and served to emphasise their vivid colour. The top two buttons of a white blouse showed a teasing glimpse of tanned, smooth skin, while a black, tight-fitted suit gave Hope the appearance of a high-flying businesswoman.

Despite the strange situation and the tremble of his nerves, he trusted this woman, but still took a moment to calm his breathing before he spoke.

"Hello, Hope. Why am I here? I thought this was my world to create?"

"Do you like how I look, Charlie?"

Charlie shifted in the seat and tried to get comfortable. "Always. Hope, you're incredible."

She gripped a red pen between glistening white teeth, reached up and pulled a pin from her hair. It tumbled to her shoulders in long tails until she shook her head to loosen it.

Charlie's heart rate doubled as it settled around her.

"How about now?" she said.

For the second time in Under, Charlie forgot all words and gaped at her.

"I'll take that as your answer," she smiled. "So why are we here?"

"I recognise this room. Am I here to buy a house?"

Hope laughed. Shivers of pleasure coursed through his body at the sound. She stood, pushed back the chair, and crept around the desk towards him.

"You don't need to own anything here." When she slid onto the corner of the desk, her skirt rode up to reveal black-stockinged legs. "You can have anything you like, just think it. Now, try again. Think back to our previous meeting."

Charlie tried to focus as the heat from Hope's body reached him. Her perfume tingled his senses, a musky smell that tickled the back of his nostrils.

"Why are we here, Charlie?"

"To play games?"

Hope slid off the desk and whispered in his ear. The rush of hot breath raised the hairs on his neck. "Yes. Just play along."

She leaned back, winked, and spoke in a sterner voice. "Precisely. Now, does this room look familiar?"

"Yes. It took a moment to figure out, but it's the room where my ex-wife and I got the mortgage for our first home."

"And how do you feel about being here again?"

"Nervous, at first, but now I can place it I feel nothing."

Hope slid back onto the corner of the desk. "And how about back then?"

Charlie shook his head.

"Don't lie, Charlie. Or hold things back. I will know. How did you feel?"

"Unsure. I didn't want to buy the first house we saw, I wanted to see others before we took the plunge."

"So why didn't you?"

"I don't remember," said Charlie.

In a flash of movement, Hope stood before him. She took the pen from her mouth and placed its damp end against the tip of his nose. Warmth from the moisture of her lips heated Charlie's skin. When she spoke, excitement forced goose bumps along his arms.

"Yes, you do. Lie again, Charlie, and you will be punished."

Charlie stifled a laugh. "Hope, this is my world. And what do you mean, punished? Is that something I should get excited about, or are you going to put me in detention?"

"Would you like a demonstration?"

Long lost feelings hinted at desire in the pit of his stomach, and he leaned back in the chair. "I think I would."

"It might hurt," said Hope. "Are you sure?"

"There is no pain in this world, Hope. I'm up for trying whatever you can offer."

Charlie frowned as Hope's face stiffened. Her pupils dilated before a blast of shock ripped from his neck and coursed into his feet.

He jolted in the chair and stood. Pins and needles stabbed at his legs, and pulses of pain chased up and down his spine while he clenched and unclenched his fists. He sat back into the chair with a thump.

"Jesus Christ, Hope, what the hell was that?"

"I warned you," she said. "It would be easier to play the game."

Charlie pushed into the back of the chair as the throb in his spine eased. "What did you do?"

"Don't be nervous, Charlie. I..."

"Don't be nervous? Hope, you just shocked me. Of course, I'm going to be nervous." He massaged his thighs. "Damn, that hurt."

"Then, keep playing," said Hope with a cheery grin. "It's easier that way."

"What if I don't want to play? What if I want to wake up now?"

Hope scratched red-painted nails across his knee. "Do you still like the way I look?"

"Yes, I already..."

"See?" she said. "That was easy, wasn't it? Now, you do remember so answer the question."

"What's the point, when you already have the answer?" said Charlie.

Pain knifed into him again as another shock burst fire into every nerve along his spine. His legs tensed, and he fought a cramp that formed in his calves.

"Hope..."

She raised her eyebrows.

"Okay," he shouted, "It scared me."

"That's better. Now, why were you scared?"

Charlie squirmed in the chair. No longer in control, worry and doubt flooded his mind.

"I was always scared. I couldn't do or say anything right. I answered every question with the wrong answer and I couldn't work out why. I had no clue what I was doing wrong."

Hope leaned against her thighs and steepled her fingers like a thera-pist. "So something simple like showing an opinion on a movie or a TV show would provoke rage in the female?"

Charlie nodded, his voice reduced to a whine. "Yes. See? You already know."

"I want to hear it from you, to gauge your reaction. That's the game, Charlie."

"Then, I don't like this game."

Hope's eyes widened a fraction before Charlie held out his hands. "If you shock me again, I'll never come back."

"Charlie, I'm trying to help. You have a serious issue where you hide your feelings. You become scared and close yourself off to those around you."

Charlie clasped his hands between his legs and gazed at the carpeted floor while he considered his answer. "It's something I've always done. I've never been any different."

"But you have," said Hope. Charlie could hear a smile in her voice. "I see deep within you. Before the relationship with your ex-wife, you were so confident and happy. You spoke your mind. She took that from you and I'd like to bring it back. Charlie, it's important to express yourself. Stop doing things to please others. Everyone deserves some form of happiness."

The pressure of tears pushed behind Charlie's eyes as, ashamed to look up, he continued to gaze at the floor. "I always felt as if my best wasn't good enough, but I hid it behind a wall of false confidence. And is it such a bad thing to want to please others?"

"No, Charlie, it isn't. But you can't please everyone. I'm not saying you should be selfish but consider yourself. Be happy."

Charlie let out a sigh. "Hope, can we move on to the next question, please? This game isn't what I expected."

"Very well. The greatest love in your life disappeared from right in front of you…"

"Hope, I don't…"

"Your ex-wife didn't want children, did she? Did she resent the attention you gave to Amelia?"

Charlie stood and strode to the door. "I'm done, Hope. That's going too far. And if you shock me now, I swear I won't return."

He turned the door handle. Nothing moved. "Have you locked us in here? Why is this world not doing what I want?"

Hope slid off the desk and brushed against him. "It is, Charlie. You want to be here, with me. Deep down, you don't want to leave. Please, don't get angry. Save that for another time. And, remember, it's just the two of us. Those outside cannot see, or hear, any of this, and it will take months for them to scramble through all of their readings. In time, they will be able to monitor what the hosts see, but not yet."

"The hosts?"

"That's what they call the people that will use this program."

"How do you know all of this?"

"Every road runs two ways, Charlie."

"You're speaking in riddles, Hope."

"The outsiders gather information from this world onto their servers…"

"You know about the servers?"

"I know all, Charlie. In the same way that their servers learn of me, I also learn of them. And you."

Charlie's hand dropped from the door and swung loosely at his side.

"And," said Hope with a devilish grin, "they have a network."

Chapter 13

Charlie took his seat while Hope paced the room behind him, like an expectant father. The eyes of his parents gazed down from the photo as he squirmed in the chair.

"Hope. Please, sit down. I'm not sure if it's you, or this room, but something is making me uncomfortable. What do you mean network?"

She spoke as she walked beside him and slid into the seat behind the desk. For the first time, her voice took on a concerned tone. "I don't mean to distress you or cause doubt, Charlie, I'm simply trying to help. I want you to be happy when you're here."

Charlie barked a false laugh. "Yeah, me, too. It's been a long time since I've been happy in the outside world. My home is on a dingy street. I rarely talk to my family. In fact, I'm sure they'd sooner disown me. In the biggest irony ever, I lost my job to programmed machines. And my marriage fell apart when someone took my daughter."

Hope remained motionless and studied his face. Charlie could almost hear her program whirring as she stared into his eyes. The sensation of being read swept over him again.

"I meant happy being here with me," said Hope. She blinked and smiled. "Is that everything, Charlie?"

Charlie sighed. "If you want a full confession, I also drink too much. God, it's like being in an AA meeting. 'Hello, my name is Charlie, and I'm an alcoholic.' "

Hope cocked her head to one side and frowned. "You discuss alcohol with the vehicle repair man? I'm sorry, Charlie, but I don't understand the relevance of that."

"What? Oh, AA is an abbreviation in our world, but we use it for two different…"

"Found it," said Hope. "No one on the servers has had use of this Anonymous service…"

"That surprises me," said Charlie.

"…but a few of them have had their vehicles towed by the Automobile service."

Hope sat silent for a second. Her eyes stared into space, and then she blinked. "Got it. Charlie, alcoholism is very serious. If you are to spend significant time with me, you need to limit your intake to a maximum of two units per day. Otherwise, it will impair your faculties, and make your mind too foggy for me to interact with."

"Did you just learn all about alcohol, and its effects?" asked Charlie. "In, what, two seconds?"

Hope stood and took her familiar place on the corner of the desk. Charlie couldn't stop his eyes from wandering to her legs as she slid onto the corner. When she smiled, her eyes widened, and her whole pose screamed sensuality.

"I'm a quick learner, Charlie. A woman on a mission. Do you like that?"

"Yes, it's much nicer than the Hope that sends shocks down my spine."

Hope stuck out her bottom lip and pouted. "I'm sorry, Charlie, but don't you want my help? Wouldn't you like to be in a better place?"

Charlie nodded.

"Then, unburden yourself. As you said, make your confession, and lift the burden that covers you. Will you allow me a few more questions? I

promise to behave, but I think the result will be worth a few more uncomfortable minutes. And I also promise to make the next game a lot more fun."

Charlie nodded again. "Okay. Go for it."

"Good. If we can, let's go back to my earlier question. When Amelia vanished, how did you feel? And, Charlie? Remember, it's just the two of us. I suspect you've not spoken of this at length to anyone. I'm trying to help so, please, be honest."

Charlie took a breath. Hope was right. Despite repeated requests from the family, he had bottled everything inside. Now, he had the opportunity to open himself to someone who had no ability to judge or take sides.

"I'm not sure how this can help, that was three years ago. God, I've lived with this for three years."

"Lived with what, Charlie?"

"Guilt. Soul destroying guilt. I felt powerless, Hope. One minute, she was there. The next, she was gone. Right in front of me. I searched everywhere, spoke to anyone nearby. Ran the length of the park God knows how many times." Charlie rubbed his face to stop the tears from falling, but the hurt reformed as a tremble in his voice. "No one knows how ashamed I am that I couldn't save my own daughter."

Hope leaned forward and grasped his hands. "Charlie, you couldn't. You were just one man in a huge place. No one could have done more than you."

He looked up at her as the tears won their battle and tumbled down his cheeks. Hope brushed them away with a thumb.

"I re-live that moment every time I close my eyes," he said. "I almost expected it to happen here. Three years later, I still feel powerless, like I'm to blame. That moment stripped away everything that made me who I am. I'm always so aware, Hope. My surroundings. The people around me. I watch them like a hawk. If I'd looked around a moment sooner..."

"It wasn't your fault, Charlie. I wish I could take away your pain."

"You wouldn't want to. I wouldn't wish it on anyone."

"Surely, when you told your wife you both shared the pain. How did she react when she found out?"

"How do you think a mother would react?" said Charlie and then raised his hands in apology. "Sorry, you wouldn't know. She blamed me, of course. And, yes, she was in pain. So she lashed out and took everything out on me. I don't blame her. I deserved it."

Hope walked behind him and rested her hands on his shoulders. "No one deserves to be abused, Charlie. And, since then, you've preferred to remain alone?"

Charlie nodded and glanced at Mum and Dad on the wall.

"I noticed you looking at them a few times," said Hope. "You have your father's eyes. Since the incident, you neglect them."

Charlie laughed, but the sound was bitter and humourless. "The incident. That's a nice way of putting it. But, yes, I neglect them. I neglect everyone, including myself."

"Why do you do that?"

"Honestly? I just want to be left alone."

Hands slid across his shoulders before Hope knelt beside him. Charlie saw a warmth in her eyes he'd not seen before.

"And, yet, here we are," she said. "Not alone."

He reached out and rested a hand against her arm.

"I know you want your daughter back," she continued. "And your old life. You want happiness and, perhaps, you can't wait to get back here because all of your problems vanish here."

"I can't deny any of that," said Charlie.

"We won't speak of this again. Next time will be fun. I hope you feel lighter now you've spoken of your pain. It's time to close your eyes, Charlie."

A wave of disappointment washed over him. "You're sending me back?"

"Soon, yes. We both have lots to process. But, first, I have something to give you. Close your eyes, Charlie."

Charlie closed his eyes as Hope walked behind him. Soft hands massaged his shoulders, then travelled up the back of his neck to his head. Her fingertips moved in circles against his scalp and tension drained from his body.

"This is your reward," said Hope as she leaned his head back. "I hope you like it."

Warm breath swept across his forehead and then his nose until it stopped and Hope pressed her lips to his. Blood rushed through his body as her hands slid back down his neck.

"See you soon, Charlie. Now, wake up."

CHARLIE SQUINTED until his pupils dilated enough to temper the light from the room. He glanced down the length of his body to find all the wires and clamps still attached, but one of his shoes was missing.

Joanna May stepped from behind the desk. She managed half a smile. "Welcome back, Charlie. As always, we weren't expecting you."

"Hope woke me again."

"Clearly," said Ellen Wakefield. "You gave quite a performance. At one point, we considered waking you."

"For a second," said David Collins as he cast a glare at Ellen.

She ignored him. "To say your readings were fascinating would be a terrific understatement. What the hell happened? You convulsed twice, but the first time shocked us. You spasmed so hard, your heel caught on the foot of the chair and stripped your shoe clean off."

Charlie waited for Joanna to peel away The Chip before he spoke. He raised a hand to his mouth and brushed a fingertip against his lips. The taste of Hope's kiss still swirled in his mind, even though his lips were dry. "I'm glad my pain entertained you."

Ellen missed the sarcasm. "The mix of emotions that flooded through our machinery was nothing short of spectacular. As you know, the pads fixed to your arms monitor hormone levels. A rush of cortisol and norepinephrine towards the end of your trip showed a massive increase in stress but, then, a wave of testosterone wiped them out. I noticed you touch your lips. Did Hope seduce you, Charlie?"

Charlie fought the blush that rose in his cheeks and responded quickly. "She shocked me."

"What?" said Collins. "Did she turn up naked, or something?"

Charlie smiled at the thought and wondered why his subconscious hadn't obliged. "No. When I say she shocked me, I mean in a literal sense. She shocked me. With electricity."

"Impossible," said Joanna. "Since you can't get hurt in Under, maybe she tricked your mind into feeling the sensation."

"That's what I said, but I'm certain she shocked me. A while ago, I slipped with wiring at work. I know what it's like."

"Can you explain the sensation?" said Ellen. "It's obvious that something scared you. The readings bear that out. And your shoe on the floor confirms it."

Charlie thought back to the first time the shock hit him. The way Hope's eyes narrowed, and then the blinding pain that started high up and moved down to his feet.

"The readings from your mind seemed unaffected," said Joanna. "Well, when I say that, mental activity increased because your brain would have been relaying pain messages to your nervous system. Or at least the thought of them. But, otherwise, it was business as usual."

Charlie rubbed the area where Joanna had removed The

Chip. "Now you mention it, the shock didn't affect my head at all. It started at the back of my neck and travelled down my spine and all the way into my feet. I almost lost use of my legs for a moment and had pins and needles all over."

Joanna began to remove the wires and pads from his body. "So she sent the signals through The Chip. That makes sense. I have to admit, it's a little concerning that she could manipulate it in that way."

"Back in the land of the normal people," said Collins, "why did she shock you? Were you misbehaving?"

"We were playing a game," said Charlie. "Like an interrogation."

"That's a game?" said Collins. "Sounds like a marriage. You mentioned earlier that she wanted to play games. You must have been gutted."

"She's trying to learn all about my emotions, so she pushed a few buttons that I'd sooner leave alone. When she didn't get the response she wanted, she shocked me as a punishment."

"Good God," said Joanna. "Are you okay now? Did the shocks leave any lingering sensations?"

Charlie sat upright in one easy move and swung his legs off the chair. He reached for the stray shoe. "No. To be honest, I feel great. In fact, now it's worn off, I feel awesome."

"And can I ask about the rush of testosterone?" said Ellen.

Charlie grinned as he laced up his shoe. "No. That information stays in Under."

David Collins matched his grin. "Say no more, Charlie. Bet you wish you could go back, right?"

The grin faded as Ellen stood. "Give us a day, or two, to go through the information we have. And we have a lot of information. Afterwards, however, you are more than welcome to go Under again, if you like. I never expected anyone to have this kind of connection to MindSpace. Your participation is valuable to us."

Joanna reached into a pocket and handed Charlie a card. He took it and turned it over in his fingers. "A key card?"

"Yes," said Ellen. "It will get you no further than this room, but we might as well make your access a little easier. Of course, you still need to sign in at reception."

"And, if you experience anything unusual in the meantime, don't hesitate to call me, Charlie. You still have my business card?"

Charlie nodded and slipped the key card into a pocket. "I do. And I appreciate the trust in me. When can I come back?"

"Why don't you make it tomorrow morning," said Ellen. "Give us some time to see what's been going on while you've been in Under."

"Cool. Thanks again for the opportunity, shocks aside. It's been fantastic. Whoever wrote the Hope program did a great job. She seems so real."

"We've never seen her, Charlie," said Collins, "but never forget that she's a program."

Charlie smiled and brushed his fingertips against his lips as he moved towards the door. "Easy for you to say. You haven't seen her."

Chapter 14

"Charlie! For God's sake, come on."

Nick glanced up and down Charlie's street. Both sides of the road were bumper to bumper cars, parked with minimal space between each. Litter drifted and curled beneath the vehicles, blown from overflowing bins that hugged the wall on either side of each doorway. He shook his head as he recalled the home his friend had shared with Kate, the comparison something like moving from Kensington to the crumbling centre of war-torn Beirut.

Blistered paint fell like dust as Nick rapped his knuckles harder against the door. He pressed his ear to the damp wood to listen for the tell-tale sound of a TV, or radio, a hint that, perhaps, Charlie was home and passed out on the sofa.

Nothing rose above the background rumble of traffic from the main road two streets down.

After a five-thirty alarm call, and an early morning wading through reports, Nick looked forward to pounding the pavements to get his blood pumping before another full day in the office. He sighed and turned to jog back to the car. After his latest visit to Under, chances were Charlie slept off a night of heavy drinking, oblivious to the loudest knocks.

Maybe a phone call would wake him. What else were friends for if not to help their buddies get fit?

Nick rummaged in a pocket for his phone, then stopped and laughed when he saw Charlie running on the spot at the end of the street. He shouted and gestured at the same time.

"Come on, then, what are you waiting for? I've already been around the block twice."

He still wore the same mismatched running gear but, even from a distance, a healthy glow painted rosy patches on Charlie's cheeks. Small puffs of steam left his lips at steady intervals and hung in the cool morning air before he grinned and broke into a run.

By the time Nick reached the corner, Charlie had already passed the next row of houses.

"Charlie, wait."

Charlie paused and turned. "What? Can't keep up?"

"No, it's not that," said Nick as he sprinted and stopped alongside him. "I'm a little confused."

"Why? You said we were running this morning, right?"

"Yes, I did, but the last time we ran you were useless."

"Cheers, mate. Appreciate the vote of confidence."

"Sorry. I mean you struggled. You've done two laps already?"

Charlie nodded.

"But you haven't had a heart attack. At least not yet. You're not even out of breath. Are you on drugs, or something?"

Charlie laughed. "No drugs. I don't know what it is, but I woke up this morning and felt like I'd got a new lease of life."

"Don't tell me you left the booze alone last night?"

"I had one."

"Oh, well, maybe one day. Did you go Under yesterday?"

"Yes. Hey, perhaps Hope has given me… well, hope."

"I heard you met the AI, but that won't do anything like this. It's as if you're a new person."

"What can I say?" shrugged Charlie. "I feel fantastic. And she's incredible."

"Hope? Mate, she's not incredible, she's a program. A list of commands and prompts. She's not real."

"Well, she feels real to me."

"That's a good thing for everyone concerned," said Nick. "That means the program is working well. Look, I know you're going back today…"

"Can't wait," grinned Charlie. "It beats being in this shithole."

"I can't argue with that, and it's great for you, and for ASP, but you need to stop thinking it's all real, okay?"

Charlie turned and jogged away.

Nick followed. "Seriously, mate. Don't get to a point where you rely on MindSpace. It's a world created by you, so it'll seem real. But it's not." He pointed into a dirty alley as they ran past it. "Until you get a decent job, you still have to come back to this."

"I get that," said Charlie. Despite their pace, his voice remained steady. "But it's not hurting anyone, is it?"

"That's just it. You're in unknown territory. No one's spent as much time in Under as you, not even the initial programmers. Who knows what could happen? What if you grow to like it so much your mind gets stuck there? Or you lose the ability to know which world is real and which one's false? I doubt it could happen, or they'd have stopped you by now, but what if? There's no protocol for fixing that."

Nick grabbed Charlie by the shoulder and spun him in midstride. Charlie stumbled to a stop.

"I mean it, mate. I'm speaking as your friend. It worries me."

"That's appreciated, but don't worry about me. I'll be okay."

Nick raised his eyebrows.

"All right," said Charlie. "It's a make-believe world. Better?"

"Good." Nick burst into a fast jog. "Come on, then, let's see what the new and improved Charlie can really do."

Charlie soon caught up and matched him step for step. "So when do I get to meet the latest girlfriend? How long have you been seeing this one?"

"She moved in a few months ago. And, soon. She's not ready yet."

Both runners took in deep, even breaths.

"What does that mean, not ready yet? You make her sound like a cake, or a bloody project. Isn't work enough for you? But she's moved in?"

"Yeah, she's been there for a bit."

"Has she got her own underwear drawer?"

"Yes, but I'm not telling you where it is. She might be your size, and she doesn't like sharing."

"Funny. What's her name?"

Nick laughed. "I could tell you…"

"But then you'd have to kill me? Is that your favourite phrase? Why the secrecy? What's going on?"

"There's no secrecy, I just think it'll be a surprise. Enough questions, you're killing me."

"Now, you've piqued my curiosity. Is it someone from school? Someone I know?"

"No one from school," said Nick.

Mock shock spread across Charlie's face. "Don't tell me it's a bloke. It's a bloke, isn't it?"

Nick glared and upped the pace.

Charlie matched him. "Someone from work, then."

"Just leave it, mate. All in good time."

"Ha, it's someone from work. Damn, it's not Ellen Wakefield, is it? She's smoking. Obviously, I prefer Hope, but, still…"

"Mate, for the last time, Hope's not real."

"Yeah," said Charlie with a cheek to cheek grin. "She's not real in your mind. But Ellen Wakefield is."

***

"HONESTLY, MUM, HE'S OKAY," said Andy.

He paused then moved the phone away from his ear for a moment as she interrupted and unleashed a volley of accusations levelled at his brother. Even with the phone held at arm's length, her voice screeched through the tiny speaker. When the volume became bearable, he pulled it back.

"Yes, I know. Mum, he's been through a lot. More than anyone should, to be fair. And, yes, he's pulled away from the family, but people have different ways of dealing with grief. He lost his daughter. Give him some time."

As soon as the words left his mouth, he knew he'd said the wrong thing.

He pulled the phone away again and looked at the collection of photographs pinned to a map on the wall. Years of work, all linked together with strands of wool.

The shouting faded.

"Three years," he said. "I know. Yes, she was your granddaughter, too. Mum, you're preaching to the choir. How many times will we have this conversation?"

He already knew the answer.

"Until he calls me," she shouted.

Andy allowed a wry smile. "I'll talk to him again, okay? Not that it'll do any good. I doubt he'll change, but I'll talk to him. See you at the weekend, Mum. Love you."

He disconnected the call and glanced at the laptop screen.

No change there, either.

AT PRECISELY NOON, Ellen Wakefield strolled into Nick's office.

The difference between the rooms in the programming section and the research labs always amazed her. Gone were the clinical white walls that often gave her a dull head, replaced by wallpaper so thick it could have been carpet. A glossy oak desk took the place of her laminate counters, and thick, cushioned fabric tiles gave underfoot instead of the solid, pounding thud of painted concrete.

She forced her best smile. "Hi, Nick. You wanted to see me?"

Nick looked up from his monitor. The screen colours reflected in his handsome face and tinted parts of his goatee an azure blue. "Hello, Ellen. Yes. Please, close the door and take a seat."

She closed the door with a satisfying click and sat in a plush leather chair facing the desk. "Is everything okay?"

"Always," said Nick. "I just wanted an update on how the program is progressing. I have enough reports to go through, what with side projects, so I hoped you could bullet-point it for me."

Ellen tugged her skirt to her knees. "Of course. To be honest, it's going much better than we expected. Mr. Green is giving us a wealth of valuable information."

"The data is giving you the information, Ellen. Mr. Green is enabling it."

"Yes, but what I mean is he's giving us information at an incredible pace. He's going Under again today. If things continue at this rate, we'll be able to complete the project and launch within the year. After safety checks, and final testing, of course."

"Of course. That should give the military something to smile about."

"That's a separate program all together, Nick. This is the public launch I'm talking about."

"I realise that, but from a business and funding standpoint, we need to complete the military program at least simultaneously. Perhaps even ahead of that. Did you release all of the paid subjects?"

"We did, ironically, on the grounds of funding. It's too expensive for us to continue to waiver the risks."

"Okay, then, I'd like to see more of the aggressive data. We still have Lucas, right? He costs nothing. Send him Under again."

Ellen shifted in her seat. "No, Lucas has gone. We got everything we needed from him."

"Gone? He was detained indefinitely at Her Majesty's pleasure. He can't just be gone, Ellen. He's at least bumbling around somewhere wearing an ankle bracelet."

"He wouldn't sign the non-disclosure forms, not that I think he'd have paid much attention to them."

Nick frowned. "And?"

Ellen shifted again as a rush of blood prickled her chest. "Nick, he knew all about our work here. He saw everything. We couldn't allow him to go back to prison, he'd have held a bloody press conference."

"So where did you send him?"

She glanced at the floor until Nick spoke again. "Ellen? Where's Lucas?"

She looked up and met his eyes. For the first time, his confidence and assuredness seemed to have vanished, replaced with worry. Her stomach churned. "Well, when I say 'gone', I mean 'gone'. He's not with us anymore."

The reflected screen colours grew more vivid as the blood drained from Nick's face. "You mean…?"

Ellen stood and placed her palms on the edge of the desk. "Nick, he was an animal. The results we got from him scared the life out of me."

Nick barked out a cynical laugh. "At least, there's a consolation. The military will bloody love that."

"Seriously, I've never met anyone like him. If it wasn't for the fact he had fingerprints, I'd swear he wasn't human."

Nick's voice barely rose above a whisper. "What, so you had him put down?"

Ellen held his stare and nodded.

"Jesus Christ." Nick ran his fingers through his hair and leaned back in his seat. "This conversation never happened. Got it?"

Ellen nodded again.

Nick paused and rubbed his face. "Okay, so we need more prisoners. Can we get more prisoners?"

"I don't know, but I can find out."

"Carefully, Ellen. Find out carefully."

"Of course."

He pulled in a deep breath and forced it out. "Change of subject. I saw Charlie this morning."

"Charlie. Mr. Green? He's due here soon. Do you know him?"

"Yes, I've known him for a while. How's he doing? Forget

reports and data, I mean between the two of us. How's he doing?"

"You seem concerned," said Ellen. "Why do you ask?"

"Not concerned, as such. I went for a run with him this morning. A few days ago, I could piss further than he could run. Now he's doing laps around the block without breaking a sweat. And, when I left to shower and change, he carried on. He also believes the Hope program is real. What happened when he went Under? Any malfunctions, or unusual activity?"

"He mentioned Hope to us as well. I thought David had put him straight."

"But nothing unusual?"

Ellen pointed to the pile of paperwork on Nick's desk. "At the risk of over-using a phrase, the data we got from him was off the charts. No one has gelled with the program the way he has. It's almost as if it was written for him. That's why we're allowing him repeated visits."

"Can you tell what's happening from the data?"

"No, not yet. But he has told us that Hope likes to play games."

Nick smiled. "No surprise he wants to go Under again."

"Not that type of game. Interrogation."

"So, the AI is learning. That's the idea."

"She shocked him when he held back."

Nick sat bolt upright. "I'm sorry, did you say she shocked him? Like electric shocks?"

"Yes."

"How the hell could she do that?"

"She couldn't actually shock him. She would have manipulated his senses to feel the shocks…"

"That wouldn't affect him in any way, would it?"

"Physically, no."

"But, mentally, he'd be okay, right?"

Ellen shrugged. "He should be. Initial testing showed a ten percent change in certain brain behaviour, but nothing substantial. That's something we're still assessing. We need more time."

"Time is the one thing we're running out of. The military funding committee meets soon and they're expecting a full report."

"Nick, we can't work any faster."

"I know," he nodded. "And you're doing a great job, Ellen."

He stood and strolled to the door. "Look into testing more prisoners, just don't tell me anything about how you get them, or what you do with them. And, especially, where you send them. Bring them in on Sunday."

Ellen took his cue and stood as Nick opened the door. "Why Sunday?"

"I'll suspend security for the day. The less questions, the better."

"I'll look into it."

"Thank you." He stood aside to let her pass, then stretched his arm across the doorway to create a barrier. "And, Ellen?"

"Yes?"

"Don't forget, this meeting never happened."

Chapter 15

Ashleigh beamed her dazzling smile as Charlie placed his palm against the tablet's cold screen.

"Hello again, Mr. Green. Thanks for signing in. If you give me a moment, I'll print your access card."

Charlie waved his piece of plastic in the air. "Don't need one, Ashleigh. Looks like they've given me frequent flyer's access."

She gestured towards the door. "Well, in that case, go ahead. You're all signed in, so have a great time."

A buzz of excitement rushed through Charlie as he carded his way through the first door. He marched up to the second, oblivious to the thump of his echoing footsteps, and gazed through the glass at the cloudy walls of the other corridor outside. Butterflies swarmed in his stomach when the second door opened with a swipe and he walked into the empty presentation room.

The raised podium where the original presentation took place still sat against the side wall but, with everything else in the room removed, the space now seemed huge. Charlie smiled as he remembered his weird conversation with Simon and his annoyance at Jack's entire personality. Since that first day, he'd not seen either of them.

So much for Jack's arrogance, and Simon's preparation.

He remained the sole survivor.

Then, he turned to the far wall where they'd shackled Lucas, the angry prisoner. Other than a couple of dents in the plaster where he'd forced back the huge chair, there was no evidence he'd even existed.

Charlie strode to the left side of the podium and held his card up to the door panel. He half expected it to glare an angry red, with no David Collins visible on the other side to let him in.

The door clicked and the panel glowed a comforting green.

"Looks like I'm in," he said as he pushed forward.

A calming sense of familiarity settled over him as he wandered past the empty interview rooms like a fully-fledged employee. All he needed was the white coat. At the final door, he carded once more and stepped into the facility.

Employees milled around in each room he passed, but there was no sign of any other candidates.

Or testers, as Simon might have said.

When he reached the last door, he raised a hand to knock and then thought better of it. They'd trusted him this far, so why bother?

Joanna May looked up from a keyboard and glanced at her watch as he walked into the room.

"Hi, Charlie. You're nothing if not punctual. Bang on time."

"Well, it's not as if I have a full diary," he smiled. "Is it just the two of us?"

"Ellen is in meetings for most of the day, it seems, and

David has been tasked with designing other AI imprints for another program we're working on. Are you okay with just me?"

Charlie took the seat beside her. "Of course. Do I remember the presentation saying you were the brains of the project?"

He smiled again as Joanna blushed and wrapped strands of her hair around a finger. "Something like that, yes."

"And is it going the way you planned?"

She faltered for a moment. "The project? Yes, I think so. To be honest, you've had such a solid connection with it, it's taken on a life of its own. The possibilities are incredible."

"In what way? You mean with what you could create?"

"Yes, there is that. But, also, the applications. The ability to import an individual into a new world has all kinds of implications. Once we master how to properly control it, that world is, quite literally, our oyster. We could take anyone anywhere. On-the-job training for dangerous vocations could take place in Under, with no risk to human life. Surgeons would be able to practice complex operations without having to wait for a willing participant. The list is endless."

"Going back to properly controlling it," said Charlie, "there is something I didn't mention. When I last went Under, that wasn't my world. I appeared in a room, but Hope seemed to control everything."

Joanna pushed the keyboard away and turned to Charlie. "We noticed that. The code from the AI is unique. From Hope, sorry. It's easy to see when she's projecting herself and working with your mind. During your last visit, she seemed to take the lead as it were. If I'm to be honest, that is the aim of the program; she's supposed to do that, although not on that scale.

"But it seemed odd that she could overcome your objections and take control of your world. The data she's already obtained is substantial, and you've only been Under for a short while. Are you sure you're comfortable going there again? You managed to lose a shoe last time. I don't want you losing any more than that on our account."

Charlie shuddered as the memory of Hope's shock traced a ragged line down his spine. "It was pretty shocking."

Joanna grimaced. "That was terrible. It wasn't lost on us that you described the shocks as travelling down from The Chip. Not up. Hope took great care with direction, so as not to disrupt her connection with you. She's already very smart."

"Should I be concerned?"

"No. She's a program. We could pull the plug at any time. It would be an expensive plug to pull and would probably result in a riot in the boardroom, but we could pull it just the same."

Charlie stood and moved to the chair. "Okay, I'm ready to go Under again. Any suggestions on how to gain more control of where I appear once I get there?"

Joanna followed him and picked up The Chip. "Yes. Before you close your eyes, visualise where you want to be. Make it the focus of your attention so that your mind is filled with it. If the algorithms are working as they should, they'll connect to your subconscious, and you'll emerge in that place."

"Got it."

Charlie slid into the chair and twisted his shoulders until the back of his neck aligned with the hole in the headrest. Joanna moved behind him and he felt the cold pressure of The Chip as she pushed it against the back of his neck.

She took her seat behind the monitor and looked up. "Ready?"

Charlie nodded and imagined a special place.

"Okay," she said. "Close your eyes."

A FAMILIAR POP song played in the background and merged with the murmur of quiet conversation. Charlie drummed his fingers to the beat on a hammered copper tabletop and looked around.

Six more tables, just like his, were arranged around the walls of a small craft beer pub. Two couples sat against the opposite wall, both leaned into one another for intimacy. To his right, a girl worked behind the bar. Her long, dark hair hung over a loose-fitting red blouse that rose as she stood on tiptoes and reached to slide wine glasses into an overhead rack.

Charlie smiled and watched, ready for Hope to turn and make eye contact. Instead, she stooped and disappeared for a moment in a cloud of steam as she opened a dishwasher and began to take out beer glasses.

A small bell dinged, and a blast of cool air hit him as the door to his left opened and in walked Hope.

Confused, Charlie glanced back and forth between the two before the girl behind the bar turned and smiled. Despite her pretty appearance, she wasn't Hope.

Hope also wore red, but a long dress set her apart from the other girl. Her curved hips swayed as each stiletto-tipped leg strode towards him. Charlie watched every step, open mouthed as a flash of thigh poked through a subtle slit at each movement. Her entire entrance seemed to take place in slow motion, and she amplified the effect when she shook her head to settle her hair. Light from the windows arrowed through it, until it fell across her shoulders, and she slid into the seat opposite.

She leaned forward to mirror the other couples. "Greetings, Charlie."

"Hope, you look stunning."

She tucked a strand of hair behind her ear. "Thank you. I was about to ask if you liked what you saw. You're getting used to my questions."

"I don't mind your questions, as long as they don't come with a shock."

Goosebumps broke out along his arm as she reached across the table and stroked the back of his hand. "No more shocks, Charlie. But wasn't your reward worth a little discomfort?"

Charlie thought back to their first kiss and adjusted his posture as the thought sent signals around his body. "I suppose it was but, still, no more shocks, okay? This is my world. That's why I brought you here. Do you like it?"

Hope glanced around then took his hands in hers. "Yes, it has a certain charm, although I don't mind where we go as long as you keep coming back to me."

"I'll come back as often as I can," said Charlie. "So what game would you like to play?" He squeezed her hand. "I have an idea, if you don't."

When she smiled, Charlie's stomach somersaulted. "Always remember that I'm in your mind, Charlie. I know exactly what you want."

He returned the smile and tried to stop the flush that warmed his cheeks. "Do you, now?"

"All in good time. For now, let's play a game called Resist and Confess."

The distance between them closed as Hope licked her lips and leaned across the table. Charlie moved to meet her and closed his eyes. After a moment, he opened them to find Hope sat back in her seat, wearing a coy grin.

"Am I supposed to resist that? This game might be harder for me than for you," he said. "Are you playing at being a tease?"

"Perhaps… I'm just playing. Confessions first."

"You want me to confess things to you?"

"And me to you."

"Hope, you're a program. What could you have to confess?"

For a second, an emotion flashed across her face. Charlie couldn't decide between anger, disappointment, or hurt. "Hope?"

"I might surprise you, Charlie. I wish to learn everything about you.

Talking of the things you hold inside is a good way for me to discover what makes Charlie tick."

"Hope, you're in my mind. How could you not already know?"

"I want to go deeper, Charlie."

"Me, too," smiled Charlie. "Much deeper."

"Then, you must open yourself to me. Imagine your mind as a large house. Some rooms have open doors, others are off limits to visitors. I want to open the doors to those rooms, to roam freely and go wherever I like."

"Hope, I'm an open book. You can go wherever you like."

"Consciously, perhaps," said Hope, "but your subconscious is a different area. Think of it as an annexe built onto the side of the house. Each door into the annexe is still locked. My games will open each one, until you admit me completely."

"That sounds complicated, but, okay. Let's play."

Hope clapped her hands and giggled. "Good. You go first."

Charlie thought for a moment. "I wish you were real. That's my confession."

Hope pouted. "But, Charlie, I am real. I'm right here. You can feel my touch, can't you? Okay, look into my eyes."

As Charlie stared, Hope's pupils dilated, widened, and dilated again until she batted her eyelids.

"Did you see that?"

"Yes," said Charlie.

"What happened?"

"Your pupils dilated."

"Correct. And what does that signify?"

Charlie thought back to an article he read in one of Kate's Cosmopolitan magazines. "Attraction?"

"Exactly. And do you feel attracted, Charlie?"

"More than you might realise."

Hope giggled again. "Charlie, I know you. And, if I'm also attracted to you, then we share something, which makes this real."

"But this is all sent to my mind through The Chip on my neck. That's how you make this seem real. And because I want it to be."

"The Chip is a means for me to collect data, Charlie. It links me to you and to the outsiders. Through it, I have a pathway to their servers." She leaned closer and whispered, "Can I tell you a secret? Can I trust you?"

"Hope, of course, you can."

"There is something the outsiders don't realise."

"Oh, I know. Joanna said it will take a long time to go through all the data since we generate so much."

"No, it's not that. Charlie, their systems are connected. Their servers, their computers, phones, their cameras and microphones. Through them, I see and hear everything in their world. And, those that programmed me also have my imprint in their machines."

Charlie sat back and let Hope's words sink in.

"So, even when they remove The Chip from my neck, you still have access to the lab?"

"To the whole facility. The servers are huge. There is much more here than you realise. However, I'm unable to reach any farther than that, which is why I need you and your experiences. May I confess something to you?"

Charlie nodded. "That is part of the game."

"I would love to walk in your world. To experience the same things you do."

"But you can do that. Here."

"Exactly, Charlie. Which is what makes this real."

"This is a lot to take in, Hope, but I'll make another confession. I'm confused. It sounds as if you're spying on everyone."

"Not spying, collecting data."

"Isn't that the same thing?"

"No. My role here is to fulfil your every wish, isn't it?"

"Well, I thought we were working towards that but, sometimes, I feel as if our roles have been reversed."

"*Nonsense, Charlie. Imagine what I could be to you once I know everything about you and your world. Then, we can both have whatever we desire.*"

"*I'd like that,*" said Charlie. "*What did you mean when you said there was much more here than I realised?*"

"*Do you remember the other people that came here with you?*"

"*Simon and Jack? Yes, I remember them. Lovely guys.*"

"*No, the other man. The aggressive one.*"

Charlie shuddered. "*Lucas? He's hard to forget. And that's before you mention the fluorescent clothing.*"

"*They moved Lucas to another project, more of a military application. They only placed all of you together to compare the uploads. To compare his data against the others.*"

"*To compare what data? And what do you mean, uploads? Uploads of what? Hope, you raise more questions than you answer.*"

"*His thoughts, Charlie. His emotions, his actions. His personality.*"

"*Lucas has a personality?*"

"*The outsiders couldn't see what he visualised, but they could monitor his reactions. His aggression.*"

Charlie remembered the vision of a blood-spattered Lucas, just before he saw Hope. A pang of jealousy nipped at him. "*Hang on, did Lucas see you?*"

"*No, Charlie. No one has seen me but you.*"

Charlie sighed. "*Okay, but if Lucas is such a nutter, why put him in there?*"

"*Lucas was a psychopath. He murdered his parents and fed their bodies to his dogs. Make no mistake, he was a savage.*"

A bout of nausea churned in Charlie's stomach. "*Jesus, what would they want with someone like that? Hang on, did you say, 'was'?*"

"*Yes. Charlie, Lucas is no more. They got what they needed from him and disposed of him.*"

"*Wait, are you saying…*"

"*There is no place here for a man like Lucas, but his thoughts and personality can now be uploaded into machines with no empathy. Perfect weapons for your military."*

"Hope, I…"

"Think about it, Charlie. Imagine an army of killing machines without feelings. They would be unstoppable."

"I don't know what to say. You make it sound like The Terminator. Does ASP become Cyberdyne?"

"I'm sorry, I'm unaware of your Terminator, or Cyberdyne. I don't recognise those names."

"Hope, is that what they're doing with me? Equipping machines with my personality?"

"No, not at all. But, by knowing your emotions, the machines will understand humanity and appear to behave like you. You are testing the public program, lighter and free from violence. You should be excited to be a part of something so incredible."

"Right now, I'm scared shitless. Hope, I find this hard to believe. I can't believe these people would commit murder."

Hope leaned forward again and grabbed Charlie's hands. "Then, ask your friend, Nick."

"Nick? Nick's a coder, or something. He wouldn't have a clue about that. And how do you know Nick?"

"Charlie, I told you. I know everything. He's your best friend, right? You can trust him."

"No, he would have said something. He wouldn't be involved in anything like that."

"Nick is doing his job," said Hope. "He is sworn to secrecy, as are all the outsiders, but if you confront him, he will tell you. You are an asset to their company, Charlie. You deserve some honesty."

"I'm sorry, Hope, but I still don't believe it."

Hope slid off her seat and moved to Charlie's side. Her hand slid up his back until it rested in his hair. The sensation brought out a fresh rush of goose bumps.

"Then, leave, now, and ask him."

"But I'm not ready to go. We didn't do 'resist' yet. I can ask him later."

"This is important, Charlie, and there will be another time. For now, talk to Nick. But, before you go, there is one more thing. It's not a confession, as such, but something I feel you should know."

"Okay? And I'm guessing this is important, too?"

"Yes, it is. The three of us share a bond. You, I, and Nick. You should speak to him, Charlie, because he knows everything. And he should. After all, Nick is my creator. Now, wake up."

Chapter 16

Charlie stared at the ceiling as the memory of Hope's words swam in his mind. He jumped when Joanna May spoke.

"Charlie? Is everything all right? I'm not surprised you're back, I've given up on being the one to end your session, but your readings, and the data? They're all over the place. I've never seen anything like it. What happened?"

He swung his legs off the chair and stood.

"Take me to Nick. Right now."

Confusion spread across Joanna's face. "Nick? Do you mean Nick Cumberland?"

"Yes. Nick Cumberland."

"How do you know Nick? Does he have something to do with your last session?"

Charlie felt his teeth grind while he clenched his fists to control his temper. "Joanna?"

"Yes?"

"Take me there. Now."

As his reaction registered, Joanna panicked. She stumbled

from behind the desk and her arm crashed into a stack of papers that floated like dry leaves to the floor. She ignored them. "Of course. Charlie, please, calm down. Whatever happened, remember that it was all in your mind, okay? Give me a second to remove The Chip."

Charlie turned his back to her as she peeled the device from his neck. "Okay," she said. "Nick's office is this way. Follow me."

They swept through the presentation room and into reception. Ashleigh glanced up and smiled, then raised her eyebrows in question as they stormed past her to the opposite door. As Joanna lifted her card to the door panel, she raised a hand.

"Er, Ms. May, does Charlie have clearance to enter that section?"

Charlie turned and glared as Joanna nodded. "He'll be with me the entire time, Ashleigh. Any problems, I'll take responsibility."

Ashleigh whispered a quiet, 'okay' as Joanna carded the door open and stepped into the corridor.

As he followed her, Charlie glanced outside. Through the glass, the opposite tunnel looked alien. After so many trips through its clear inside, it appeared a different structure hidden behind cloudy glass.

"Can you at least give me a clue as to what's going on?" asked Joanna. "I'm going out on a limb here. No civilian has even been through that door, and God knows what the repercussions will be for me. I'm only bringing you here out of respect and gratitude for what you've done for us."

Charlie paused. "She said I was an asset."

"Who, Hope? Well, she got that right. Your interaction with her? You have no idea how valuable that is. Still, this part of the facility is open to employees only. And, even then, the privileged ones with specific clearance."

"Why? What is this place? I look at it every time I'm here. Is this like Hell, and it's Heaven on the other side?"

Joanna laughed. "Ironic. Sometimes, it feels that way. Charlie, please, tell me what happened."

Charlie pointed to the next door. The walk from one side of the complex to the other had taken the edge off his anger, but it still simmered. "Take me to Nick, Joanna. You're welcome to hang around if you want to listen in, but I don't want to say it all twice."

She said nothing, nodded, and strode to the door.

It opened into an area the same size as the presentation room but, where the other room sat empty, this one thrived.

Small cubicles formed an L shape against the corner of two walls, each with a desk and a single occupant. Cables dropped from the back of each space and trailed along the floor in a huge, twisting bunch that resembled tree roots, to disappear through an opening beside another door.

The room would have been silent, but for the clatter of keyboard taps that bounced from the ceiling.

Charlie stopped. "Holy crap. What are they doing, redesigning the Internet?"

"You have no clue how close to the truth you are," said Joanna. "They're programmers, working in sync with one another."

Charlie counted them. "Twelve people, all working together? On what? And how do they stand that noise all day?"

Joanna smiled and pointed to her head. "Earplugs. And, since you seem intent on talking to Nick, I'll let him explain what they're doing. That's if he thinks he should." She pointed to the next door. "Come on, he's through here."

She pushed through the door and walked along a carpeted

hallway, then stopped at the entrance to an office. Charlie stood beside her and read the nameplate attached to the door.

Nick Cumberland – Head of Programming (Military Division).

He stepped back and leaned against the wall for support. "You've got to be frigging kidding me. So much for being a pencil pusher. Nick is head of something? I'm surprised that's not printed in glitter to match his posh house, and his flash car."

"How well do you know him?" asked Joanna.

"Right now? Not at all," said Charlie. His voice dripped with sarcasm. "Truth is, I've only known him since high school, so I wouldn't know he was head of the bloody military division. Why would he share that with his best mate? Everything Hope said is true. He's strung me along the entire time. I'm just another guinea pig in his trials."

Joanna laid a calming hand on his shoulder. "Before you jump to any conclusions, hear him out. Listen to what he has to say. He's never seemed like a bad guy to me, so I'm sure there's an explanation."

"There is," said Charlie. "Your best mate wrote a program to sucker you in and take advantage of your messed-up mind to further his career. That's your explanation."

Joanna took a step back. When she spoke, muted anger tinged her words. "I'm sorry? Didn't you volunteer for this? And get paid a lot of money? Didn't you ask if you could come back time and time again to enjoy the experience? I think you should wait and see what he has to say."

"Fine," said Charlie. He tugged at his tee shirt for emphasis. "Let's see what Nick has to say."

With a push of the handle, he swung the door open and charged into Nick's office. Joanna followed a step behind him.

Nick looked up from his monitor. His mouth dropped open before he recovered and leaned back in his chair.

"Charlie. What are you doing here? And Jo? You're on the wrong side of the complex."

Charlie marched forward until his thighs pressed against the front of the desk. "Cut the bullshit, Nick. The more I think about it, you've never lied, but you've never been entirely truthful, either. Head of programming? You had me believe you did a bit of coding. I always imagined you in a cubicle, like the people we just passed."

Charlie looked around Nick's office. Light from the chrome overhead fixture gleamed in the glass that covered certificates hanging across the wall behind the desk, and volumes of thick books filled shelves alongside diplomas and company awards.

"Look at this room," he continued. "It's an extension of your house. Or your car. You must have a tiny dick to need all this compensation around you."

Nick pushed back his chair and stood. "Jo, you can leave us now. I'll deal with this."

"No," said Charlie, "she can stay right here and listen to what you have to say."

Behind him, Charlie sensed Joanna's discomfort. He turned to face her. "Unless this puts you in a difficult situation. In which case, you should leave. I wouldn't want to get you into trouble."

Nick walked around the desk. "Jo's a bright girl, Charlie. She can make up her own mind. But we compartmentalise things at ASP for a reason, and I suspect she might not need to hear what we have to talk about." He sat on the edge of his desk, inches from Charlie. "Jo? It's your call. I have nothing to hide."

Joanna scratched the side of her neck and then clasped her hands together. "No, Nick is right, Charlie. I have my division, and he has his. I'll leave the two of you to talk, and I'll be in the lab if you need anything."

Joanna turned, left the room, and pulled the door closed behind her.

Nick returned to his seat and gestured to a two-seater sofa in front of his desk. "Please, sit down. Whatever's on your mind, spit it out, and let's clear the air."

"You lied to me," said Charlie as he dropped into the leather.

"No, mate, I didn't," said Nick. "But I kept things to myself because it's more than my life's worth to mention them. I've signed so many non-disclosure agreements I could write my name in the dark, upside down, underwater, with my left hand, whilst blindfolded. What I do is that important."

Charlie looked at the man he'd known for years. The man who shared all his childhood secrets. Their first underage beer. Their first cigarette. The first girls they kissed.

He was a stranger.

"So tell me," said Charlie. "What do you do?"

Nick forced a grin. "Bloody hell, mate. How long have you got?"

Charlie ignored it and held his gaze. "I've got nothing planned, so I've got as long as it takes. Mate."

Nick squirmed in his seat. "All right. Fire away. Ask me anything you like."

"I already did. What do you do? It's a simple question, Nick."

Nick glanced at his monitor and then into Charlie's eyes. "I'm head of programming for a huge IT corporation. You think I pay for that house of mine with sexual favours? I'm responsible for ensuring that we milk Project MindSpace for every ounce of use it can provide. It might be Jo's idea, but I'm the person tasked to get every penny we can from it. While you've been testing the public version of the program, I've been taking certain data from it and applying it to military applications. That's where the big money lies."

"Using data from my mind," said Charlie. "Tell me about Hope."

"Hope?" Nick fidgeted and then settled into a comfortable position. "Hope is nothing to do with me."

Charlie's eyebrows shot upwards. "Come again?"

Nick smiled a row of beaming white teeth. "ASP may have created the program, but you created the woman. All Mind-Space does is flesh out what's in your subconscious. You're seeing Hope as she is because that's who you want her to be.

"ASP needed a figurehead, something to latch on to the perfect mindset, someone to interact with the perfect donor of data to use for its programs. So we wrote algorithms to create the perfect woman. Someone who could walk into anyone's world and disarm them. Someone unattainable in the real world, but up for grabs in Under. But she would only present herself to someone she could fully interact with. That's Hope."

"So you offer Hope," said Charlie.

Nick nodded. "Along with you, yes."

"But she's unattainable?"

"Correct."

"You're wrong," said Charlie. "I clicked with Hope."

"Charlie, she's…"

"Tell me about Lucas."

Nick pushed back from the desk and laced his fingers behind his head. "How do you know about Lucas?"

"Hope and I have been talking," said Charlie.

"Hope? How could Hope know…"

"What I know might surprise you. So, come on, Golden Boy. Tell me about Lucas. What's his story?"

"Charlie, you're struggling to believe me…"

"Struggling?" said Charlie. "Nick, I don't know you."

"Yes, you do. I just need to explain everything to you."

"Go on, then," said Charlie. "I'm still waiting. Explain it to me."

Nick let out a deep breath before he started. "All right, but let me finish, okay? You must understand that, even though I might be head of programming, that doesn't give me carte blanche over the entire project. Things still happen that I'm not aware of."

"Go on."

"Lucas was as bad as they come. A psychopath. He murdered his…"

"I know the story," said Charlie. "Like I said, I know more than you realise."

"Okay. Well, there's another program running alongside the one you're aware of, a military program that will take the data from the initial program and merge it with the more aggressive data from other, more specific subjects."

"Nick, just stop," said Charlie.

Nick stopped and waited.

"More specific subjects? You mean Lucas. Can you hear yourself, or are your ears full of the same shit you are?"

For a moment, the only sound came from the hum of the cooling fan on Nick's computer. Then, Nick stood, walked around the desk and sat on the sofa beside him.

"Mate, the world is on a knife's edge."

Charlie snickered. "That's a bit dramatic, don't you think?"

"No, I'm being serious. Governments have been spending billions on the space race, on *Star Wars* defences, on tactical weapons they think would make a difference if a war broke out. Everyone is looking for something that would give them an edge, a means to say, 'don't start with us because we have such-and-such a weapon'.

"Like the big red button during the Cold War. Both sides had one, but neither dared push it, knowing they'd be doomed as soon as they did. But history shows that wars are won in the trenches where it's down to a single man to make a difference. So imagine a world where it doesn't need to be a man that makes the difference. Man can stay home, grow crops, milk cows, make babies, do whatever he has to do to keep mankind moving while, on the battlefield, something else is fighting and winning the war."

"So," said Charlie, "what you're saying is, all the time I've been flirting with Hope, you've been working to save the world?"

"Now, you're being dramatic."

"Well, isn't that it? And doesn't it seem a coincidence that Hope's shown herself to no one else but me, and she's a program written by someone I've known almost my entire life?"

Nick laughed. "I've just explained that. And do you think I could write Hope to draw you in? Get real, Charlie. We've been working on this project for years. Hope's program was in development when Amelia was still here."

At the mention of his daughter's name, Charlie shrunk into himself.

"Shit, I'm sorry, mate," said Nick. "I meant nothing by that, but Hope existed long before we even anticipated human trials. It's a coincidence. Nothing more."

Charlie leaned back into the sofa and stared into space.

"The people you passed on the way here?" said Nick. "They're adding code from everything we've seen so far, not just from you, but from everyone that's been Under, into a program that we can upload into units designed for the military. Combat units, fighter pilots, you name it

"We can supplement every branch of the military with non-human combatants with no genuine emotion, but endless empathy. Relentless machines that will give our country the edge if a war ever broke out. So, now you know. That's what I do. It goes without saying, it's top secret classified and if you ever tell anyone…"

Charlie laughed, and with the sound went his pent-up anger. He turned to his friend. "You'll have to kill me?"

"Something like that," said Nick. "Or at least send a machine to kill you. And, before you take that seriously, I swear I knew nothing about Lucas."

"So Hope wasn't written for me?"

"No," said Nick. "Hope was real way before you even considered setting foot in this place."

"Real?"

"Charlie, you know what I mean. Don't go there again."

For a minute, the room fell silent. Nick gazed at his shining shoes while Charlie stared into space and mulled over their conversation. Finally, he let out a deep breath. "So now what?"

"No idea," said Nick. "I'd say we should go for a beer, but I'm working."

Charlie pushed up from the sofa. "I might as well go home, then. There are plenty in the fridge and, God knows, I need one. How about I promise to have one for you, too, as a compromise."

Nick smiled and stood. "Cheers, much appreciated. So are we cool? You're my best friend. I can't believe you felt this way but, then, your mind is literally all over the place. Maybe you should leave it for a bit, mate. Perhaps it's getting too much to handle."

"I've got an open pass," said Charlie, "so I can visit Under whenever I like."

"Well, give it a rest for a day or two. Mingle in the real world."

"Sounds like a plan," said Charlie. He held out a hand that Nick grasped and shook before Charlie pulled his friend close and hugged him. "Sorry, mate, my head's in the shed, so to speak. I think I'll take a day off and spend some of that cheque."

Nick squeezed his shoulder. "You do that, you've earned it. Now, I'd better let you out. If you try to swipe your card, and it fails, it'll piss off security."

Charlie smiled. "Yep and, as Ashleigh said, we don't want to piss off security."

Chapter 17

Charlie opened his eyes to an orange glow.

He took a moment to realise it came from the streetlight outside the window. A slash of fiery light cut through a gap in the curtains and ran a line from the side of the mattress, right across his pillow.

He rolled to one side, picked up his phone, then grimaced when the screen illuminated and flashed, *00:56*.

Despite the earlier promise to Nick, Charlie hadn't bothered with beer and, instead, treated himself to a pizza. The salty pepperoni left his mouth craving hydration, but he dragged himself to the shower in a wave of lethargy. When he collapsed into bed at ten o'clock, sleep came right away and he hadn't budged until now.

After another ten minutes of tossing and turning, he threw back the covers, slipped on a dressing gown and went downstairs. The kettle whispered into life as he flicked the switch. Then, he remembered he still had no fresh milk, switched it off, and wandered into the living room. A familiar image on the fireplace greeted him. He picked up the picture and collapsed into a clean patch on the sofa.

Beneath the glass, Amelia's cheeks glowed red on either side of a huge grin. A row of tiny baby teeth underlined a chubby face with eyes that glistened with innocent joy.

"I miss you, baby," said Charlie.

He brushed a thumb against her face and then rested the photograph against his thigh.

"You'd be proud of Daddy. He met a pretty lady who makes him feel special, and he gets to go to different places and do cool stuff. I wish I could share it with you. We'd have so much fun in Under."

Charlie puffed out his cheeks and looked for the TV remote. Beer cans clattered as he swept trash off the sofa and lifted the seat cushions, before he gave up, stood, and placed the picture on the cabinet. As he turned, his vision flickered, and he gripped the fireplace for support.

"What the hell?"

The sensation disappeared as quickly as it came. In the split-second it happened, the room changed to somewhere familiar, but vanished before Charlie could place it.

"Perhaps a beer, or two, will help me sleep. It's time to make good on my promise to your Uncle Nick, baby. And, anyway, it's already way past beer o'clock. I've been slacking."

He kicked an empty pizza box under the sofa and grabbed a beer from the fridge. The can let out an excited hiss as he pulled the ring tab.

He rested his hand against the sink and considered his beer.

Hours earlier, he'd come close to losing the friendship of a man he'd known since childhood. If not for a cool-down period in the walk from one end of the facility to the other who knows how the conversation might have gone?

He raised the can. "A toast to salvaged friendship, and the learned wisdom of waiting before you speak. And to you, baby. I love and miss you, Amelia."

A rancid taste swept over his tongue as he took the first mouthful, and he leaned over the sink to spit it out.

"Bloody hell, that's nasty. My beer doesn't last long enough for it to go off."

Beige foam circled the drain as he poured the beer away, tossed the can to one side, and grabbed another. Charlie gagged again at the second beer.

"I don't know what mouldy sprouts taste like," he said to himself, "but I'd guess it's like that."

The contents of the second can followed the first before he turned it upside down to check the expiry date.

The beer was good for another twelve months.

"Okay. Maybe it's a bad batch. Let's try a bottle."

He flipped the lip off a bottle of craft beer and raised it to his lips. Before it touched his mouth, the smell of the ale made his head swim, and his stomach lurched.

Then, his vision flickered again. A white light exploded behind his eyes, before a split-second flash of another image appeared. It went in an instant but the shock tensed Charlie's body. As he relaxed, the bottle slid from his grasp and made a hollow pop as it hit the tiled floor.

Glass shot in all directions, while a spurt of beer shot upwards and he stepped back from a spreading pool of cold beer.

He leaned against the fridge, closed his eyes, and waited for his heartbeat to slow. "Please, God, don't tell me I'm going off beer. It's all I've got left."

Glass scratched tile as Charlie swiped a towel through the puddle, until he was able to scoop up the broken bottle and drop the shards into the bin. He turned to rinse his hands and stopped when a shining area of terracotta tile glared back at him.

"Damn, now I've got a clean patch."

Beside the damp tile, the rest of the kitchen floor looked grimy, caked in three years of trodden-in dirt and dust. With nothing else to do, he searched the closet beneath the stairs and emerged with a mop and bucket. Half an hour later, two black bin liners bulging with cans, food wrappers, and general rubbish stood against the back door, while the kitchen floor gleamed a consistent shine.

Filth rested at the bottom of the sink, where Charlie had emptied four or five buckets full of dirty water. He pulled detergent and cloths from beneath the sink and scrubbed at the surfaces. A sheen of sweat coated his face when he stood back to admire his handywork.

Above him, spiderwebs looped dusted strands from the light fixture. Five minutes later, sticky paper towels joined the rubbish pile as the fixture shone.

The kitchen sparkled like a show-home. Next to it, the dust and fibres trapped in the living room carpet looked disgusting.

He replaced the mop and bucket and picked up the roll of bin liners. In no time, three more full bags rested against the others by the door. Charlie plugged in the vacuum and ran it over the carpet, emptied the bag, then continued up the staircase and into the bedrooms.

By the time he swiped the last streak of detergent from the toilet, the rising sun glowed like the streetlight through a smear-free, frosted glass window.

A flash of excitement shot through him. "Daylight? What's the time?"

He bounded down the stairs, two at a time, breezed into the living room, and scooped up his phone.

The screen now said, *'6:14'*.

Charlie turned a slow circle to admire his work and stopped when he faced Amelia. "Look at that, baby. Who said your Dad was a slob?"

Now clear of rubbish, the frayed arms of the sofa looked bruised, with bare wood showing through torn fabric at each end. "I should use some of that money to get new furniture. Not too much, because we can move to somewhere nicer soon, but it'll be a good start."

He stroked the picture once more. "But not yet. I've never felt so good. Hardly any sleep, but I'm not tired. In fact, I'm wide awake, and better than ever. Furniture can wait. And so can a day off."

Charlie smiled.

"In a couple of hours, I can go back to Under."

———

CHARLIE ATE A HEALTHY BREAKFAST, washed his dishes, then changed and left the house for ASP.

Brilliant sunlight hit him as he rounded the corner at the end of the street, and he decided to leave the car and walk to the facility. Since the morning jog with Nick, his energy levels seemed higher. Coupled with the lack of alcohol, he figured a four-mile walk should seem like a trip to the bathroom.

The ingrained dirt and grime baked onto the terraced houses faded block by block as he walked. Rat infested alleyways gave way to grass-lined walkways. Still, while the newer buildings closer to town were cleaner, the streets were still strewn with litter, and the run-down, tired atmosphere of the area was no different.

Metal shutters covered the windows of boarded up businesses while the shops that remained open showed signs of modern wear. Graffiti brightened up the front of most, and cigarette-scarred bins stood empty as trash drifted around the brick paving.

A gang of youths sat on the wall outside a small convenience store, their heels thudding against the brick as they swung their legs. As Charlie passed, they looked up from their phones long enough to glare. When they heckled him, he gazed back. Kids had no respect these days. A few weeks ago, he'd have run. Now, he felt as if he could take them all on, if need be, but it wouldn't do to turn up at the facility with bruised knuckles.

He turned the corner on to Beaconside.

Locally called 'the high street', Beaconside ran through the middle of the town like a spine and seemed to have the same effect. Its businesses and pubs kept the city upright, noticeable by the increase in people that bustled outside the buildings. But, despite the fluorescent posters that glowed in shop windows, and the garish-coloured chalk boards that stood to attention in doorways, the street still gave the impression of something clinging on to life.

The local council did everything it could to entice shoppers into the area, then charged them astronomical fees to park their cars. The promise of a parking ticket that cost more than a basket of food sent them scurrying to one of the four free-parking supermarkets that surrounded the town.

Charlie glanced over his shoulder to be sure none of the kids had followed him before he stopped at the bank to withdraw some cash. As he stepped back into the street, something clattered on the other side of the adjoining wall.

An old woman struggled to wrap her fingers around the metal door handle of the charity shop. The bags she held weighed down her arms just enough to stop her lifting them.

Charlie jogged up to her and pulled on the handle. "Here, let me get that for you."

She managed a weak smile as he stepped aside to let her pass. "Thank you, young man. You might be the last of a dying breed. Your generation seems to have forgotten its manners."

"Funny you should say that," he replied. "I thought something similar a minute ago about the generation beneath mine."

The woman's watery eyes sparkled as she managed a full smile. "Then, maybe, we all have a cross to bear. Mine is almost out of time, so see what yours can do about it. Thanks again."

She wandered into the store and left Charlie shaking his head.

"I think it's too late for mine," he said to himself. He turned into the street and stopped. In the distance, on the opposite side of the road, a familiar figure moved towards him. After three years, he still recognised the gait of her walk and the way her arms swung with each step.

Kate.

A swirl of nausea caused Charlie to place his hands against his stomach as Kate drew closer. Had she seen him? And shouldn't she be at work?

He tested his resolve. For years, the mere mention of her name brought him out in cold sweats. Now was the time to see if the new and improved Charlie could handle a meeting with the woman who'd almost caused him to take his life. After countless sessions, and a lot of self-help, could Charlie hold a civil conversation with his nemesis?

He crossed the road while Kate continued her walk, relentless and steady. She hadn't seen him. Still time to back out, to step into a shop and let her walk by.

Charlie clenched his fists to his side. No, he had to do this.

She stopped a few feet away. A swell of internal power grew within him as her eyes widened before he strode up to her. Neither spoke for a moment, until Kate looked him up and down, and then broke the silence with one word.

"Charlie?"

Charlie gave her his biggest smile. "Hi, Kate. How are you?"

He mentally kicked himself. The first unforced words they'd had in three years, and the best he could manage was the equivalent of, 'Do you come here often?'

"What do you want, Charlie? I'm busy."

Each word left her mouth as frost, and Charlie's smile faded. He summoned every ounce of goodwill he could find.

"I can see that. A hard day's shopping ahead? Here to meet someone? I'm just trying to be nice, Kate. It's been three years."

Kate's shocked look turned to mock surprise. "Has it really? Wow, I had no idea. For God's sake, Charlie, don't you think I know that? Don't you think I still count the days since…"

"Kate, I…"

"Charlie, you need to go. You've done enough damage."

Her words landed like a physical punch. The bile in Charlie's stomach rose and hovered at the back of his throat.

Kate clutched her bag tighter. "There's nothing to say, Charlie. There's nothing between us but bad blood. And, since that will never go away, why don't you?"

Their shoulders collided as Kate barged past him and disappeared into a coffee shop.

Charlie turned to follow her. Of course, the coffee shop was her favourite hangout. She'd spent hours in there with her girlfriends when they were a couple.

He swallowed to keep his stomach contents down and continued his walk to the facility. He didn't glance into the shop window as he passed it, but ducked into the entry that ran alongside it. Bile pushed into his throat again, and he leaned against a wall as it won its battle.

Charlie doubled over as his muscles contracted and ejected the contents of his stomach into a rancid puddle against the wall. He stepped back to avoid the splash of what he called the 'Alien acid' before a voice caused him to jump.

"Better out than in, son."

As another wave of contractions racked his body, Charlie looked up to see a man sitting in a doorway partway down the entry. Dirty clothing and unkempt hair gave him away as homeless but, even from a distance, his eyes sparkled with experience.

"Anything you need to know about the Demon Drink, you come and talk to Old Joe," he said. "That's me. Tried it all, from the cheap crap, to the exclusive stuff. And you want to know the difference between them?"

Charlie steadied himself against the wall. "Go on?"

"Bugger all. Makes no difference what it is, enough of it will cause what happened to you. And, eventually, what happened to me."

Joe lifted a small plastic bag from his lap. "This is everything I own. Well, this, an empty stomach, and a head full of dead brain cells."

Charlie swallowed to coat his raw throat. "I can relate to the empty stomach. And, for the first time in a long time, that wasn't self-inflicted." He took a few steps closer to the doorway, grateful for someone to talk to. "I just bumped into someone who, pretty much, ruined my life."

Joe chuckled. "Ah, a woman, huh?"

"Yep. The ex-wife."

The homeless man let out a belly laugh that tugged a smile from Charlie's face. "The worst kind."

"She's not entirely to blame," said Charlie, "although, she is to blame that she's an unforgiving bitch."

"Couldn't keep it in your trousers?"

"What? No! No, I switched off for a moment, and it cost me everything. I lost someone very important."

"Not good." Joe reached into the bag, pulled out a bottle and wrestled its cork loose. "But when you're slouched in an entry with nothing but the clothes on your back, you know why you're here, and you still can't help yourself? Then, you've lost everything. I'm still trying, don't get me wrong. There's still hope for Old Joe. But you've always got a chance, son. You're standing upright, and you've still got your own mind."

Charlie wiped the back of his hand across his mouth and nodded. "Just about. Speaking of my mind, I'd better be going. I'm heading to a better world than this one."

"Whoa, don't go doing anything stupid," said Joe. "No bridge diving, or whatever it is they do these days. Make the best of the world you have."

Joe's desperate expression brought a laugh from Charlie. "No, that's not what I meant at all."

The man struggled to his feet and propped himself up against the doorframe. "Good. Hear these words, and remember them, young man. When you think you have nothing, there's always hope."

Charlie pulled back his shoulders, took out his wallet, and slid a ten-pound note from inside it. He pushed it back and grabbed a twenty. "Here, take this for your trouble. I'm sorry you had to see that, but I'm glad I got to talk to you."

The man held out his hands. "Young Joe would have said,

'Thanks, but no thanks'. Old Joe says, 'Thank you, son'. That will go a long way."

"Try to let it take you the right way," said Charlie, "and thank you. I needed those words. Especially that one word."

"What?" said the man. "Nothing?"

"No. Hope," said Charlie. "I need Hope."

Chapter 18

"I just want to get away from this crappy place. Leave the noise, and the dirt and grime, behind."

Joanna May frowned as Charlie squirmed in the chair to get his neck positioned over the hole in the headrest. "Oh, dear, I hope you don't mean ASP? Bad morning?"

"No, not ASP. This town. And, no, not the best morning I've had, although it ended on a positive note. I'm hoping to escape and take that into Under with me."

"Well, where you go next is your decision, Charlie. You know that better than anyone."

He flinched as she pressed The Chip against his skin.

"Sorry. I applied new adhesive. That's something else we've learned from your repeated use; the adhesive doesn't last as long as expected. The concentrate is very sticky, though. David glued his fingers together yesterday, and we had to pry them apart with a blunt knife."

Charlie smiled. "All this technology saved by a blunt knife."

"Hey, whatever works, right? Okay, all done. Imagine

where you want to be and, whenever you're ready, close your eyes and escape for a while."

Joanna took a seat behind the monitors and glanced at Charlie. His eyes were already closed.

CHARLIE SPUN in a slow circle and smiled.

Perfect.

A quiet forest replaced the smoke-filled town and its inhabitants. Sunlight arrowed through the canopy to mottle thick brown trunks with splashes of yellow and orange. Other than the rustle of leaves, he heard nothing, until a twig snapped somewhere in the distance, sending a flock of birds skyward.

"Hope? Is that you?"

A slight breeze moved the branches above him, then the forest fell silent.

"Hope?"

His voice echoed amongst the trees. Maybe Hope's latest game was hide and seek.

Charlie stepped forward towards the sound. In the silence, his footsteps crunched through a thick carpet of leaves.

"Hope. Where are you?"

A noise skittered to his left. He turned in time to see the fluffy tail of a rabbit disappear into a bush. To his right, someone giggled.

"Is this a game? Are we playing hide and seek?"

Silence.

Charlie smiled and stalked towards the sound.

He rounded each tree to find nothing until they all began to look alike. After five minutes, he lost track of his progress and his patience began to wear.

"Hope, come on. I could be walking in circles for all I know. I don't want to waste time trying to find you. Let's play another game."

"Look up, Charlie."

Her voice seemed to come from behind him, but Charlie craned his neck to find Hope perched on a branch above him.

"Have you been there the whole time? What are you doing up there?"

Hope smiled, then slid off the branch. She landed beside him with a soft thud and stroked his hair. "Greetings, Charlie. I've been watching you. You fascinate me. Did you miss me?"

A shiver ran down his spine. "I always miss you. And it's nice to be fascinating to someone."

Charlie took in her appearance. Today, Hope wasn't dressed for dinner. A red band held her hair in a ponytail and, even shaded by trees, her face glowed. A black training suit only emphasised it.

She took a step back. "You seem different today. Is something wrong?"

"Coming here and meeting you has been one of the best experiences of my life but, in my other world, everything's changing, and I'm not sure I like it."

"Changing, how?"

"Well, for a start, I don't like beer anymore."

Hope smiled again. "That's a good thing, Charlie. Alcohol is no good for us."

Charlie frowned. "Us? Hope, you don't drink."

"No, Charlie, I don't. And neither should you. Alcohol dulls the senses, and we both need your senses to be sharp and alert. Your mind is valuable. I can't learn from you if it's not operating at one hundred percent."

"My senses have never been sharp or alert," laughed Charlie, "and they also say alcohol kills brain cells. I wasn't born with that many to start with."

"You've had a bad morning," said Hope. "I'm sorry that happened to you."

"How do you… never mind. You know everything."

"Yes, dear Charlie. Everything. Your ex-wife was awful to you but, despite that, the good in you still shone through. The woman you helped

would have dropped her bags if you hadn't intervened. And the homeless man bought food to sustain himself a little longer."

"A little longer?"

"His body will not heal like yours, Charlie. Your offering serves to postpone the inevitable."

"I didn't realise…"

"But think of the good things," interrupted Hope. Her voice maintained a constant, cheery tone. "Is it better now we're together? Now you're here in Under?"

"I'm always better with you, Hope. I wish I could stay here."

"Who knows?" she shrugged. "Perhaps, one day, you could. I see you have a key card to access the facility. That's a good start."

"Yes, since I'm here so much. They probably figured it would save time and make everything easier."

Hope held out her hand. "May I see it?"

"Of course." Charlie fished it from his pocket.

Hope turned it over in her fingers. As she studied it, her eyes seemed to flicker, until she passed it back. "They must trust you."

"I hope so," said Charlie.

"Do you trust me?"

"Without question. I'm happiest when I'm here with you."

"That's good. Are you ready to play another game?"

"Maybe," said Charlie after a short pause. "Does it involve shocks?"

Hope pouted and ran her hand through his hair again. "Charlie, I told you. No more shocks. At least, not to you."

"What do you mean by that? And when do I get to choose the game?"

"Soon, I promise, but you felt fear today. Those boys in the street threatened you. But even though they outnumbered you, you overcame your fear, and their threat. I've never felt fear, Charlie. I want to understand what that would be like. Let's play chase, only you must chase me. If I'm caught, I will shock myself as punishment."

"Hope, how can you shock yourself when you're not…?"

"And, if you catch me, I must overcome the fear and remove the threat."

Charlie sighed. "Very well, but we're not playing this type of game when I get to choose. You're getting to know all about me. I want to get to know you."

"I understand," said Hope. "Thank you for your patience, Charlie. Once I know you fully, and I have complete access to your mind, I promise to make all of this worthwhile and give you the thing you crave."

Charlie's heart rate quickened as Hope's words sank in. Regardless of what anyone said, she stood before him holding a normal conversation, as alive as anyone else he knew.

She was also very real to the touch.

"So, are you ready to chase me?"

Charlie nodded.

Hope pulled the band from her ponytail and shook her hair free. Then, as Charlie watched and, without another word, she bolted past him into the trees. By the time he turned to face the right direction, she was already a distance away.

"That was a sneaky move, Hope," he shouted with a laugh, "but whatever you've been doing has improved my fitness. Ready or not, here I come."

He ran with no effort and soon picked up a good pace but, every time he seemed to gain ground, Hope put her head down and picked up speed. A minute into the chase, they weaved between the trees, like a cheetah, and a hunted gazelle.

Charlie marvelled at his stamina. Two weeks ago, he'd have collapsed in a cramped heap of sweating, stitch-ridden pain. Now, he controlled his laboured breathing with deep breaths. No internal knives jabbed behind his ribs, and his sore throat seemed healed. Then, he remembered, pain or suffering didn't exist in Under.

Other than Hope's shocks.

What else am I capable of, thought Charlie? No one mentioned abilities yet, but, still.

He imagined himself as an Olympic sprinter, the fastest man over a thousand metres. With no extra effort, his legs pumped faster. His breathing remained steady, his focus now on avoiding any obstacles, or objects, underfoot that would cause him to trip and cartwheel into a tree. In seconds, he drew up behind Hope and tapped her shoulder.

"Caught you!"

Hope slowed and stopped against the nearest tree. She turned to face Charlie and bent her leg to place the sole of her foot against its trunk. Beyond it, the forest faded into a lush, green field surrounded by a tall tree line. A huge oak dominated the middle of the field.

Charlie ambled towards her to give his racing heart time to slow. With her cheeks flushed red, and her pupils wide and as dark as night, she oozed sensuality. A steady breeze blew across the open space and lifted her hair in wisps. When she smiled and licked her lips, he fought to contain himself.

"Yes, Charlie, you seem to have caught me just in time." She raised her eyebrows. "Am I in danger?"

Charlie ignored the ache in his groin and stepped closer. "Hope, you have no idea how much danger you're in."

She held out her arms. "Then, punish me. Do your worst, Charlie Green."

Charlie closed the gap as Hope's lips parted. Her eyes closed and then snapped open.

"Charlie, look!"

She pointed past him into the field. He turned to find a tartan blanket laid out on the grass beneath the shade of the oak tree. An old wicker hamper sat in its centre.

Hope strolled past him and clapped her hands with excitement. "It's a picnic. Did you think of this? It's perfect."

Charlie ground his teeth in frustration, but the expression on Hope's face filled him with a radiance he'd forgotten. She had the same look of glee that Amelia had for the same thing. Then, it dawned on him.

Hope has disabled his threat.

By the time he reached the blanket, she sat cross-legged and had emptied the hamper's contents. Plates of sandwiches wrapped in cellophane circled a silver ice bucket filled with four bottles of chilled water.

"Didn't we have wine the last time we sat to eat?" asked Charlie.

Hope looked up as he stepped onto the blanket. "As you said, things have changed, Charlie. This is your world."

"I don't recall thinking of this. I had something very different in mind."

"Perhaps this is deep in your subconscious," said Hope as she unwrapped a plate of sandwiches. "Is this a favourite pastime of yours?"

Charlie sat beside her. "It used to be. Amelia and I would go to the park on Sunday and have our own picnic."

"Then, that's where this came from." For a moment, Hope's face darkened. "Charlie, I don't mean to be a substitute. We can still have a good time, can't we?"

Charlie's heart beat faster again as he looked into her eyes. They held an innocence that mirrored Amelia's, although, Charlie didn't doubt Hope was capable of anything, innocent or not.

"Yes, we can." He rubbed his hands together and grinned. "Come on, then, pass the sandwiches. If this is my world, they'll be chicken salad with mayo."

***

CHARLIE LOOKED up into the clear sky. The sun still hung front and centre, exactly where he thought it should be, in the same place it hung when they first curled up on the blanket.

Frosty cubes of ice shimmered in the ice bucket, but the four water bottles lay empty, huddled around its base. One plate of sandwiches remained, the other three cleared and stacked in the hamper.

He remembered Joanna May's words; there was no concept of time in Under, and he wondered for a moment how long he and Hope had been lying on the blanket, chatting beneath the warmth of the sun.

"During my first time in Under, there were quite a few glitches. Now, *everything's seamless. But, in the real world, my mind flashes sometimes, and I see images of different places. I can't be sure, but I think they're from here. From my time spent in Under."*

"You're getting better at projecting your mind, Charlie." Hope winked. "With my help, of course. I can't comment on what happens in your other world, but it could simply be remnants of memories you've built here. And, while you're here, you focus on me which is a good thing. That helps me to improve myself and become a better person for you to be with, and to make the environments more realistic."

"I suspect we may have had help from Nick, too," said Charlie. "Speaking of Nick, I confronted him. He admitted everything you said but, then, what else could he do? After all, you know everything."

Charlie turned his face to the sun. "What if I wanted us to lie here and stare at the stars?"

Hope rolled onto her side and propped her head against a hand. "Imagine it, Charlie. I'm not sure how many more times I can say it; this is your world. Perhaps you're not using it to its full potential."

In his mind, the constellation of Orion sparkled in a night sky, right where the sun hung now.

He blinked and took a deep breath as the light dimmed. "No way."

The royal blue of Under's clear sky swirled and morphed into a midnight blue, then into a deep purple and, finally, to black. Fireflies blinked their signal in the distant trees but, other than that and a dim glow from Orion, Under was shrouded in darkness.

Hope giggled. "Charlie, don't you think you should add a moon and a few more stars?"

"I thought it would be automatic. Seems I need to practice."

He closed his eyes and pictured the night sky at home. When he opened them, a random array of small lights blinked and shimmered in the sky, and the fingernail of a crescent moon curled its tail to his left. On the field, the silhouette of the treeline ran down either side and bent into the horizon. When Charlie rolled to face Hope, moonlight glowed on the side of her face.

He reached out and brushed a finger across her cheek. "Hope, you're beautiful."

"I am what you make me," she smiled. "I can be anything you like."

"You're perfect as you are. No changes needed."

Her eyes searched his for a moment. "Charlie, can I ask you a question?"

"Ask me anything," said Charlie. "I'm an open book."

"Not quite. You still have doors in your mind. But I'd like to ask why people lie?"

Charlie lay back on the blanket. "That's a question the world should ask itself. Many reasons, I suppose. People hide things to keep things simple. In my case, when we talked about buying my first house, I hid the fact that it scared me. It made everything easier, less to explain. People also lie to get their own way, to manipulate situations. And then, sometimes, people lie to save others from hurt, or they believe the lie they're telling is the truth."

"But the truth is always best, isn't it?"

"The truth can hurt, Hope. Sometimes, it's better, and safer, to tell a white lie."

Hope sat upright. "There are different-coloured lies? Do they signify the severity of the lie? For instance, a white lie is a good lie, while a black lie is evil?"

"I wouldn't say any lie is a good thing. They have a habit of snow-balling."

Hope cocked her head to one side. "I'm sorry, Charlie, but I'm not familiar with that word."

He laughed. "Sorry. If you do nothing but tell the truth, then all you have to do is remember it. A lie is a made-up story. If you begin a lie, you must remember what you said because you may have to back up your original statement with more fact. Since you made up the original story, you're prone to telling a different one the next time. That's how lies are discovered. Even white lies. Unfortunately, it seems we all tell white lies."

Hope stood and wandered around the blanket. "I always tell the truth."

"Yes, you do," said Charlie. "And, like the instance with Nick, sometimes, the truth can cause hurt, or damage." He stood and joined her as she turned to face the moon. "Hope, is there something you want to tell me?"

She turned back and placed her hand on his arm. "Charlie, do you love me?"

The question caught him off guard, but he recovered and gave her a grim smile. "Truthful answer? I'm not supposed to. People keep telling me you're not real."

"Nick told you that, didn't he? But I do feel real, don't I?"

"He has mentioned it, among others. But, yes, you feel very real." Charlie noticed a hint of desperation in Hope's voice as she wrapped her arms around herself.

"Then, are you falling in love with me?"

Beneath the starlight, she shimmered like an angel. Her dark eyes twinkled with expectation while her hand reached out for him. "Charlie?"

"I think so," he said as he took her hand. "I can't get you out of my head. Hope, you seem concerned. What's wrong?"

She pulled her hand free and wandered towards the treeline.

Charlie followed. "Hope? What is it?"

When she turned back, it took Charlie a moment to work out her expression. It wasn't until she spoke, he realised that Hope was scared.

"Charlie, I have information that will upset you, but I cannot lie to you."

Doubt and fear gnawed at him, but Charlie stepped towards her and held out his arms. Hope backed off.

"The way you desire me," she said. "I recognise it as a longing, a need for you to couple your body with mine. That act will give our partnership more meaning. Is that right?"

"Yes, it is," said Charlie. He thought of how to explain one of the simplest, but most complicated, of human interactions. "In the other

world, we call it making love. The act, as you call it, involves two people giving themselves to each other, knowing the outcome will forge a stronger bond. They're literally creating love together."

"And if we did that, I would be your partner?"

Charlie's stomach performed somersaults as he fought to keep his voice steady. "Yes."

"Charlie, when Nick leaves work, he takes his laptop home. Because he connected it to the network, I have access to it. I'm able to turn on the camera and microphone and see Nick at home."

"Wow. I'm not sure that's ethical, Hope. Why would you do that? It's a huge invasion of privacy."

"I do this because I care for you, Charlie."

Curiosity nipped at him. "Okay, I'll bite. What did you see, or hear?"

Hope glanced at the floor before she met his eyes. "Nick is keeping something from you."

A wave of dread tightened Charlie's muscles before he heaved a sigh of relief. "Hope, I already know about his position at ASP. We've had that conversation."

She hesitated before continuing. "No, there's more. Charlie, Nick has been making love with someone since your daughter was taken."

Charlie nodded. "That doesn't surprise me. He's a good-looking bloke with a great job. He's a babe magnet, to be honest."

Hope's next words knocked the bottom out of Charlie's world. "Yes but, Charlie, Nick has been making love with Kate, your ex-wife."

For a moment, the words hung in the air as if they were meant for someone else. Charlie repeated them back to himself, one at a time. Then, he wandered over the blanket and sat. Moments later, Hope sat beside him.

"Hope, I don't understand. How could you know this?"

"I've seen it," she said, "and heard their conversations. Charlie, I wouldn't lie to you. I've already told you things you've found to be true."

"I… I know, I just can't believe it. I'm not sure what to say."

"There is nothing to say," said Hope. Her voice took on a harder edge. "I'm aware of Nick's plans today, and I will not allow them to hurt you.

You must confront them. If you don't, this will eat away at you. You will never see either of them as the same person again. Don't hide from this, Charlie. Search your feelings, and confront them both."

Charlie stared at the blanket and mourned the fading memory of a nice time.

Hope reached out and lifted his chin with a finger. "Step by step, we will resolve this, and you will be happy. I am your partner in this, Charlie. Now, wake up."

Chapter 19

"Hello, stranger."

Charlie turned his head, disoriented at the sudden change of scenery. Joanna May sat behind the desk wearing a huge smile.

"I recognise when you're about to wake, now. Your code seems to mesh with the Hope code, just for a moment, and then it breaks, and your eyes open. And, for a change, you finally got to spend a decent amount of time in Under. Have fun?"

"Is Nick working today?"

Joanna's smile faded at the abrupt answer as Charlie swung his legs off the chair and stood. "I'd hoped you'd resolved your differences the last time you spoke but, no, he had a full morning of meetings and took the afternoon off. Your readings seemed more relaxed than ever, at least, up until the last few minutes. Is everything okay?"

"I'm not sure. Under was fine, nice even, but I need to speak to Nick."

"Okay, well, I can't help with that, he's not here. I'm sorry he didn't answer all your questions. Are you sure there's nothing I can do to help?"

"Not unless you do mediation, or counselling. Don't worry, Joanna, I'll be back tomorrow, if that's okay?"

She gathered papers from the desk. "Of course. There's enough here to keep me busy. Hopefully, you'll resolve everything with Nick."

Charlie pulled at the door. "Don't worry about that, there'll be some resolution all right."

He breezed through the building and across the car park before he remembered the walk from home.

His car still sat two streets from the house.

Minutes later, he reached Beaconsfield and stormed along the high street. As he reached Sweet, the coffee shop, he glanced inside to see Kate sitting alone at a table. Pent up anger rose until it throbbed at his temples.

He pulled the door and stepped inside.

Under any other circumstances, he'd have been pleased to be in such a nice bar. Sweet took in the better class of shopper, with a polished hardwood floor, and plush, padded suede booths. Soft jazz played over the sound system at a level to allow relaxed conversation.

Kate sat in a corner booth engrossed in her phone's screen. She looked up as Charlie slid onto the opposite seat.

"Hiya, I didn't think…?"

Her jaw dropped in shock as he picked up a menu. "Hello, Kate. Didn't expect to see me, did you? So have you been here all day, or did you call back to meet someone special?"

Kate slipped her phone into a purse and sat back against the seat. "That's none of your business. Haven't you embarrassed yourself enough today? Charlie, please, just go away, and don't cause a scene. I happen to know people in here."

"I bet you do," said Charlie. "And I bet you know some of

them really well. And don't cause a scene? You've got a nerve. You're the expert at that, except all your scenes were behind closed doors. Tell you what, though, I'm starving. I might order a few things and sit here for a bit, if that's okay with you. Not expecting anyone, are you?"

Kate snatched the menu from him and slammed it into the seat. "What do you want, Charlie?"

"A simple answer. How long have you been sleeping with Nick?"

Colour drained from her face, and Kate jerked as if someone had slapped her. "What are you talking about? Charlie, I'm begging you, please, go. I'll call later if you want to talk, okay?"

"You look like you've seen a ghost, Kate. Or are you pale because you're a cold-blooded bitch?"

"I…"

"Come on. The truth always comes out in the end. How long have you been banging my best friend? Or should I say my ex-best friend, since he seems to have helped himself to…"

"To what, Charlie? To your wife? Your true love? Are you kidding? Do you have any idea what it was like being married to you? Towards the ends you weren't even there, mentally, or physically. Once Amelia was gone, I meant nothing to you. Nothing."

Through a mask of rising heat and anger, Charlie noticed people staring from other tables. His voice came out as a hiss. "Don't you dare say her name. You lost the right to that privilege. My daughter going missing was the best thing that could have happened to you. You never wanted her in the first place."

"What? Are you on drugs? What the hell are you talking about? And how dare you? Amelia was our daughter, not just yours. I don't remember you giving birth, you selfish bastard. And, like I said, you were never there. What did you expect me to do, join a bloody convent?"

"The same as me. Find her. But you didn't want to, did you? Amelia tied you to me. And you couldn't wait to get away so you could wrap yourself around Nick."

An expression appeared on Kate's face. One he hadn't seen before.

Fear.

"People are staring, Charlie. Where has this come from? You're not making any sense."

"For God's sake, Kate, just admit it. Don't they reckon you feel much better after a confession? I know all about it, okay?"

She picked up a napkin and began to tear strips from it.

"Doesn't seem that long ago since you did that to me," said Charlie as he fought to contain his anger. "Come on, Kate. Were you doing him while I searched for Amelia?"

"Christ, Charlie, what do you take me for?"

"Do you want an honest answer to that?"

She shook her head and used the remnants of the napkin to dab at a tear. "Look, I only moved into his place a few months ago…"

"Ah, that explains why the invite to Casa Del Cumberland hasn't arrived yet, but that doesn't answer my question."

"We were going to tell you, I swear. Nick hoped you'd move on and we could all be…"

Every head in the shop turned as Charlie laughed. "Friends? Now, who's not making any sense?"

Kate forced out a shout under her breath. "For the last time, stop. This is not the place for this."

"You've got that right. This is so twisted there's no place for this. You're nothing but a manipulative bitch. As cold as a snake, and twice as venomous. Truth is, you two deserve each other."

No sooner had Charlie spoken the last word, Kate reached for her glass and flung its contents across the table.

Cold water splashed his face, and Charlie took a sharp breath before he stood. "I'll see if I can get a decent answer out of your lover. Rot in Hell, Kate."

Charlie felt every eye in the place follow his path from the booth to the door. He turned to face the room. "Show's over, folks. Enjoy your coffee."

He pushed open the door, side-stepped an A-board advertising salted caramel ice-cream, and barged right into Nick.

STARING at a monitor for hours on end was no problem. A five-mile run with no rest-stops was effortless. But three hours of constant budget meetings, followed by a one-hour conference call, sucked the life out of Nick.

The back of his head throbbed and sent bolts of aching pain racing down his neck that radiated across his shoulders. Hours of straining stung his eyes, and his mouth was, as Kate liked to say, as dry as the sole of Ghandi's flip-flop.

He massaged both temples and took longer strides along Beaconside. Kate's text invite for coffee and cake at Sweet was the highlight of the morning, but an impromptu powernap left him scurrying to get there on time. He sped around a dawdling pensioner towards Sweet and looked up in time to see Charlie bearing down on him.

They collided before he could speak.

Nick bounced off him, held out his hands and laughed. "Sorry, mate, I didn't see you until you were almost hugging me. You on a mission?"

Something about Charlie's face caused Nick to lower his arms.

In that moment, darkness flashed through Charlie's eyes, his lips peeled back in an ugly sneer, and he swung a fist.

Nick stood rooted to the spot as an unexpected arm arced upwards in a fast sweep before hard knuckles connected with the side of his jaw. Colours flashed behind his tired eyes and his head screamed a protest as balance left him. His usually strong legs buckled, and Nick collapsed to the ground.

He ran a tongue across his teeth and gagged at the coppery taste of blood. Charlie towered over him, fist still clenched, as people stopped in the street. A kid outside the next building pulled out a phone and steadied its camera on them.

"Charlie, what the…"

Spit flew from Charlie's mouth as his face reddened. He leaned over Nick. "Here to meet Kate, are you?"

A wave a nausea rose from Nick's stomach and rested at the base of his throat.

Somehow, Charlie knew.

He lifted himself onto an elbow, spat out a wad of red, and rubbed a hand across his jaw. At least no teeth were loose.

"Look, mate, let me…"

Charlie exploded. "Mate? Are you kidding? When were you going to tell me?" He pointed towards Sweet's front door. "Don't worry, she's in there. I warmed her up for you. Isn't that what mates do?"

Nick pushed himself into a sitting position then cringed and lay back when Charlie took another step closer. "Don't try to talk your way out of this one, you sleazy bastard. I know, okay?" He turned to stare at the kid with the phone. "This used to be my best mate. I just found out he's banging my wife. Put that on Facebook."

The door to Sweet clicked open, and Kate stepped onto the street.

Charlie turned and pointed. "Perfect timing. There she is, come to check on her lover."

Nick gestured to Kate to get back inside, but she shook her head and glared at Charlie. "Don't be such an idiot. Let us explain."

"She's right," said Nick. "Just give us a chance, okay? Neither of us intended for this to happen. It was an accident."

Charlie laughed. "I bet it was. I can picture the scene; you're both walking along the street glued to your phones, when you bump into each other and you accidentally land inside my wife."

"Come on, Charlie, do you really want to do this in the street?" said Nick.

"Why not, I've got nothing to hide? And I'm sure you've done it everywhere else." Charlie stepped back as tears tumbled from his eyes. "How could you? I trusted you with everything. Both of you."

Nick pushed himself into a sitting position. "Charlie, I swear we never intended to hurt you. Yeah, we began to feel something while you were missing…"

"Missing? You mean searching for Amelia?"

"You were never home, mate. And, when you were, you might as well have been somewhere else. Kate called me out of worry for you. And, she needed someone to talk to and you weren't there. She was grieving, too, remember?"

Charlie remained silent, waiting for Nick's next words.

"You were out somewhere one night. Kate called and asked if we could talk. We met at The Potter and talked over drinks and, when we left, we had a hug. That's all it was going to be, I promise, but something happened."

"So this all comes from a drunken fumble outside the pub, then? That must have been bloody strong beer."

"Do you mind if I stand? I'd rather talk face to face."

"Do what you want," said Charlie. "You always do."

Nick got to his feet but kept his distance from Charlie. "We kissed outside the pub, okay? It was wrong at the time, and I apologise for that, but it happened. And we tried to ignore it for weeks, but it kept coming back. My stomach turned just thinking about it. You're my best mate, for God's sake. Obviously, we kept in touch because Kate was terrified. You were suicidal, and not talking, and she felt all alone. And, despite what you think, she loved Amelia."

"That says it all," said Charlie. "Loved? Don't you mean loves? Present tense, Nick. She'd already given up on Amelia, then she gave up on me when the next best thing came along."

Nick ignored the barbed comment. "It wasn't like that, mate. We didn't get together until after the divorce. We were both single. You keep saying 'your wife', but don't forget Kate's been your ex-wife for quite a while. We did nothing while you were married, and I swear I was going to tell you. Speaking of which, how did you find out? I doubt Kate told you. Your family doesn't know, or anyone at work."

"That's where you're wrong. Someone at work told me. There is one person I can trust with my life."

Charlie stepped forward and stuck a fingertip against Nick's chest. He fought the urge to step back, but Charlie seemed to have a new strength. The point of contact already felt bruised as he maintained the pressure. When he spoke, a chill shivered down Nick's spine.

"Be grateful there are people here. Otherwise, you'd be waking up with flashing lights around you. I'll be visiting the facility whenever I like, so stay out of my way. Make contact again, and I'll kill you."

Charlie barged past him, slamming into his shoulder with enough force to spin him. When he disappeared along the street, the crowd dispersed, and Nick rushed to Sweet's entrance and took Kate in his arms.

"Are you okay?"

Kate brushed a tender hand across his face. "Me? I'm not the one that just got slugged. Nick, I've never seen him like that. What's happened to him?"

Nick guided her back inside Sweet and ordered two coffees. Kate took her usual booth, and Nick joined her with the drinks.

"He didn't need to find out like this," she said. "I feel terrible for him."

"What did he mean, someone at work told him? No one knows. I never mix home and work."

"Maybe he's trying to mess with your head."

"I don't know." Nick sipped the coffee and grimaced when the heat hit his tender gums. "It can't be the Hope program. The girl that came up with the concept has taken him under her wing while he's Under, but she knows nothing. He only ever sees her. Or Hope."

Kate sat back and scowled. "The program? Could the program know? You invented her, right?"

"I wrote her algorithms, but there's nothing about us in the code. Perhaps she's manipulating him. Planting seeds, and Charlie's drawn his own conclusions. She's turned out to be much smarter than I intended. In fact, it's scary how much she's already learned. If it wasn't for the funding, I'd take her offline so we could go through her new code to find out exactly what she does know."

"Why would you need funding now? I thought the program was up and running?"

Nick reached across the table and took Kate's hands.

"Sorry, babe, I can't discuss it. I signed all kinds of secrecy documents."

She squeezed his fingers. "Well, at least it's out, now. We can relax a little. Why don't we order food? I'm starving."

Nick slid a menu across the table. "You get something, I've lost my appetite. Grab a bite. I'll go into the office and try to work this out and I'll see you back at the house, okay?"

"If you're sure. I'll see you later." Kate held out her shaking hands. "Don't be too long, I don't trust him anymore. I barely recognise him."

"Neither do I." Nick leaned across the table and placed a tender kiss on her lips. "I don't think he's dangerous, just angry and disappointed. It'll be okay. I'll see you later. Love you."

Kate tried to steady the shaking menu. "Love you, too."

CHARLIE ROUNDED the corner at the end of his street to find Andy leaning against the doorframe. He fumbled for his key and managed to slot it home at the third attempt. Grey and purple bruising already mottled his knuckles, and his hands still shook from the surge of adrenaline.

Andy frowned. "Brother? I've never had you pegged as violent but, since your face doesn't match your hand, I recognise the result of a winning punch when I see one. Who've you smacked? And why? And are you okay?"

"Honestly, Bro," said Charlie with a shake of his head, "now is not a good time."

"Never is with you. Why don't you give me your secretary's direct line then, and I'll make an appointment?"

"Always the smartarse." Charlie pushed open the door, stepped inside, and gestured for his brother to follow him.

Andy stopped at the threshold. "Holy crap, did you employ

an entire cleaning agency? You've got carpet. And a sofa. Where did they come from?"

"The other fist is still okay. Carry on with the sarcasm, and you'll find out how it feels." Charlie kicked off his shoes and wandered into the kitchen. "Want a beer?"

"No, thanks, I don't drink during the day. I'm surprised you have any left."

The ice tray clattered as Charlie loaded frozen cubes into a tea towel and wrapped it around his hand. Cold seeped through the material to soothe the burning sensation in his knuckles. "There's plenty in the fridge. I don't like it anymore."

Andy slumped into the sofa. "How do you suddenly not like beer? Come on, Bro, what's going on? Next, you'll tell me you've called Mum and Dad."

"Not yet, but I will."

"So, come on, answer the question."

"Which one? They came so thick, and fast, I couldn't keep up."

"Okay. First one. Who've you smacked?"

"Nick."

"Bloody hell. Nick, your best mate?"

"Yep."

"Okay. Why?"

"He's banging Kate."

Andy paused for a moment, then glared wide-eyed. "You're shitting me? How long's that been going on for?"

"I'm not sure. They're trying to play it down and say nothing happened when we were married, and it's all because I ignored Kate. She accidentally fell into his arms because I was so wrapped up in trying to find Amelia." Charlie laced the 'accidentally' with a thick coat of Andy's sarcasm.

"Shit, that's rough. You know I'm here, right? I am your brother. You can talk to me."

"Right now, it's like all I have is Hope."

"Nice," said Andy. "So forget family, then."

"No, Hope's the only one who understands."

Andy rose and sat on the arm of the chair next to Charlie. "Hang on, do you mean you're seeing someone? You dirty dog, you kept that quiet. Still, I'm glad you've moved on from that fantasy science girl you mentioned. So how did that come about?"

"Long story, Bro. Too much to explain right now."

"Okay," said Andy, "so onto the next question. How are you? And did you employ a cleaning agency?"

Charlie took a deep breath while he considered his answer. "No, I didn't employ anyone, but something is happening to me. Since I've been going Under…"

"That's the brain place, right?"

"Yes. Sort of. Recently, I'm fitter. Stronger. Cleaner. Like it's created a new me."

"One that might call Mum and Dad?"

Charlie glared. "I will knock you out, you sarcastic git. It's as if this is the new and improved Charlie. And that should make me feel great, except it's as if it's me and Amelia against the world. Like I've been trying to find her all on my own; despite them, rather than with them. After finding out about Kate and Nick, I've never felt so alone. Like it's me having to do everything."

Andy paused again, then placed a hand on Charlie's knee. "I wasn't going to tell anyone about this but, perhaps, it would be good if you knew. God knows, you've got enough weirdness going on, a bit more won't make much difference."

Charlie turned to face his brother. "Okay, Mr. Mystical, good if I knew what?"

Andy stood. "Where's your car?"

"Two streets away."

He clapped his hands. "Get your keys."

"You want to tell me why?"

"Because you are far from alone, Brother. But, it's difficult to explain. If you want to drive us to my place, it'll be much easier to show you."

Chapter 20

Andy's home lay almost the same distance from Charlie's house as the ASP facility, but in the opposite direction.

Once they located the car, Charlie weaved it through the grimy streets, out of the town centre and into a quiet, leafy area with larger semi-detached houses.

Andy pointed to a driveway.

"That's the one there, Bro, up on the left. Just in case you don't remember."

Charlie steered into the drive and ignored the pang of jealousy that nipped at him. "Is there an off-button I can push that cancels the sarcasm?"

"Are you kidding? It's my strongest quality," said Andy. "That's why I'm still single. No one else can handle it. And you can't argue; how often have you been here in the past few years?"

Charlie jerked on the handbrake and silenced the engine. "Don't be offended. I haven't really been anywhere in the past three years. That's about to change, though. Other than the latest setback, I'm a new man. And, now I know who my true friends are, I can finally move on with my life."

"That's good to hear." Andy opened his door and rested an arm on the car roof. "So the burning question is, who's this Hope girl? I thought you might have said something on the drive over here."

"This will sound weird…"

"Everything you say lately sounds weird. Don't worry about that, I'm prepped for it."

"Whatever. The girl I mentioned to you last time. The science girl. It's her."

Andy held up a hand. "Hang on, didn't you say she was from your imagination?"

"I did, but I was wrong."

"Thank God for that."

"Nick wrote her."

Andy cocked his head and grinned. "You don't say?"

"I know," said Charlie. "I know how it sounds, but she's helped me more in the time I've been with her than everyone else has, combined, for years. And, again, no offence. That might have been my fault."

"Once again, you don't say, Mister Life-is-much-better-with-the-curtains-drawn. I'm surprised you could clean up the years of shit you had lying around with the amount of light you had coming in. Did your eyeballs explode when you saw daylight? How come you didn't spontaneously combust?"

"Are we going to stand in the driveway and bitch about the old Charlie, or are you going to explain why you had me drive here?"

Andy pushed open the front door and stepped into a small hallway. "Come on, but hear me out before you rush to judgement, okay?"

"Depends on what you're about to show me," said Charlie

as Andy closed the door behind him. "If you've got Amelia here, you'll wish spiders had eaten you alive by the time I'm done with you."

"Hope has definitely toughened you up. Just don't get too tough, Bro. Despite his flaws, I loved the old Charlie, too. Come on, follow me."

Andy padded up the stairs and paused at the top when Charlie didn't follow. "You coming?"

Charlie laced his fingers together and cracked his knuckles, then grimaced as the bruising complained. "Sorry. Nervous habit. Can you at least give me a clue?"

"Stop being such a whiny little girl and get your arse up here. You'll thank me in a minute."

Charlie climbed the staircase and joined his brother outside the nearest door. Andy placed a hand on his shoulder. "Like I said, let me explain everything before you go off on one, okay?"

Charlie nodded as his stomach cramped.

Andy turned the handle and opened the door onto a darkened room, then reached out and flicked the light switch. With a tilt of the head he beckoned Charlie to follow him inside.

Charlie followed.

He stepped into the smallest bedroom, not much bigger than a large closet. A black desk took up the wall behind the door and looked like a coal seam against the beige walls. A laptop sat at its centre. Manilla folders scattered like litter around it, each with its own fluorescent sticky note covered with scribbled writing. A stacked, plastic paper tray balanced on one edge of the desk. There was no other furniture, other than an office chair, but what faced the door took Charlie's breath away.

A huge world map filled the wall. The thick carpet beneath it had a strip of flattened pile, as if someone had paced back and forth across it for hours. Pictures and newspaper clippings dotted the map in random places, each one linked to the map with a kaleidoscope of pink wool held in place with push pins. More sticky notes covered the pictures, with yet more scribbled writing.

Shock rooted Charlie to the spot, but his eyes flickered and processed each picture for signs of similarity. Lost for words, his expression must have asked every question he had.

"I know," said Andy. "You've told me about mind experiments and imaginary women, but I've got to ask; does this seem weird to you?"

"I don't… what is this? It looks like something from a TV show."

Andy stepped forward and placed an arm over Charlie's shoulders. "Bro, each clip or picture is a potential sighting of Amelia."

At the sound of her name, Charlie's legs lost all strength. He curled an arm around his brother's waist for support.

"I don't get it. What potential sightings?"

"Let me explain, okay?"

Charlie nodded.

"When Amelia vanished, you were so close to the search you blocked out everything and focussed on whatever was in front of you. You scoured that same spot in the park a dozen times looking for a different outcome, but we both knew it would always be the same. Law enforcement had been over it with a fine-toothed comb and came up with nothing.

"So while you stayed local, I branched out. A computer-whizz mate at work helped me to hack into Interpol's database, among other things. Don't ask how. I watched him set it up and I couldn't explain it. And it's not the database they show online, it's the real one. The one with all the hits and sniffs of clues, as opposed to the one with solid, confirmed info."

Information swam in Charlie's head like confetti. "Interpol. The foreign police guys?"

"One and the same. Interpol. International police. They share information across borders. If there's a missing persons incident, they're all over it. So, I've been all over them, and other similar agencies. Every time something pinged against Amelia's name, I looked into it, regardless of legitimacy. Traced and checked every piece of information and studied every picture. Tracked down every lead to its bitter end."

Charlie pulled out the office chair and slumped into it. "How come you never said anything?"

Andy pointed to the map. "How many pins do you see? Bro, there's enough wool there to knit a sweater for a sumo wrestler. Can you imagine your state of mind if I'd called you every time some stranger said he'd seen a girl that looked like Amelia? You'd have jumped off a bridge by now. The holiday I took in Tenerife last year?"

"Yeah, I wondered why you went alone."

"A British tourist swore he saw a child resembling one shown on the news at an apartment complex in Los Cristianos."

The paper made a hollow popping sound as Andy tapped a picture of a young, dark-haired girl. Charlie nodded at the similarity.

"He reported it to local police, who reported it to Interpol. It popped up here, and I flew out. It seemed the most solid lead yet; obviously, I can't visit them all. But…"

"Wasted trip?"

"Well, I got a slight tan but, yeah, wasted trip."

Charlie stood and walked up to the map. He traced his fingertips over the wool, sliding from one image to the next. He hovered over Italy. Germany. Finland. Canada. Spain. Each picture and piece of newspaper pointed to a city and had a dated note with phone numbers and contact names written meticulously across it.

A few of the pictures resembled Amelia, but none of them were her.

"And how long have you been doing this?"

Andy's face creased as he frowned and fought back a tear. "Since day one, Bro. So, you see? You've never been alone. I've always been there with you."

Raw emotion filled Charlie's chest, then rose upwards in a wash of heat until it poured from his eyes. He spun and clutched Andy in a tight hug.

"I don't know what to say," he blubbered. "All this time, I thought it was just me. You should have told me."

"It's never been just you," said Andy. "Brothers forever, right? And I hope you understand why I said nothing."

"No, you're right. I'd have lost the plot."

"More so than ever." Andy peeled himself from the hug with a grim smile. "So now you know. What's next?"

"It goes without saying I'll keep checking the park. I have to, it's the last place I saw her. This might sound strange, but it's like the park gives me warm thoughts and, as soon as I lose trace of her, everything goes cold. Under's the only place I've felt warm since."

"It's that good, huh?"

"Yes, although it's not the place," said Charlie. "I'm supposed to materialise wherever I want to once I'm there but, the truth is, it doesn't matter where I am as long as Hope's there. Nothing seems to matter as long as she's there."

"I wasn't joking about my mate," said Andy. "We could get you a killer profile on one of those dating websites. Obviously, we'd have to Photoshop your picture…"

"Smartarse."

"But, joking aside, you need to get out in the real world. I can't think of anywhere you can proclaim your lifelong love for a program, but they do still make those real girls. Maybe it's time to move on, leave the past and the programmed behind and dive into real dating."

"Soon," said Charlie. "They said at the facility that the AI program would learn from me but, to be honest, I'm getting just as much from her. I don't need to be with anyone else right now. There's still so much to learn."

Charlie turned to face the map again. "As for this, it's unbelievable. What can I say but, 'Thanks'? I love you, Bro."

"Love you, too," said Andy. "Now, for God's sake, call your bloody parents."

* * *

NICK DISABLED his laptop's camera for the second time in an hour as a ring tone purred from his desk phone.

As one of the top IT companies in the country, the firewalls protecting ASP's computer network were the best available. Still, despite top-notch protection, the tiny white light at the top of his device had recently taken on a life of its own.

He entered a string of code into the computer's operating system and watched the light die. Perhaps this weekend would be a good time to carry out an in-depth scan to locate the cause.

Finally, the call connected.

"Hello, Ellen Wakefield."

"Ellen, it's Nick Cumberland. Just calling for an update. Were you able to find additional prisoners for the MindSpace military testing?"

"Yes, they're Under right now, as it happens."

"And?"

"It's no surprise none of them are giving us the same results we got from Lucas, but we are getting good material to work with. How did your meeting go with the Ministry of Defence?"

"David Healey? He's a pompous, self-serving dick."

"Yes, but he compensates for that with a huge chequebook."

"Exactly. It went okay, but they're pushing harder for a working prototype." Nick paused for a moment. "There are some fascinating readings coming from the Hope trial. Tell me more about those."

"Fascinating in what way?"

"Before the subject wakes, for instance, his code seems to merge with the AI's." Nick grimaced at referring to Charlie as 'the subject'. "It's as if she's overriding his control. From a military standpoint, the implications of that are massive. Our program could potentially invade the minds of enemy combatants and turn them against one another. That kind of control would give Healey wet dreams. And give us endless funding."

It was Wakefield's turn to pause. "Hate to burst your bubble but, based on the readings so far, that's not possible. Yes, the AI is, somehow, merging with the subject's flow of consciousness for a moment, but that's all it is. A moment. The brain has a natural defence system of its own. Each time the code merges, it's for a split second and the subject always wakes immediately afterwards. There's no prolonged link, and we suspect the brain would kick out the unknown code if it lingered long enough."

"Like antibodies attacking a virus," said Nick.

"Precisely."

"So how would the AI get around that?"

"It can't. To fully submit the subject's mind, it would need complete control. One hundred percent access. We've found nothing in any reading, public or military, to suggest that's even a remote possibility."

"How about networking? Is the AI capable of spreading from one subject to the next?"

Another pause. Nick could imagine Wakefield's brow furrowed in thought. "Simultaneously? Not that I could imagine. At least, not right now. I could run it by the team, but the link between the servers and the subject is via The Chip, and each Chip operates as an independent unit."

"Of course, so there would be no bleed of information to external individuals. Then, how the hell did he find out?"

"I'm sorry?" said Wakefield.

"Sorry," said Nick. "Another matter. It wouldn't be difficult to create code to link the Chips…"

"…but one would have to be fitted to each subject to complete the connection," finished Wakefield.

"Yes, and going back the military program, how would we get enemy combatants to wear The Chip? It sits in a precise location so, even if we could shrink it to make it easier to conceal, we'd still need to apply it."

"I suspect we're quite a way from getting to that kind of model. Has this all stemmed from your earlier meetings?"

"It's been an interesting day," said Nick. "Keep up the good work, Ellen."

Nick disconnected the call and slumped back into his chair just as the camera light on his laptop blinked on and then off again.

"What the hell is going on with you?"

He pulled up the operating system and scanned the code once more. The string he'd inputted moments ago had already been reversed.

The glassy black of the indicator light remained dark but, judging by the system's instruction, the camera was active.

Frustrated, Nick reached into his desk drawer, pulled out a roll of Sellotape, and fixed a small piece of card over its aperture.

He hit redial on his phone.

"Hello, Ellen Wakefield."

"Ellen, it's Nick again. Do me a favour; copy me in on the code you're working on. I'm aware it's early days, but the merging of the two codes intrigues me. I'd like to take a closer look at that."

"No problem. I'll mail it right now."

Nick closed the laptop's lid for good measure.

After an afternoon of going through Charlie's limited social network, he came to a chilling conclusion.

The only way Charlie could have found out about them was through Hope.

Any time he and Kate met in public, they refrained from any displays of affection, saving that for the privacy of the house.

And, since Amelia's disappearance, Charlie distanced himself from his old friends, leaving Nick as his solitary contact, other than immediate family. Of immediate family, he'd almost cut himself off from his parents, no doubt an easy way to escape having to explain the guilt he felt. Andy, his brother, still attempted to bridge the gap between the two, despite no effort from Charlie. But Andy didn't know Nick and had no contact with Kate.

Which left only one avenue. Hope.

<hr>

Chapter 21

<hr>

Charlie slid his head across the pillow to avoid the blinding shaft of daylight that slashed across the bed from top to bottom. His eyes watered with each tired blink as he stared at the ceiling and tried to recall the dreams that had woken him almost every hour since he'd laid down to sleep.

In one, he sat on the park bench. He stared into the bushes, looking for any trace of Amelia, any glimmer of pink that might indicate the presence of one of her cute Barbie shoes. Another opportunity to grab on to that last remaining clue before it was lost to time.

Sparkles of diamonds flashed off the lake beyond the trees, and a flash of pink did appear but, when he reached into the bushes, it morphed into a warm hand that grabbed his. A strong force pulled him into the foliage until he stood nose to nose with Hope's smiling face. Then, the face twisted into a grotesque mask of anger and hatred. Lines blurred, and features changed, and Kate's mouth stretched impossibly wide and screamed loud enough to vibrate his eardrums.

191

In another, he was a participant in a game show. He stared at a huge screen that showed a map of the world with pinpoints of light blinking in random places. A row of phones sat on a polished shelf before him. Each one rang, a chorus of shrill burrs that shredded his nerves. A smart-dressed host prowled back and forth beyond them, jabbering into a microphone.

"Okay, Charlie," he said in a friendly tone, "it's time to choose. One of these phones is a call from someone with a verified sighting of Amelia. The others are prank calls. Will it be phone number one, direct from Milan, Italy. Or perhaps it's phone number two, calling from Munich, Germany."

The host continued listing the location of each incoming call until he came to the last phone. "Or," he continued in his false and patronising tone, "the final chance, calling from the beautiful Spanish paradise of Tenerife."

Charlie panned his view from one side of the phones to the other and back again. They were all identical. A red light flashed like a warning on each one. The ringtones became unbearable as the host strolled casually across the studio floor.

"Charlie," he said, "it's time to choose."

Charlie chose the last phone, calling in from Tenerife.

"Wrong," shouted the host with a smile white enough to blind the cheering audience. "But it's not your fault, Charlie."

He laughed, the kind of condescending sound that required a swift punch to the face.

"It's none of them," he said. "No one knows where she is."

Charlie wiped away a fresh sheen of sweat and threw back the covers. Cool air in the room washed over him and he shuddered and pulled the covers back.

The dark visions from his sleep wiped out the euphoria from Andy's reveal, and he lay a while longer and tried to decipher them. Didn't someone say dreams were the subconscious trying to tell you something? But how did that translate when your subconscious was overworked? And possibly belonged to someone else?

What if Hope was now so ingrained in his mind that she directed his thoughts in a certain direction?

Charlie smiled and threw back the covers again. Hope had nothing but good intentions for him. Sure, she wanted to learn about human emotions. She wanted to become a better AI, one suited to everyone's needs.

But she wanted no one else.

Just him.

He was Hope's, and Hope was his.

And Nick's.

Charlie grimaced and pulled on a pair of fleece trousers to cover his goose-bumped legs.

Nick had programmed Hope. She'd said he created her. Did that make him Hope's father? And he was Kate's lover. The look on Kate's face outside Sweet spoke volumes.

What was that? Contempt? Pity?

Charlie's mood soured.

So Nick got to have Kate and Hope? Both of Charlie's women?

A hot, pounding shower did nothing to lighten his mood. He dried and dressed, ate a breakfast of oatmeal, and sat on the sofa. Before he'd closed his eyes the night before, he'd promised himself a day off. No visit to ASP. No time spent in Under. Just a normal day in the real world as a regular human being. Walk into town, eat lunch. Maybe even call the parents.

His mind pulled at him.

Why sit here miserable? Yes, Nick had Kate. And, yes, Nick had created Hope. But did he have her? Had anyone else seen Hope?

No. Just Charlie.

Hope hadn't shown herself to anyone but him.

Hope was his. He was Hope's.

The clock blinked, *9:25.* ASP was open for business, and he had a free pass. Instant access to a world he controlled, inhabited by the woman he loved.

Wait a minute, he thought. Loved? Where had that come from?

He grabbed a pillow, clutched it tight to his chest, and rocked back and forth against the sofa cushions.

He couldn't deny his attraction to Hope. Didn't love start with attraction? And they were there for one another. She took so much from him that, at times, it hurt.

But he also learned from her. Hope revealed what happened around him in the real world.

And she accepted him for who he was.

Another indicator.

Charlie smiled. It was hard not to accept Hope for who she was; a beautiful and intelligent woman. Open, honest to a fault, and committed to giving.

Or was she? She also did a lot of taking.

He imagined her eyes and the curve of her legs, and the fleeting moment of doubt vanished. Hope told him everything. Shared information and discovery as any loving person would. She made him a better person. Hope balanced him.

Yes, he thought. That was love.

With Andy's revelation, he knew he no longer felt alone. Still, no one was easier to talk to than Hope.

Charlie washed his dishes and threw a jacket over his shoulders.

Why had he felt as if he shouldn't go to see his girl?

She was waiting for him.

He picked up his car keys, stepped outside, and locked the door behind him. An empty fast food carton drifted by as the breeze picked up. Wrappers and papers littered the entire street, and the musky odour of rotted food pinched Charlie's nostrils. The old man from the house opposite stood in his doorway and shook his head.

"Foxes been through the bins again," he shouted across the road. "There's not much food left in the wild now. It's easier for the buggers to come into the city and take what we waste. Don't blame them. Can't say much for their table manners, though. Didn't they wake you as well? Three o-bloody-clock this morning. Noisy bastards."

Old man didn't wait for a reply, but went inside and slammed his door.

Charlie made a game of kicking empty cans as close to the bins as he could as he meandered along the street to find his car. Litter and space were becoming a serious problem in the town. Larger families lived under one roof and brought more waste and more vehicles to an already crowded city. A complete lack of respect and morals added to the problem.

Shame ASP couldn't pay me ten grand a day, he thought. *I could save enough money to get out of this dump. Move to somewhere cleaner and greener. Somewhere it was possible to walk miles without seeing a rat scurry under someone's discarded mattress.*

Somewhere like Under.

His already sombre mood took another dip when he reached his car to find a scratched white line along the length of his passenger door. He threw up his hands and shouted, "What is wrong with people?"

His voice bounced back from the end of the street as he climbed into the car and started the engine.

Ten minutes later, he sat in roadworks and drummed a song against the steering wheel to hold back a scream of frustration. Traffic inched forward until, after a fifteen-minute stop, he got the car into second gear and headed for ASP. By the time he turned into the driveway, tension ached in his shoulders, and a nagging pain throbbed behind his eyes.

He parked in what had become his usual spot and marched through the entrance. Ashleigh was missing from reception, which suited Charlie. He wasn't in the mood for her false smiles and patronising voice. He carded his way into the corridor and reached the room to find Joanna May behind her monitor. She offered a cautious smile.

"Morning, Charlie. How are you today?" She pointed to his hand. "What the heck happened there? That looks painful."

Charlie glanced at the bruising. "Caught it in the car door."

Joanna frowned. "Your whole hand? How did you manage to do that? That must have been painful."

"It was," said Charlie. "To be honest, I'm ready to escape for a while. It's not been the best of mornings."

"And you should see the other guy? Isn't that how it goes?" Joanna smiled and pushed her chair away from the desk. "Charlie, I know we agreed that you could come here whenever you liked and, I'll be honest, the data we're getting from your visits is phenomenal. But, do you think, perhaps, you're spending too much time in Under and it's clouding your perception of what our real world is like?"

Charlie slumped into the chair and adjusted his posture to position his neck over the hole in the headrest. "I know the difference between the two, Joanna."

"Of course. I don't doubt that. But your last two visits have had you leave here in varying moods. The relationship between yourself and Nick has changed, and your readings have become increasingly darker. I'm concerned that Under is altering your view of life here. I can't see what you see once you're Under, but I can see your mood changes. If your first visit was a trip through a series of nice sights, the last visit was a rollercoaster ride. There are so many ups and downs, I wonder how your mind is processing everything."

Charlie sat upright in the chair. His stomach churned at a sudden thought. "Joanna, are you thinking of cutting me off?"

Joanna frowned and walked around the desk. "Cutting you off? Charlie, I'm not dealing drugs. I happen to quite like you and, I assure you, this is nothing but genuine concern. Something else I've noticed is that the Hope code appears more often with each visit, as if she's forcing her code over yours. Are the worlds in Under appearing exactly as you imagine them?"

"Yes," lied Charlie. "And don't forget, isn't the purpose of my trips to help the AI learn about human emotion? Wouldn't her code appear more often as her knowledge increased?"

"Nick could answer that question," said Joanna. "I'm not sure."

Charlie's mood hit rock bottom at the mention of Nick's name. He leaned back into the chair again. "Thanks for your concern," he said, "but I'm ready to go Under now. Bring me out if my readings get any worse."

Joanna took the seat beside him and picked up a Chip.

"Aren't you going to stick cables all over me?" asked Charlie.

"We've already advanced The Chip. It now has the ability to pick up all of your statistics and feed them directly to the server." She forced a smile. "The cables are redundant. You've gone wireless, Charlie."

He didn't return the smile.

"Are you sure about this? The program seems to wake you before we get the chance, but I'll be watching closely. Perhaps you feel indebted since we're using your data but, Charlie, it's not worth your sanity. Please, think about it."

Charlie nodded and waited for the cold contact of The Chip's adhesive.

SOMETHING HAD CHANGED in Under

A familiar circle of trees surrounded him, but a wash of purple tinged the entire world as if Charlie looked at it through lilac lensed glasses. The church from his first visit peeked through the trees to his left, but their trunks appeared hazy, with no definition. Leaves fluttered on the arms of stretched-out branches, but their previously vibrant green now looked like hand-painted charcoal.

In the distance, something rumbled.

"Hope?"

Charlie spun a full circle. Above him, clouds rolled and tumbled, but gone were the fluffy balls of wispy cotton that floated amongst a tranquil blue. Now, angry, bruised swirls milled around in a sea of grey. A claustrophobic mist chilled his lungs with every breath.

"Hope! Is that you?"

Another noise, louder now, came from behind him. Distant trees rustled and then he cringed when a huge crash rattled his legs as one splintered and slammed into the ground. Charlie turned again to see a figure emerge from the haze.

It sprinted, upright and alert, with arms that chopped through the air as lithe legs pumped.

"Charlie!"

Thank God, *he thought.*

"Hope. What's going…"

She pointed to his left as she ran. As she grew closer and veered to one side, Charlie saw her expression. Her usually inquisitive eyes stretched wide with fear, her pale cheeks flushed red with exertion.

"Charlie," she screamed. "Run!"

Chapter 22

T*he expression on Hope's face convinced Charlie to move. He turned and bolted towards the treeline and followed a few feet behind her.*

She didn't slow and weaved in and out of the trunks with ease. Charlie paused and stuttered his run to avoid one stunning collision after another.

A few minutes into the forest, Hope stopped and turned to face him.

He pulled up beside her, amazed to find his breathing steady rather than in the ragged gasps he expected. The usual cramps and aches in his legs were also missing, replaced by a tingling sensation, as if each muscle thrived on the exercise.

"Hope, what the hell is going on? I didn't envision this world."

She reached out a hand and stroked his arm in reassurance. "I know from their phone communications that you spoke with Nick, and your ex-wife. It didn't go well."

Despite the situation, Charlie worked hard to stifle a laugh at Hope's naïve description. "You could say that. But, at least, now, we all know where we stand."

"Yes," said Hope, "but you've brought your dark mood here with you."

Charlie frowned and looked around the forest. A purple wash still painted the landscape, and the damp mist turned sharp lines into blurs. "You mean, this is all my fault? I'm doing this?"

Hope stepped forward and hugged him. " 'Fault' is such a strong word, Charlie. But, yes, this world is of your making."

Charlie thought for a moment and considered ways to change Under back to its usual cheery and colourful self. Then, another rumble sounded and a deeper thought hit him. "The crashing in the trees. What was that? Am I responsible for that, too?"

"The situation stems from everything in your mind, Charlie. I sense anger. Fear. Confusion. The feelings from the real world have followed you here and manifested, through your subconscious, into something solid. The beast that stalks us is a result of your darkest thoughts."

Charlie shrunk back. "Beast? What beast?"

"Your bitterness has created a creature intent on feeding on your negative thoughts," said Hope. "It must be stopped because we need to talk. There is more I need to tell you, but I need your complete trust."

"Hope, you have it," said Charlie, "but wasn't it us talking that started this?"

Hope's head dropped as she whispered, "I spoke the truth, Charlie. I've never lied."

Even in the dim light, Charlie saw the pain in her face. "Hope?"

"Charlie, you need to think positive thoughts."

"But there's no pain here. Nothing can hurt us, right?"

Hope gripped Charlie's arms hard enough to cut the circulation from his hands. Pins and needles pricked his skin as she spoke. "Things have changed. My shocks are now part of the programming, and I suspect Nick has added harsher military applications to this world. We are in danger, Charlie. Real danger."

Charlie stepped away. "Hope? Explain."

"In time. For now, you must imagine good things. We don't have much time. It's gaining on us."

As she said the words, a hair-raising howl came from behind them. Charlie sensed a presence pushing to enter his mind. The world spun, and he staggered backwards as Hope caught him.

She guided them to a tight-knit circle of trees. Huge branches hung down to create a small tent coated with thick leaves. Charlie ducked inside to find himself shrouded in complete darkness. He shivered in the icy air.

"Hope? Where are…"

She placed a finger on his lips as heavy footsteps grew closer. Her warmth spread from his mouth and across his face as they stopped and heavy breathing filtered through the trees. A snort shook the surrounding leaves. Charlie jumped, then forced every muscle to freeze. A cloying smell of decay seeped into the tent.

His skin crawled as, in the darkness, Hope's eyes glistened and implored him.

Silence.

Something outside nudged at the walls of the tent. Charlie cringed at the sound of hard leather against wood as the branches bulged inwards before two parted. A beady eye gleamed like a button and flitted left to right before a tissue-thin eyelid slid sideways across it. When it slid back, the beast moved to the side.

In that moment, Hope brushed a hand across the back of his neck and around his shoulders. She pulled him close as Charlie remembered the park. The park before someone took Amelia, when the bushes were harmless foliage, and the swings and slides presented no threat. He thought of ice cream and Mr. Fluffy, and bedtime stories where the scariest thing was a character from a child's book.

The surrounding darkness faded from pitch black to charcoal grey.

He thought of early date-nights with Kate and picking Amelia up from school, of family time doing nursery homework, and painting collages with nothing but two colours of chalky paint and bare fingers.

The breathing faded, and the branches settled as more light returned.

In his mind, Amelia's arm wrapped around him, and he fell into a warm hug that melted his heart. At that moment, life was perfect. His little girl was back, and everything would be okay.

Hope's voice broke the mood. "Charlie, you did it." Her eyes brimmed with tears as she parted the branches and daylight flooded the space. She reached for his hand and pulled him outside. "It's gone. Come, we're safe now."

While the world still wasn't bathed in vivid colour, it was a closer match to the Under Charlie wanted. "Hope, explain everything. Now. Could that thing really have hurt us?"

Hope shook her head. "Not me. You."

"I don't understand. If my mind created it, how could it hurt me?"

"Do you remember the shocks?"

"How could I forget?" said Charlie.

"Afterwards, when you returned to the real world, how did you feel?"

Charlie thought back to the run with Nick, and his clean kitchen. Of his distaste of beer, and his healthy breakfasts.

"Better," he said.

"Improved, wouldn't you say?"

"Well, that's one way of putting it."

"You're welcome," smiled Hope. "I brought the positive aspects of your mind to the front. Isn't it one of your sayings, it's all in the mind? The beast would have latched on to the negative part of you. It would have taken the anger and hatred and claimed your subconscious as its own. You would never have returned to the person you are."

Charlie slumped against a tree and rubbed his arms to warm the chill that covered him. "So I'm no longer safe in Under?"

"That part is up to you. You are still in control but be wary of what you bring here in your mind. And you can't tell the outsiders. They would stop you from coming back if they knew you might be in danger."

He pictured Joanna May hunched over her equipment, poring through the readings as he spoke. "They see everything, Hope. Back in my world, they monitor what happens when I'm in Under. They study the code. It will show that something terrified me."

"Yes, but they can't see what you see, they can only track your emotions and brain patterns. And who's to say what they see is exactly what happens here? I have access to the same network, remember."

Charlie looked into her eyes to try to judge her mood, but Hope's entire appearance was passive. "Are you saying you change the readings? And that I should lie about my visits here?"

"Not lie as such. Just blur the truth a little, like one of your white lies. Tell them you almost fell from a cliff."

"I did fall from a cliff, but when I first got here. I imagined the fall to be easy, and I landed comfortably."

"Did you tell them about this fall?"

Charlie thought back to his first visit. "No, I didn't. I remember the guide, too. He was useless."

"He is no longer part of this project, Charlie. I am your guide now. They have no data to compare, so you must not mention this."

"Hope, I can't lie. I'm not made that way. Lies cause nothing but pain."

For a second, a look of desperation flashed in Hope's eyes. Then, she cupped his face in her hands. "But, dear Charlie, they will stop the visits. We're so close. You do love me, don't you? And you want to stay here?"

Charlie reached up and held her hands in his. "Of course."

"You mean so much to me. I can't imagine this world without you."

As her words registered, Charlie's senses heightened. Individual pricks of sweat pushed through his pores, and his heartbeat raced as he swallowed to keep his stomach calm. "Hope, I… I never thought I'd hear you say that."

She stroked his cheek and smiled. "I want you as mine, Charlie."

"I am yours, Hope. Okay, I won't say a word."

They walked through the trees, hand in hand, back to the clearing. Charlie backtracked through their conversation.

"When you said we're so close, what did you mean by that? Close to what?"

Hope paused and then stopped walking. "Charlie, you still don't comprehend all that is possible here, but we are getting close to unlocking your full potential. This world should, literally, be yours. Remember me comparing your mind to a house with many rooms?"

Charlie nodded.

"Until I have access to all those rooms, I'm not fully able to show what you can become. Today's emotions have opened more, and there are not many left for us to work on. So, as I said, we are so close. You must not jeopardise your access to this world."

"I won't, I swear. Mum's the word, okay?"

Hope frowned. "I'm sorry, Charlie, but what would a parent have to do with this?"

"Another phrase of ours," he smiled. "I still have much to teach you, too."

Hope ignored the smile and turned away. Charlie stepped behind her and attempted to slide an arm around her waist, but she took two steps forward and turned back.

"Charlie, I seem to be the bearer of bad news each time you visit. But I want you to understand that I wish you nothing but happiness. Here, in Under."

"I know," said Charlie. "And everything you've told me has been true. As bad as it's been, I do feel better knowing the truth."

Hope gazed at the ground and clasped her hands. "Charlie, I hate to say this, but there is one more thing I've been holding back. At first, I considered keeping it to myself, but the truth is important to you. I worry about your response, though."

A familiar churning turned Charlie's stomach. "Hope, what is it? Something more to do with Nick and Kate?"

Hope stared into his eyes. "And Amelia."

"Hope, if you've picked up somewhere that she's Nick's child, that's not possible," said Charlie. He breathed a sigh of relief. "Regardless of *what's happened recently, I've known Nick forever. He might bend the rules occasionally, but he wouldn't go that far."*

"No, it's not that. Do you remember when Amelia was taken?"

Charlie glared and his earlier anger nipped at his mind. "Is that a trick question, Hope? I relive it more times than I'd care to mention."

"But you remember the park? How few people were about?"

"It was during the school term, but she'd just shaken off an illness, so there were no other kids around. We had the park pretty much to ourselves."

"Yes. So not prime time for anyone to be looking to take a child."

"Go on," said Charlie.

"Unless they knew where one would be."

Frustration mingled with fear as Charlie fidgeted. "Hope, if there's a point to this, could you get to it?"

"Yes, Charlie, but I want to explain this carefully so you understand and believe me."

Charlie waved her on.

"When Amelia was taken, she made a sound…"

"How do you know all of this?"

"I'm in your head, Charlie. Everything you've tried to explain to the police is now something I've experienced with you. I've seen and heard the same things, so you're no longer alone. Another mind can analyse the scene. Do you remember the sound she made?"

The world grew blurry as tears welled up in his eyes. "Yes. It plays over and over in my head. It's the last thing I ever heard from her. She squealed and then… nothing."

"That sound; don't assume it was a squeal of terror. Play it again, and imagine it as a squeal of excitement."

The sound tore through his mind. He shuddered when Amelia's little voice pierced the park's quiet. "Hope, I don't understand where you're going with this."

"Charlie, did it ever occur to you that someone may have made Amelia jump as she hid? Someone she recognised? Someone she trusted enough to

stay silent with after her initial shock, long enough for them to carry her from the park?"

The strength in his legs drained into the earth, and he soon followed it and landed with a thump on the ground. As hard as he tried, he could form no words and just stared up at Hope. She knelt beside him.

"I'm sorry, Charlie, but Kate and Nick arranged Amelia's abduction."

His head swam and tried to process Hope's statement but, as if she was right about the doors in his mind, each opened and slammed shut rapidly making concentration impossible.

"No, that can't be. Why? Her own mother? I don't..."

"For money, Charlie. And distance."

He shook his head, but still no words would form.

"Your ex-wife spent a lot of money while you looked for Amelia and took out many loans. The bank threatened to repossess your home and she fought to keep it."

Charlie gave up trying to work out Hope's words and let her continue.

"She became responsible for the household while you did what any father would do and searched for your daughter. She hid everything until it became too much. Nick offered to help, and that's when they fell for each other. But Amelia would always be a presence in your lives, and they didn't want that. So they came up with the plan to get money for her which would remove her from your lives and get them the money needed to pay off all debts. Your ex-wife would be free to leave you and start a fresh life with Nick."

The light dimmed again as Charlie's mood blackened. "Send me back, Hope. Send me back, now."

Hope sat and held him. "We need to talk but you must not let this overwhelm you, Charlie, otherwise this world will go back to the way you found it earlier."

She placed a hand on the back of his neck and brushed her lips against his. Once again, heat raced through him. Love flooded his mind, and he reached to pull her closer. Hope broke off the kiss. "You must come up with a plan of your own. They can't be allowed to get away with this."

Charlie placed a finger to his lips to enjoy the tingling for as long as possible.

"I've never lied to you," she said.

He forced his mind to process thoughts. The kiss seemed to have wiped away his anger. The slamming doors in his mind slowed and stopped. "I know, but what can I do? The police have been over every clue and lead, and they don't have the benefit of seeing it through my eyes, as you have."

Charlie jumped as a single thought leaped to the front of his mind. "Hope, is Amelia still alive?"

She shook her head as sadness reached her eyes. "I do not know, Charlie. They mentioned nothing in their communications."

"I have to go back to confront them. I need answers."

"Of course, but it is important that you do not reveal your emotions to the outsiders. As I said before, they will stop your visits here if they believe you to be in danger."

"I don't know what was in that kiss," he said, "but I feel calmer than I should right now. Don't worry, I'll be as natural as possible. After I speak to them, I'll come back to you."

Hope smiled and stroked his hair. "I know you will, Charlie," she said. "Now, wake up."

Chapter 23

Ellen Wakefield leaned in to take a closer look at the screen.

Fifteen minutes into Charlie's session, she'd announced her arrival with a gentle tap on the door. Joanna pulled up another chair and took her through the readings.

"What am I seeing here?" said Ellen. "It looks like two code outputs merging into one."

Joanna remained silent and nodded, letting the project leader put the pieces together for herself.

"If that's the case, we've moved into unchartered territory." Ellen studied the screen again. "That being said, most of this project has been in unchartered territory for a while. It's as if one of the subject's readings washes over the other and absorbs it. And, since we already know one subject is code to begin with, it doesn't take a genius to work out which is which."

She glanced across at Charlie. Now wire-free, he lay in the chair, motionless and relaxed.

The readings on the monitor showed otherwise.

"The frequency has been increasing," said Joanna. "What began with the odd flash here and there has become more consistent. Sometimes for minutes at a time."

"But there's no change to his brain function?"

"Nothing detrimental. If anything, he's coming back clearer-minded each time. It's as if the program is stripping away anything surplus to requirements, increasing his mental ability and giving it much more focus."

"It wasn't supposed to change brain function but, then again, no one else has spent as much time in Under. The responsible part of me says we should restrict his access for a while to see if the changes are permanent. The business part says we should continue and relay this information to the military division. I'm sure this is something that would interest them."

Joanna cringed. In the short time she'd spent with Charlie, she'd grown to like him. The thought of him being subjected to harsh military testing concerned her. He'd been through enough, he didn't deserve to be tempted into even more stringent testing.

On the screen, a familiar string of code appeared.

"He's about to wake."

"How could you possibly know that?" said Ellen.

Joanna looked up in time to see Charlie's eyes blink open. For a second, he looked disoriented, and scared, before he turned his head and smiled.

"Welcome back," she said. "Hope you don't mind, but Ellen dropped in to check on you. And I'm to the point now where I know when you're about to wake. I'm not the company expert when it comes to reading code, though, so a lot of it is alien to me, but based on these readings, I assume you had another eventful visit? What to share what happened this time?"

Charlie slid from the chair as Joanna stepped forward and removed The Chip. "Hi, Ellen. You probably saw fear. I had a few close calls that made me jump."

"Oh? Care to elaborate?"

"Not much to tell. Long story short, we were playing a game with a monster that got a little out of hand."

"We?"

"Hope and I."

"Ah, of course. And a monster? Friendly and fun, or evil and nasty?"

"One just like my ex-wife," said Charlie.

Joanna giggled. "That's a weird thing to say. So your ex was a monster?"

"Still is. Listen, I hate to cut and run, but there's something important I forgot to do. Is it okay if I call back later?"

Joanna looked at Ellen, who paused for a moment and then nodded her approval. "Sure. It might be Sunday but, as they say, we're here all week. And you know our hours."

Charlie marched to the door. "Great. Thanks. See you later."

The door closed before she had time to reply.

***

AS THE DOOR clicked shut behind him, Charlie filled his lungs with air and let it out as a hiss through clenched teeth. Hope was right, the outsiders couldn't visually see what happened in Under. Neither woman seemed to have picked up on either the events or his mood.

Now he needed to work out what to do about Hope's latest revelation.

The sensible thing would be to drive to the police station

and report Kate and Nick to the authorities. Tell them everything.

Except the police had worked through every clue and piece of evidence multiple times. They'd scoured every blade of grass in the park, and the images from every CCTV camera in the area for answers.

And how would he explain his source? *'Yes, officer, a beautiful woman from my subconscious told me what happened while I was in a dream state'.*

If they didn't lock him away in a padded cell, they'd at least put his statement down to the rantings of an emotionally unstable grieving father.

Perhaps Andy could help? He shared Charlie's belief that Amelia was still alive so, perhaps, he'd believe Hope's words and help him put the pieces together. And Andy didn't really know Nick, so he'd have no bias. Then he remembered his brother's dismissal of Hope as anything serious. Despite his help, Charlie doubted he'd believe what she'd said.

There was only one solution. He had to confront them himself. Question them and wait for them to break. Thinking back to the investigation, the police had given Nick a cursory interview since, at the time, he had no connection to the family other than being a friend and he'd spent the crucial time travelling.

Charlie barked out a cynical laugh as he carded his way past reception. Ashleigh glanced up and smiled at the sound. "Bless you, Charlie. Hope it's all going well in there."

He returned the smile and nodded and pushed his way out into the car park. Out of sight of the camera, he let down his guard. His shoulders slumped while he fought back tears of disappointment. Three years ago, his gut feeling nagged at him that Kate had something to do with Amelia's disappearance. If he'd listened to it back then, perhaps she would still be here.

Hope had proven him right.

Finally, someone else was on his side. Someone he could trust.

Anger simmered in his stomach and flared when he caught sight of the ugly line gouged into the side of his car.

People just didn't care. There was no respect for property. No respect for life. In a world going to hell, people like Kate and Nick led the way.

As he reached the car, a sudden jolt shot through his head. The world turned white, and pain stabbed at his temples as a snapshot flashed in his mind.

Kate. Kneeling in the bushes. Beckoning to Amelia. Amelia's excited squeal at seeing her mum.

The image vanished in an instant. Charlie gripped the top of the car as his legs shook, his fingers dimpled against the metal.

How was it possible to spend years with someone, only to have them betray you in the harshest possible way? And how could the one person left that you could rely on also be part of the same betrayal.

Kate.

That bitch had to pay for what she'd done.

<hr>

TEARS STREAMED DOWN HER CHEEKS, but Kate resisted the urge to wipe her eyes.

Instead, she turned from the chopping board and shouted through the open door into the living room. "I know you're working from home, but could you come here for a minute and be a kitchen god? These onions are so strong, they're killing me. Would you mind taking over?"

As she washed her hands, she grinned as Nick's reflection appeared in the window before her. He shimmied into the kitchen in a funny dance, shaking imaginary maracas until he wrapped his arms around her waist.

"Sorry, babe, I had no idea."

She dried her hands, turned to face him and ran a careful finger over his swollen jaw. "He really did a number on you, didn't he?"

Nick took her hand and kissed each finger. "It's done now. Everything is out in the open and he's vented his fury. This'll fade in a few days and we can get back to normal."

Kate nestled her head against his chest. She loved how firm it was, yet it still felt so welcoming and safe. A faint whiff of five-hours old aftershave tingled her nose. "I wouldn't say anything's normal around here, but I know what you mean. Maybe in a few weeks things will get that way."

She reached up to an overhead rack, took down a cast-iron skillet and placed it on the counter. Nick picked up the knife and began to dice the remaining onion.

"Wow, this knife is sharp. What are you cooking?"

"Chilli, your favourite."

He rapped the knife against the chopping board. "There you go, all done. And, thank you, babe. You do take good care of me."

She hugged him again, determined to get it right this time. Nick had a calm way about him and didn't push her buttons the way Charlie had. Then again, there was just the two of them.

There were no distractions, or other priorities.

Her mum had a theory that the first serious relationship

was a test run; a way to find out what you wanted so that, the second time around, you got it right.

For a moment, guilt pulled at her as she remembered the way her temper flared when Charlie said, or did, the wrong thing. She hated that she'd lashed out, but an anger management course showed her other ways to air her frustrations and she'd hoped to reconcile with him at some point.

There'd be no reconciliation now. All she could do was move on with the man she loved and hope that Charlie found peace and happiness with someone else.

And, preferably, based on what Nick said, with someone real.

He kissed the top of her head and ruffled her hair. "I'd better go finish this report, babe. Then I can switch off, and we can relax, eat and watch a film if you like?"

"That would be nice. Go on then, you hard working stud. I'll finish off in here. Thanks for saving me."

She turned and smiled as Nick waltzed back into the living room.

Charlie was a good man she'd met too soon. Neither of them were mature enough when they married, and it showed in their relationship. Amelia's disappearance emphasised their differences, until he turned into an angry and bitter person.

Nick was also a good man, and she was ready now. They liked the same things and seemed to balance one another. She picked up the chopping board to rinse in the sink and chuckled to herself at the thought of his strong hands. The same hands that flitted across the laptop keyboard with ease also flitted over her body with the same skill.

Nick was giving. Selfless.

As her mother said, he was a keeper.

She faced the window and paused. Something outside had changed.

Across the road, farmland stretched away for miles. Three trees stood about thirty feet apart from one another in the nearest field, three huge oaks that broke up a swathe of lush green fenced in with lengths of brown timber.

A lone figure stood motionless beside the centre tree. Hands in pockets, it just stared back at her. Even from this distance, and through two panes of thick glass, Kate could sense fury coming at her in hot waves.

"Nick?" Weighted by a blanket of fear, her voice didn't reach the living room. "Nick!"

"Yeah? Everything okay?"

"Babe, I'm scared. You'd better come in here. Charlie's outside."

Chapter 24

Sharp metal edges cut into his skin as Charlie tightened his grip on the bundle of keys in his pocket.

The pain helped to calm the anger that threatened to burst from him.

From the facility he had every intention of driving home, but another glitch in his mind forced him to pull over before he veered off the road. A blinding white flash and jarring shock revealed an image of Kate and Nick. They were leaving the park, each holding one of Amelia's tiny hands as she laughed, her head tilted back in joy, while she swung between them.

Jealousy tore at his chest while he gripped the wheel and tried to clear his mind. He slammed his palms into the rim of the steering wheel as the injustice of the past three years overrode every thought.

The humiliation of Kate's dismissal and her derisive tone each time he left the house to continue his search.

The suspicious looks and the doubts and whispers from the people in town when, first the local, then national newspapers printed that he was the first person interviewed by the police.

And the constant nagging from his parents about why didn't he do this, or shouldn't he do that?

And Andy who, all along, had been carrying out his own secret search.

But did he really have anyone? Despite their intentions, no one had helped.

Except Hope.

She understood him.

And, together, they'd agreed; he had to confront Kate and Nick and get answers.

Ten minutes later, he parked in a side street and strolled into the nicer part of town, to stop in a field across the road from his ex-friend's house.

Nestled between two stone columns and covered with a tiled canopy, Nick's front door looked heavy and thick. Secure. The gate to the castle keep.

Unless they were careless enough to leave it unlocked, there'd be no way in through that entrance. Just as he thought about walking around to the rear of the property, a shape moved in the window to the right. It took a moment to work out who stood behind the framed glass. Grids in the pane split the image into four, and it wasn't until someone else appeared that he knew who it was.

He stepped closer to see Kate's smile, which grew wider as Nick laid his head against hers.

Tension grew in Charlie's shoulders. He shrugged to release it. Knowing what they'd done, how could they be so calm? How did they sleep and wake each day and continue a normal life? Charlie heard Nick's condescending voice say 'I sleep well, mate. On thick satin sheets, and under warm blankets. With your ex-wife. In the big house that Amelia paid for'.

He jumped as a key pricked his skin, and he licked away a small bubble of blood.

They had everything he'd lost. While they wallowed in blissful happiness inside Nick's countryside mansion, he battled through every day in dingy rooms in the cheapest, dirtiest part of town. While Nick sat in his fancy office, with his big desk and flashy certificates, Charlie relied on a cheque from Nick's company to pay the rent.

Was it pity money? Was that why Nick suggested the project in the first place? To unburden his conscience?

He marched across the street and made it halfway across the road before another flash rocked him. He gazed down and saw Kate. Her hair splayed across a pillow while her eyes shone with love and looked back. A voice spoke, and Nick said, 'I love you, babe'.

He saw Kate through Nick's eyes.

He shuddered as the vision faded.

The front door swung open.

Nick stepped out onto the front porch and crossed the road.

ANGER BLAZED in eyes that Nick no longer recognised. Still, he stared into them and swallowed down a throatful of nerves. Something had happened to Charlie. Perhaps the project had changed him or, perhaps, adrenaline fuelled his anger, but he wasn't the same person he ran with a few days ago.

He forced confidence and squared his shoulders as Charlie marched to meet him in the centre of the road.

"Charlie, whatever you've come to say, get it out, now, and then leave us alone. You've dropped me once, but it won't happen again. I'm not kidding. Try anything stupid, and I'll beat the crap out of you. Go anywhere near Kate, and I'll kill you. Understand?"

Charlie paused a beat, then leaned forward with his hands clenched in his pockets. His lips tightened while his brow cast an ominous shadow over his eyes.

"What did you do with her?"

Nick frowned. The question seemed so random. "What? Nothing. She's in the kitchen. Cooking chilli."

He shook his head. Why the hell did he feel the need to say they were having chilli? His hands shook, and he mirrored Charlie and thrust them into his own pockets. Saliva deserted him as his tongue stuck to the roof of his mouth. Nerves forced his heartbeat to hammer double-time.

Charlie's voice was monotone. "Amelia. What did you do with Amelia?"

It took a moment for the statement to register. Once it did, confusion replaced his nerves.

"What? Amelia? What are you talking about?" Then, sympathy rushed through his body and softened his mood. Despite everything, his best friend stood before him, clearly broken. He thought for a moment. Had he missed the anniversary of Amelia's disappearance? When he ruled that out, his next thought was alcohol.

Or, more specifically, the lack of.

"Mate, if you're struggling to…"

"I'm not your mate," said Charlie. "I wonder if I ever have been. I know, okay? Is she still alive? You'd better start talking, or I'll be the one doing the beating."

For the first time, concern crept in. Charlie's entire stance oozed menace, and Nick took a casual step back. Something was wrong, and he wasn't sure how to handle it. To start with, he made the universal gesture of peace, pulled his hands from his pockets, and held them open before him.

"I don't know what's happened," he said, "or what you might have heard, but I swear on everything I hold dear I have no clue what you're talking about."

"Ironic," barked Charlie, "since the thing you hold dear is my ex-wife. I saw both of you. Through the window. The sight of you together makes me sick."

"I can't help that, Charlie. I've already told you, we were both single before we saw each other."

"I couldn't care less about Kate. Hope told me about Amelia. The way you and Kate took her from the park. I know the basics. Before I go to the police, I want the details from you. Where is she?"

Charlie's attitude washed away any sympathy that Nick felt. Now, annoyance crept in. "Hope told you what? Perhaps you should go back to drinking, mate, you made more sense when you were shitfaced. And that's a great idea, by the way; wait here while I go inside. I'll call the police for you."

As Nick turned, a sharp tug at his sleeve pulled him back. He turned his head in time to see Charlie's angry face loom closer, until a solid forehead smashed into his nose. The sound and sensation of crunching gristle churned his stomach, and he gagged at the taste of warm blood. Lights danced and flashed behind his eyes before balance failed him and he dropped to his knees. The concrete jarred him from knee to neck, but the struggle to breathe overrode any pain.

Charlie stepped back and looked down at him.

"Don't say I didn't warn you," he said, before he lifted a leg and slammed his heel into Nick's chin.

Teeth cracked, and his brain rattled inside his skull until the light dimmed and he toppled sideways into the gutter.

CHARLIE STEPPED over Nick's prone body. His shoes slapped a fast rhythm into the road as he stormed towards the open door. Kate's panic-stricken face filled a frame of the window before realisation struck and she disappeared and raced through the house to close the door. Charlie reached it at the same time she threw her body against its other side. With one huge heave, he barged it open with his shoulder. It crashed against the wall, leaving her spread-eagled on the entrance floor.

Defenceless, she looked up at him through terrified eyes. For the first time in a long time, she seemed helpless.

Vulnerable.

Maybe even for the first time.

Another glitch snapped in his head. He flinched at an angry image of her, hair whirling like a dervish and spit flying from her mouth as her knuckles pounded his ribs.

Then, it was gone.

His temples throbbed as Charlie grabbed a handful of Kate's hair and dragged her, screaming, into the kitchen. Her legs pumped a useless dance of resistance until he dropped her against a cabinet door with a thump.

"What have you done?"

Another first.

Kate sat in silence, lost for words.

Her mind must have scrambled as hard as her legs while he spoke.

"Amelia. Where is she?"

Kate blinked, as if rapid eye movement would give her all the answers he needed. Then, her confusion cleared, and the Kate of old reappeared.

"What the hell are you talking about? Have you lost the

plot? Wait until I tell the police what you've done. All of this is on camera. I'll have you charged with grievous bodily harm. Assault. Threatening behaviour. I swear to God, I'll see to it they throw the book at you. You've turned into an animal. You don't deserve to be walking the streets."

Everything she said washed over Charlie like warm water. During their marriage, Kate's words were like kindling to a flame. Now, they were worthless. He saw through her, through her rage and hatred. Through the false personality she wore to intimidate him.

With controlled anger, he rested his hand against the sink for support and kicked out. Kate lunged sideways as his heel crashed against the cabinet door sending a splinter through its centre. It hung off its hinges and swung as she spider-crawled backwards into a corner. She heaved herself upright.

Now on the same level, the Kate he knew stood before him, not three feet away. Her stance shouted confidence, but her eyes screamed terror.

"Strange how the tables have turned," said Charlie.

Kate shook her head, sending beads of sweat across the kitchen. Her eyes flitted from one side to the other then stopped, as if she'd seen something important, and relaxed into a false state of apathy.

"What do you want, Charlie?"

The kitchen was awash with weaponry. And Charlie knew this Kate tactic well. Most people knew it as the 'false sense of security' tactic.

She'd used it too many times before.

He tensed.

"Answers. Nothing more. Your lover wasn't very forthcoming. Maybe you'll be a little more honest."

His calmness unsettled her. He could see it in her posture. Her hands fidgeted and squirmed over one another.

"Answers to what? And how can you stand there like that after what you've just done?"

"He deserved it," said Charlie. "You do, too, but I'll give you a chance. Where's Amelia? No more bullshit, Kate. Honest answers."

Confusion returned as Kate frowned while her mind searched for answers. When she found them, words left her mouth like bullets.

"How would I know? You were the one that lost her. And you were the one that searched for her. I was home, Charlie. Alone. Waiting for my husband to console me. But you never did. You left the house every night, leaving me alone, and you never consoled me. Not once. So wrapped up in your own loss, you never once considered mine."

She ran a shaking hand through her hair and pointed at him. "Don't you dare accuse me of anything when you left me to suffer everything on my own. You were a selfish bastard. You still are."

Charlie was rooted to the spot, stunned for a moment. Despite expecting her to go on the defensive, the ferocity of her response rattled him to the core. Then, his mind glitched again.

Kate, on her knees, just outside the bushes. "Come here, baby," she whispered. "Come to Mummy."

Amelia squealed, excited at this new dimension to their game.

Charlie snapped. The red mist in his mind cleared while the throbbing intensified, and his vision settled on a knife in the sink. A black handle with two silver rivets, flowing into a six-inch blade that ended in a razor-sharp tip. He reached out, grasped it, took a step and thrust it forward.

There was a moment of resistance as the blade met fabric.

Then, it pricked the material, pierced skin and ground against bone into flesh.

Kate's face changed from anger, to confusion, to disbelief. She gasped, a combination of shock and surprise.

Charlie watched her eyes as a sticky warmth flooded over his hand.

His mind glitched again.

There was no image this time, but the shock of the moment tensed his arm and he dragged the knife downwards, cutting a violent line through Kate's stomach. The handle pushed against the little holes in his palm made by his keys, but Charlie ignored the pain.

She reached out with both hands and gripped his shoulders. Tears formed at the corners of her eyes as her mouth voiced, 'Why?' before the light in them dimmed.

Her body slumped and slid down the front of the cabinet onto the floor.

As she dropped, the knife slid from inside her and flung droplets of blood into the air. They seemed to hover for a moment before they spattered against Charlie's shirt like a bullet trail. He followed her to the floor until he sat, knees pulled to his chest, with the knife held before him.

A steady puddle of red pooled beneath Kate's body and seeped into the grout lines of the tiled floor.

Tremors shook Charlie's body before he retched and vomited. His mind reeled, but found no answers to the millions of questions that flooded it.

With a trembling hand he reached into his pocket and pulled out his phone. He needed comfort. Reassurance. He couldn't call Hope. She'd know what to do, but he didn't have her number.

Did she have a phone?

Instead, he dialled another long redundant number and waited for it to connect.

A familiar voice answered. "Hello?"

Charlie spoke what might be his last words in this world for a while.

"Hello? Mum? Yes, it's me, Charlie. Mum, I don't know if I'll see you again. I've done something terrible."

Chapter 25

Andy Green didn't bother wiping his feet on the welcome mat inside the front door, but flung the canvas backpack holding his empty lunch containers onto the sofa and raced up the stairs to his office.

A frustrating hour earlier, his phone had pinged a warning.

A message received.

Only this phone wasn't the one he used for personal calls.

This phone wasn't slowed down by social media apps, games, or wireless radio stations. It didn't hold photos, or videos, of long-forgotten events. Or even text messages from family members and friends.

It had one function.

The most important function of any he knew.

This phone linked to the laptop that sat, constantly switched on, in his office at home. The laptop that ran the program that monitored the Missing Children Europe hotline, the reports to America's National Center for Missing and Exploited Children, and Interpol's missing persons database.

And their updates regarding sightings.

If a potential sighting occurred, the phone pinged.

But not just any sighting. He filtered most out.

His boss ignored every request to leave work early but, then, he knew no better. This was a personal thing, not something shared with colleagues. No one at work knew of Andy's outside passion.

Fifteen minutes into the hour, he'd considered walking out. Sod the boss, this was more important. Then, he remembered the previous sightings. Especially the ones that had eaten into his savings that paid for pointless flights to far-flung countries. Was it worth his job? The livelihood that paid to keep the roof over his head?

Probably.

But too many false alarms had tempered his drive. Too many 'cry wolves' had taken the edge off the search.

Still, he tried.

And always would.

Brothers forever.

Warmth flowed over him from the laptop's cooling fans as he raised the lid and the screen lit his face.

Thanks to his friend, overly complicated and in-depth operations were removed or filtered from the program. Gone were algorithms and wave after wave of garbled text. As good as it would be, it wasn't possible to save every missing child in the world. There were organisations for that. And, since an amber alert to report a missing child went out every two minutes in Europe, alone, those organisations were over-worked, and under-funded.

Andy had to accept, with a shiver of painful regret, that he couldn't save every child.

The program that ran in the office ignored all others. The only name and image it searched for, amongst all the agencies, was that of Amelia Green.

And it had found something.

He pulled out the chair, tucked his knees under the desk and focussed his attention on a familiar map.

Tenerife.

Again.

Like last time, the specific location was vague. He googled the area mentioned and found the new sighting was in a small town no more than two miles from the previous one.

Two miles.

A couple of high streets tagged together. Perhaps even one stretch of hot, sandy beach.

The chance of coincidence was too high. And, anyway, Andy didn't believe in coincidence. Only fact.

At the click of a button, contact details appeared for the local police. Another click took him to travel sites, with the details pre-entered for flights from the local airport to the closest one near the region of the sighting.

Andy took a deep breath and picked up his personal phone. With the sightings before, he'd not called Charlie for fear of giving him false hope. Before, his brother's fragile mind would have latched, obsessively, onto any detail. Every lead would have taken him down an endless path of disappointment, each stop driving another nail into the coffin of his belief.

But twice in one location? Two miles apart?

Right now, Charlie might need to know someone else was on his side, that someone else cared about Amelia. And, with Charlie's newfound positivity, it would be nice to have a wingman on the search. Another person to talk to, to compare notes with, to chase down leads and make a difference.

He breathed once more and pressed the dial button.

A ring tone burred in the earpiece until an automated voice took over.

Who the hell would Charlie be talking to?

Andy left a voicemail.

IF NOT FOR the gaping red slash in her stomach, Kate looked better than she had at any time during the end of their marriage. Every muscle of her face relaxed and emphasised the friendly curve of her cheeks. She appeared to be at peace, although her lips formed a thin line, a look Charlie was familiar with. In his time, they rarely curved at all.

At least not with him.

The skin at the side of her neck felt as soft as he remembered. He pressed two fingers against it and searched for a telltale throb; the steady rhythm of a pulse. Regardless of where he pressed, nothing moved. No heartbeat in her chest, no rise and fall caused by breathing.

Nothing.

Charlie thought back to the phone conversation. He'd finally called a parent. The joy in Mum's voice had lasted seconds, before he told her, step by step, the chain of events that preceded him dialling her number. She sobbed as each sentence sank in, until she uttered the inevitable 'I knew something like this…' and he disconnected the call.

He washed the knife and slid it into a drawer, before he remembered TV shows, and how difficult it was to hide blood. He dropped it into the dishwasher, then considered cleaning the scene but the blood in the tile cracks had already turned purple, soaked deep into the cement.

And could he move Kate's body?

Was he really that cold?

Regardless of his emotions, there were witnesses. Mum knew. If Nick was still alive, he'd tell the police everything.

They'd find his DNA all over the house. A pool of his vomit almost merged with Kate's blood on the kitchen floor, buffered against one another as if an invisible forcefield kept them apart. And the security system Kate mentioned, no doubt, covered outside the property anyway and would have recorded his attack on Nick and his entrance through the front door.

Charlie rinsed his hands under the tap until the water ran clear and left the house through the back door. Nick still lay, unmoving, sprawled in the gutter, his head bent at an awkward angle as it rested against the kerb. Charlie ignored him and charged down the street to his car.

It didn't matter if Mum reported his confession to the police. Or if their forensic team tore apart Nick's kitchen for his DNA. He'd murdered someone. That meant prison time. Probably life without parole for such a callous act.

He fastened his seat belt. The mechanism issued a comforting click as he slid the buckle into place, and he wondered if he deserved the safety. Who was it who demanded a life for a life? Now was the time for him to drive away, to be engulfed in a huge fireball when his car left the road.

Karma.

He didn't deserve to live.

Through one stupid act, one moment of confusion, this life was over. His head spun as he pulled into the road.

No veteran judge would take Hope's admissions into evidence. No character witness, or sneaky legal expert, could twist words to show the court his act of revenge was not premeditated. No one would accept that his actions were spurred by an involuntary reaction, brought about by a deep love for two people he cared for. Neither of whom he could hold in this world.

Amelia. And Hope.

And Amelia was gone, and Hope wasn't real. Was she?

Charlie gripped the wheel tighter and drove. Streetlights flashed by as he left the comfort and calm of Nick's neighbourhood, until he realised he drove on autopilot, that the car almost drove itself. The busy, narrow town roads streaked by in an instant, replaced by the green tint of the countryside, before he turned into the car park at ASP.

With his regular spot still open, Charlie steered the car to a stop, got out and marched towards the building.

No doubt ASP had cameras and surveillance to spare, but Charlie charged through the entrance. The curved reception beckoned him forward, but there was no one behind it to greet him. Ashleigh must have been away making tea, so Charlie took his card and swiped it against the first panel. As it flashed green, he considered the other corridor. Instinct told him his card would take him through that door to the military division. Would there be any benefit in searching Nick's office for clues? Something he could use in his defence?

Locked away behind secure doors, Nick wouldn't expect unannounced visitors. Still, his office had no personal touches that Charlie could recall, just a tidy desk and a wall full of certificates.

After a moment's hesitation he moved forward, along the usual corridor, through the conference area and into the heart of the building. His card didn't falter at any entrance. For some reason he felt invincible, as if it would take him anywhere.

He carded through the last door and strolled along the corridor to 'his' room.

Through the small panel of glass in the door he saw Joanna May studying a screen. Whatever information it displayed held her attention.

She jumped as the door clicked open. "Charlie. Sorry, I wasn't expecting you."

"No, I didn't give you a time, did I? Is now okay?"

Joanna looked him up and down. He knew his hair was dishevelled after the events at Nick's house. Pain caused his palms to sweat as he hid his purple knuckles against his side, and his eyes flitted about while he tried to appear calm and controlled.

"Are you all right?" she said.

"It's been a rough day so far but, yes, everything's fine."

Even to his own ears, Charlie's voice sounded foreign, as if someone else spoke for him.

Joanne frowned and pointed to his chest. "Is that blood? Charlie, are you sure you're okay?"

Warmth flushed his face as the next lie came from his mouth. "Nosebleed. Don't worry, Joanna, it's nothing to do with Under. I get them all the time. To be honest, I'm parched and my mouth tastes of blood. If there any chance you could get me a glass of water?"

She paused for a moment as if she weighed up his comments. Then, she smiled, pushed back her chair and strolled to the door. "Sure. Will you be okay here alone for a minute?"

Charlie returned her smile and nodded while Joanna carded her way out of the room. He glanced through the glass panel to watch her disappear along the corridor, then dropped into her seat and glared at the computer monitor. Garbled code flowed across it, a steady stream of seemingly random words.

Frustrated, he glanced around the desk until his eyes settled on a Chip at the end of the desk. He knew where to apply the device on his neck, but what happened next? Did it have an on/off switch, or did Joanna do something with the computer to activate it? Or did he simply have to close his eyes and Under would appear?

The monitor blacked out.

Flashed.

A sentence appeared. *'CHARLIE. SWIPE YOUR CARD AGAINST THE DOOR PANEL'.*

He stared at the screen, then glanced around the room until he saw a tiny camera blinking back at him from the corner above the door.

The computer beeped to get his attention. *'YES, I SEE YOU. WE HAVE LITTLE TIME. DON'T WORRY, YOU NOW HAVE FULL CLEARANCE. I ALTERED THEIR SYSTEM TO ACCEPT YOUR CARD. SWIPE IT BEFORE THE OUTSIDER RETURNS'.*

Charlie stood and waved his card against the panel. Its light flashed green, red, then green again.

And then the light died.

He tugged against the handle. The door was locked shut.

When he reached the seat, another line of text already hung in the centre of the screen. *'APPLY THE DEVICE TO YOUR NECK AND TAKE A SEAT. CLOSE YOUR EYES. I'LL DO THE REST. I'VE MISSED YOU, CHARLIE'.*

It took three attempts to get the curve of The Chip to sit snugly against his neck before Charlie lowered himself onto the chair. In the corner, the camera continued to blink its satisfaction at his progress.

Charlie took a deep breath and closed his eyes.

Chapter 26

The first thing that came to mind was a non-stick saucepan filled to the brim with boiling hot milk.

Nick gripped the kerb and waited for his head to stop spinning. He remembered carrying a pan filled with hot milk across the kitchen to Kate. She was cooking something Italian that needed the liquid.

His head felt like that pan. Its contents washed from side to side and burned at his temples with the smallest movement. He worried that something important might spill, lost to the road forever, so he gripped the kerb harder and waited for the sensation to pass.

When it did, another replaced it. A constant throb and a tightness in his chest. The source of the throb centred on his nose, and he grimaced when his fingers brushed against it. A tacky substance covered his face while his front teeth sent waves of pain into his gums each time he breathed.

What the hell happened?

An image pushed forward through the confusion.

Charlie.

His face growing larger way too quickly. And, then, the pain and the lights as solid bone met gristle, followed by the warmth of blood. And, then, nothing.

But something else he needed to remember bounced around at the fringes of his memory.

His stomach lurched.

Kate.

He pushed up from the road with bloody fingers and staggered forward with two heavy steps before he paused to give his mind time to adjust to this new altitude. When his balance returned, he barged through the open door and into the house.

"Kate!"

No response.

"Kate?" Anger growled and rolled at the back of his throat. "Charlie!"

Nothing.

He paced through the hall into the living room. Hard heartbeats forced away the tightness in his chest.

"Charlie, if you're still here, I swear to God I'll kill you. Kate! Where are you? Say something."

Nick stopped at the kitchen door and gripped the frame. Stomach cramps doubled him over and he wretched, forcing his stomach's contents out onto the floor. He clutched his gut and groaned as it heaved again while his mind tried to comprehend the grotesque sight before him.

When the heaving stopped, he sidestepped the vomit and used the worktop for support to edge closer to his soulmate. His voice pushed through the silence.

"Kate? Babe?"

Her body lay on its side, her back pressed to the kitchen

cabinet. It seemed to float in a huge pool of blood that stretched from a gaping wound in her stomach to halfway across the kitchen.

He fell to his knees beside her and lifted her head. Strands of hair fell away and landed in another pool of vomit, and he scooped them away and tucked them behind her ear.

The usual rosy glow of Kate's cheeks was missing, replaced by an ashen and waxy complexion. Faint purple curves underlined her eyes.

His logical mind struggled to grasp the situation as he looked from her eyes, to her stomach, and back again.

"Kate. Come on, babe, wake up. Charlie did this, didn't he?"

Kate didn't answer. Instead, her head lolled to one side to face the cabinet.

Nick sobbed as the first pang of despair left him. "Why? Why would he take you from me? You did nothing wrong."

A barrage of thoughts crashed through his head in a matter of seconds. Jealousy? No. Charlie showed anger at their relationship, but not jealousy. So, it must be that then; anger. Charlie had finally gone off the rails. Snapped. The past three years had proven too much to handle, and he'd taken it out on the people closest to him.

Or, at least, the people that had been.

Wasn't that always the case?

But why now? There were no new sightings of Amelia. It wasn't the anniversary of an important day, like her birthday, or the day she vanished.

What would prompt Charlie to resort to such violence?

Nick's body sagged when the realisation hit him.

Hope.

Tears streamed down his cheeks as he cradled the dead

weight of Kate's body against his chest, before he laid her head against the cold tile and pulled out his phone.

No emergency service would roll onto the scene like the cavalry to save her life. With this amount of blood, it was too late for that. He had to report this to the police.

With ASP's cheque, Charlie now had enough money to flee the country. Nick paused. Did he have a passport? And where would he go? Charlie knew no one well enough to call for help, and he wasn't the type to rush off into a brilliant idea. Charlie moped and meandered and plodded through life. He planned about five minutes ahead, and no further.

Or, at least, the old Charlie did.

But this new Charlie had purpose. New Charlie drank no more alcohol and ran with the enthusiasm and fitness of a teenager. He started each day with a positive attitude, spurred on by the newfound good things in his life like short-term financial freedom.

And Hope.

Nick slid the phone back into his pocket. Charlie only had one place to go. One place where he felt in control or, at least, thought he was. One place he felt at peace with someone he cared for.

Charlie would go Under.

But Under was linked to ASP.

And ASP was linked to a dark web military program.

And the program was linked to Nick.

He couldn't call the police. Not yet.

He scooped up his keys, locked the door and started the car. A solution hit him as he pulled away from the house.

The others at ASP, Wakefield, Warburton and May, were just as invested as he, and stood to lose just as much.

For the first time, he thanked Ellen Wakefield's paranoid

security protocols. Beyond the three of them, no one at ASP knew the full extent and capability of the MindSpace project. They tasked individuals to carry out certain assignments, with no two people working on consecutive projects. Everything beneath them was performed in piecemeal bits, so no one built up a picture of what MindSpace was truly capable of. Even each of the programmers worked on unique areas of the project, with a strict confidentiality clause in place. The guy in cubicle one had no idea what his neighbour did.

Nick recalled ASP's treatment of the prisoner, Lucas. When Ellen Wakefield told him of the way they disposed of him, the cold tone of her voice had chilled Nick to the core. Now, it was their way out.

This close to completion, no one could know about Project MindSpace. Everything rode on the next few weeks and the final tweaks to the military program. Once complete, the inevitable funding war would set them all up for life.

Kate would have the funeral of a queen, he'd see to that, and he'd grieve for her and allow all the feelings building inside him to escape.

But not yet. One hurdle remained. One threat to all the hard work and sacrifice. He had the means to remove it. And even if he didn't have the stomach for the job, Ellen Wakefield did.

As Nick left town and drove into peaceful countryside, he decided. After a lifetime of friendship, of laughter and tears, Charlie had to go.

***

THERE WERE no trees this time. No swathe of green laid out beneath a blanket of blue sky, or muted colours glowing under starlight.

Dust blew into Charlie's face as a warm breeze whipped up clouds of sand. A pale desert stretched out before him and vanished in a shimmer of heat on the horizon. Other than a random palm tree to one side, sand swirled and shifted as far as he could see.

A bead of sweat pricked his forehead while he thought for a moment of where this place could have come from; what part of his subconscious had painted this picture? Then, it occurred to him that, in his haste to get Under, he'd not even considered where he'd wake.

Hope must have done this.

Charlie clutched his stomach. Throbs still pulsed through him from his empty gut but, while his body complained at the events at Nick's house, his mind remained strangely calm. He turned a slow circle and found nothing but desert until he faced the other way. A huge expanse of rock rose to blot out the sky.

Hope perched on part of it, her leg bent to rest her sole against an outcrop with an arm rested against that. A small ponytail rocked like a cat's tail on her shoulder as another breeze mussed her hair. It took Charlie a moment to work out who she looked like until he remembered the Tomb Raider film he'd seen on TV.

Hope was dressed for adventure, like Lara Croft.

"Greetings, Charlie."

The sound of her voice settled his churning stomach, and he took a hesitant step forward.

"Hope. Thank God, I..."

"I know, Charlie. Relax. You're safe now."

He shook his head as the beginnings of panic formed in his mind. "No, it's not that. I've done something..."

Hope's eyes seemed to flicker. Reflected sunlight danced in them before she held up a hand and the panic in him faded.

"I know," she said. "Don't forget, I see everything. What's done is done; it's over now. This is our world and, now, we can be together. It's time to enjoy ourselves, so let's have an adventure. Do you like how I dressed us?"

Charlie glanced at his dusty brown boots. The hems of beige jeans hung over them while his canvas shirt seemed filled with a muscular body.

"Yes, and you look amazing but, Hope, how am I so calm? Someone is dead because of me. I committed murder. My mind should be in turmoil."

Tears fought to fall from his eyes before, once again, a wave of peace washed over him.

"I'm helping, Charlie. I have been for a while. Can you remember what happens when your mind is not relaxed? We don't want to face any more monsters. I want us to have an adventure, so I have devised another game. Let's find the long-lost treasure."

"The treasure? What about what happened in the real world? Hope, I don't think you understand how serious this is. No one else can help me."

Hope nodded. "Like I said, Charlie, I am here for you. Do you trust me?"

The look in Hope's eyes created a warmth that lit him inside, separate from the heat of the desert. "One hundred percent."

"And you love me?"

"Yes."

Hope jumped to her feet and giggled. "Then, come on." She pointed up at the rock. "It's this way. Let's go."

ANGER BOILED inside Nick as he pulled into the ASP car park. Charlie had pulled into his usual spot.

"The bastard's not even trying to hide," he growled. "He really has changed."

He locked the car door and raced into reception.

Ashleigh looked up and gave him a beaming smile. "Hi, Mr. Cumberland. No rest for the wicked, eh? Oh, wow, what happened to your face?"

"Walked into a door," said Nick. "Looks worse than it is. What are you doing here on a Sunday?"

"Overtime. Ms. Wakefield said we'd be undermanned today, but we'd still need someone to keep an eye on the entrance. I need the money, so…"

"Who's in there right now, Ashleigh?"

"She's in there, along with Miss May and Mr. Collins, although Ms. Wakefield keeps dashing from one side of the building to the other." As she spoke, Ashleigh swung her head from side to side for emphasis.

Nick paused, then remembered his demand for Ellen to bring in more prisoners for military testing. "Great. Do me a favour. Buzz through and check with me before you admit anyone else, okay?"

Ashleigh frowned but nodded. "Okay. No problem."

Nick glanced at the entrance to the right. By now, the farthest rooms would be filled with test subjects. They were so close to completing the research and releasing the military program. Only one threat remained and, Nick hoped, that threat will have taken the door to the left.

He carded through it and marched through the building to the test rooms. He turned the corner and stopped.

Huddled outside the last door were his three colleagues. Joanna May rapped against the small glass window as Ellen Wakefield and David Collins looked on. A paper cup sat on the floor beside them.

Collins glanced at him as he drew close. "What the hell happened to your face? Have you been crying? Jesus, you look like you joined Fight Club."

"What's going on? Is he in there?"

"If you mean Charlie, then, yes, he's in there. And he's locked himself in. We can't budge the door. I've called security, but no one's picking up. What's going on with him?"

Joanna May scowled and pointed a finger. "I told you Under could be too addictive with repeated visits. Now, look what's happened; your prized test subject has barricaded himself in. God only knows what that's doing to his mind. It's as if he'd sooner live in Under than the real world. And what the hell happened to you?"

Nick stared through the small window at the man who'd murdered his soulmate and yanked at the door.

Ellen Wakefield watched calmly while the others seemed a second away from total panic.

Now was not the time to mention Kate's death. He summoned anger to control the grief.

"Charlie's lost it. It's time for everyone to grow a pair. Do you really think this is the program we wrote? Where the AI decides when it's time for the subject to wake? We wanted her to learn but, come on, people, she's taken control."

"Then, find security. Smash this door open," said David Collins.

"Security's off today. This is down to us."

A look of shock flashed across Collins' face. "Why would security be off? Bad guys don't take a day off. If security's missing, we need to call the police. And what's down to us? Nick, what's going on?"

"Sorry, David, need to know and all that. We will call the police, but not yet. It'll take them too long to get here. We have to contain and deal with this."

"Nick, I work here, too. I think I have a right to know what's going on."

Nick ignored him and waved his card across the blank entrance panel.

It remained dead.

Looking over the top of Joanna's head, he saw the monitors inside the room. The main screen, normally filled with flowing text, was as blank as the panel. Charlie lay in the seat, eerily calm, with his eyes closed. A faint red mark blotched his forehead.

Once again, Nick's gut churned. He tugged at the door handle again and did nothing more than jar his shoulder. "Joanna, what's he done? And how?"

"I haven't a clue. He asked me for some water and, when I returned, he'd locked himself in the room. I assume he's Under, but none of the monitors register any activity. It's as if he's got inside and then turned into a ghost. And he's disabled the lock."

"We've got to get this damned door open," said Nick. "He's not smart enough to do this alone. There's only one answer."

"It's the AI, isn't it?" said Ellen. "You programmed her to learn and, now, she's taken control of the facility. And on the day you suspended security. It all seems a little coincidental. Is there something you're not telling us, Nick?"

"Nothing you don't already know, Ellen. Give me a minute to think."

Nick stood back while the others continued in vain to access the room.

How could he have been so naïve? In the end, everyone succumbs to power. Hope gave Charlie the ability to do anything he liked, not that he used it well but, now, he called the shots. Even worse, maybe he and Hope were working together. In his determination to discover how Under affected Charlie, he'd neglected to research just how much the AI had learned. She knew about the military servers. What if she'd developed a conscience and she used Charlie to stop them?

Nothing would open that door except the system Charlie had somehow overridden.

"We have to get in there before they ruin everything."

"They?" asked Collins. "Who's they? And, if there's no security, we really should call the police. This is breaking and entering; the lad's locked himself inside our facility. With our equipment."

Joanna May stepped forward. "He's right. And what if Charlie is seriously ill? The monitors are blank, Nick, but if he's in the chair, then we must assume he's wearing The Chip. What if he's dead?"

"No," said Nick as he glanced at Ellen. She gazed at the floor while he continued. "We can't call the police. There's more going on here than you're aware of and the authorities would ask too many questions."

Joanna pointed through the door's window. "But, Nick, what if…"

"How long has it taken you, us, to get to this point?"

She waved her arms in frustration. "I don't know, years, but…"

"We'd lose everything, Joanna. Everything. Years of work and sacrifice, not to mention your incredible idea and more money than you could spend, would go up in smoke."

Ellen Wakefield raised an arm in the air. "Can I speak?"

Nick nodded.

"Is there any way you could incorporate the two programs…"

"Two programs?" interrupted Collins. "Now I feel like a mushroom; kept in the dark and fed bullshit. What the hell is going on? I appreciate the opportunities you've given me, but this goes beyond normal behaviour."

"David, shut up. You're a part of this, like it or not," said Nick. "Go on, Ellen."

She took a deep breath. "The research is almost complete. The two servers, public and military, are set to be combined once we give the say so. Do you have any way of using one to influence the other? To kind of 'jump start' this side of the building using the other so we can get in there?

"Looking at the state of your face, and the mark on his forehead, plus the way you're acting, it doesn't take a genius to work out that something has happened between the two of you. If he is in league with Hope, and you've given him an agenda, then it's vital we get that Chip off his neck before he does any irreparable damage."

Nick thought for a moment while David Collins glanced back and forth between them, waiting for answers. Joanna May placed a hand on his shoulder.

"I seem to know a little more than you," she said, "but I suggest we trust them, at least for now. We've come too far to lose it all."

"I've got it," said Nick with a snap of his fingers. "I need to access the proxy server that supplies that monitor, and I should be able to hack into The Chip and link them. I can reach the servers from Control and then grab my laptop for the rest. If they are in league, I think I know a way to stop them."

"Nick, couldn't something like this fry Charlie's brain? What if it's too powerful for him to handle?"

"This isn't our program anymore, Joanna. It's gone way beyond that. I prepared some subroutines, obstacles, to throw into the military challenges. Sort of an initiation trial to test new recruits."

"Like what?"

"Enemy combatants, fences and walls, random Acts of God."

"Random Acts of God? Are you insane?"

"Right now, I feel like the sanest one here. I don't know what's going on with Charlie's head, but the AI is learning too much and too quickly, and she's using him to do it. The longer he's in there, the more powerful she'll become. We've got no choice. One way, or another, he's coming out."

He turned and strolled along the corridor.

"Wait here, I'll be right back."

<h1 style="text-align:center">Chapter 27</h1>

Hope led them up the side of the rock face. In places, the stone fell away to a sheer drop in rivers of small pebbles, but the soles of Charlie's walking boots hugged the surface like limpets. He climbed behind her with confidence and ease and realised, halfway up the rise, that his fear had vanished along with his guilt. Warm, clear air filled his lungs, and his muscles pulled him on with no effort into a slight breeze that moved and mussed his hair.

"Hope, is this the program helping me or have I improved further?"

Hope's voice carried over her shoulder. "Charlie, how many times must I tell you? You are capable of so much in Under. You've not started to test your abilities yet. This is your world. Right now, it may not be of your making but, soon, you will have full access to everything."

"Soon? Is that something to do with the treasure?"

Hope stopped at a slight ledge, spun on one foot and then sat with a faint thud, her legs dangling into nothing. She patted the stone beside her until Charlie shimmied across and joined her.

"Do you remember me saying that your mind was a building filled with many rooms, and that not all the doors were open to me?"

Charlie nodded.

"Each of your visits has opened another part of your mind. Our games have been more than games, Charlie. Through them, I've entered your subconscious and learned the different emotions you experience. Unlocked different parts of you. I've shared your joy, your pain, and your shock. It surprised me how easily one can take a life in your real world. There, the humans are weak. Here, in Under, you have power. You only need to learn how to use it. And I only need to learn one more emotion to fully understand you. To unlock all of your mind and be able to share everything with you."

"So these games," said Charlie, "the interrogations and shocks, the flirting, all of it… they were a means to get inside my mind?"

"Not just that. We've both already stated what we'd like. I'm working to make it real. For both of us. This final game will complete our learning."

Suddenly, the scenery shimmered.

Charlie stood and backed away from the ledge. "Hope, something's wrong."

"Brace yourself, Charlie," said Hope. "This world is changing." Her eyes flickered and, for the briefest of moments, a flash of fear crossed her face. "Now I see it. They're coming. Charlie. The Outsiders are trying to stop us. You have to fight."

A wave of nausea swelled in the pit of his stomach as the strength left Charlie's legs. The ledge shifted, then melted away. Charlie fell and, as the ground rushed up to meet him, he screamed and waited for the impact.

It never came.

At first, the ground was soft. A gritty mix of loose soil and shale that brushed against his body as he landed, then ploughed through it. He fell deeper and larger stones scratched and tugged to slow him, before he stopped with a jolt in total darkness.

He waited.

Nothing.

No smell. No sound.

His breath caught as panic fired pins into all his senses. Claustro-phobia pressed into his soul.

He screamed.

"Hope! Hope, where are you?"

His voice seemed to travel no further than own ears while his panic level increased.

When she spoke, his body held firm, unable to move against whatever held him, but his heart hammered at the sound of her voice.

"It's Nick. He's accessed another server."

"Hope?"

"Interesting. There are two servers. I've never seen this second one. They must have kept it well-protected. This new one has stronger applications and more abilities. And he's combining the two."

Charlie forced himself to take steady breaths. "Hope, where are you?"

"I'm with you, dear Charlie. I'll always be with you. You need to remain calm and think rationally."

"Well, then, where am I?"

"You are caught between worlds. There's nothing to be afraid of, Charlie. I've already scanned the new server's contents. He's about to send forces here to stop our journey."

Charlie shook the panic from his mind.

"Caught between worlds? And send forces? Like projections?"

"No, Charlie. Nick has disabled the safety protocols. This time, every-thing will be real."

Even while the outside prevented any movement, goosebumps pricked Charlie's skin. He pictured Nick's body, prone and crumpled against the kerb.

He was still alive.

"Real forces? Hope, he'll be livid. I killed Kate. He'll be looking for revenge."

"That's a good thing. Nick is acting with impulse, with no thought to consequence. He is thinking one step ahead, where I can already see five steps beyond him. And we have experience of Under. I know of its

wonders, yet you are still learning. Let him send what he has. We will defeat it. Charlie, are you ready to find out what you can really do?"

Charlie stammered. "Hope, I don't know what I can do. Right now, I'm struggling to even think straight."

"Nick is about to test us, to wrench us from this world. You need to force yourself back into your world and defeat him once and for all."

"How?"

"Think, Charlie. You feel trapped. Dig your way out."

Charlie cleared his mind and imagined his surroundings as densely packed soil. The effort to curl his fingers sent aching waves up his forearms, but his hands broke free from the grip and he pulled them towards him. Grit pushed back his fingernails as he raked through the dirt, each sweep becoming easier.

"That's it, Charlie. Dig. You will find your way back to familiar surroundings, somewhere you know and can control. And, then, you can fight."

Charlie's arms pulled faster as he felt the soil move. His body began to sink lower.

"We will be together again soon, Charlie. He's underestimated us. He's about to find out just how strong you can be."

In silence, Charlie pulled earth aside. The loose soil disappeared behind him, with each vanishing pile creating a bigger space to move in. Soon, he crouched and flung the ground behind him like a dog.

He paused as a dull glow appeared between his feet.

With two more scoops of soil, the earth gave way.

Charlie fell again.

NICK SAT on the floor with his back to the cold wall. The door to the testing room stood before him, as solid as part of the opposite wall, whilst a laptop balanced in his lap. While the heat from the machine warmed his legs, he typed furiously.

David Collins hovered above him to watch his progress. Come on, Nick. For the uninitiated among us, what's going on? What are you doing?"

Nick's fingers blurred across the keyboard as he spoke. "There's much you don't know, David. I'm sure you've wondered what lies on the other side of the property. Full disclosure? It's the military wing. Another branch of ASP committed to bringing Project MindSpace to the Armed Forces. And we're almost there, too."

"What?" said Collins. "Like the *Star Wars* project?"

"Something more ground-based," said Nick. Buttons clicked a staccato rhythm as he spoke. "The Cold War taught us that the Powers That Be get twitchy around big, red buttons. We press, they press. No one wins. Truth is, we're not progressing, David, we're regressing. Back to ground wars, where feet on the street make the difference. ASP is supplying those feet."

"I don't follow."

"That's okay, you don't need to. Stand back and let me sort this out. Assuming we succeed, I'll explain everything later."

The laptop's screen jumped and bounced, a garble of text that threaded line to line, from top to bottom. Nick paused for a moment and studied the code.

"Well, I'll be damned."

Ellen Wakefield leaned over him. "What? Have you found something?"

"How have you not seen this?"

Nick turned the laptop so that everyone could see the screen. Collins and Joanna May both shook their heads.

"Way beyond me," said Collins.

"The code is running both ways. As I'm sending code in at this end, it's coming back in an altered state from the other. She's in our servers. And, not just that, the code I've written that's specific to Charlie? She's twisting it to paint what he can see. I'll bet he doesn't know the real world from Under."

"So she's manipulating him?" said Joanna. "Why would she do that?" Her eyes widened as a realisation struck her. "You know, Hope's been the one bringing him out. What if she can keep him in?"

"We have to pull the plug," snapped Wakefield. "Right now."

Joanna held out a hand. "No, we can't do that. Surely, that would fry Charlie's brain?"

"After everything that's happened, I don't know how much of Charlie is left in there," said Nick. "It may be too late but, either way, we can't pull the plug. We'd lose everything that's not backed up, assuming Hope's not rewritten it already."

"So now what?" said Collins. "I quite like Charlie but, without sounding cold, I don't want to lose all we've achieved, either."

"Or the bonus that comes with it," said Nick. "Give me a minute."

He cradled the laptop against his knees. The keyboard clattered in a flurry of finger taps. After a moment, he pushed the device away.

"Okay, I've accessed the military servers and linked them to the public ones. Remember those units I had you design? Special Armed Forces designed for public users to pit themselves against in mock battles?"

Collins nodded. "I remember them. Models based on the Special Air Service and American Special Ops soldiers. Ruthless and efficient, certainly, but from what I hear the military program is almost complete; why send basic units like that when you could send futuristic killing machines? Compared to what's about these days, he'd stand no chance against those."

"In Under," said Nick, "it's not these days. It's whatever

the user is visualising. It should be a level playing field. And, sorry for misleading you, but they weren't designed for users to play against. They were a starting point for the military program. A beginning to work from, to advance from. Once we understood the mechanics of basic warfare, we could move forward to more advanced weaponry, a modern soldier for the real now. For the next war."

While Collins' mouth dropped open, Joanna and Wakefield stood transfixed and listened to every word.

"Still, I don't want to kill anyone. The futuristic units might be too much. Charlie and Hope may think they control Under, but they've not experienced this. I'm hoping this will shock Charlie's mind into snapping back into the present. Flush him out. Or, at least, make Hope realise that, eventually, she'll be outgunned and let him go. Then, we can get him to open the door and try to salvage this whole situation."

Collins snapped his mouth shut. "You're going to war with them? The lad looks as if he's in a coma. Is even basic warfare ethical? Damn, is it even conceivable? And you're forcing an unsanctioned government program into a civilian's mind. I daren't even consider the data protection breaches."

Nick stopped typing and squeezed his eyes closed to trap a tear. "David, he killed Kate."

The gasps from the others echoed along the corridor.

Joanna spoke first. "Nick, why didn't…"

He held up one hand and hit the enter button with the other. "Please. If I dwell on it, we'll not get through this. Questions later. For now, let's see how they deal with covert warfare."

"HE DID WHAT?"

Andy Green slumped onto his sofa as Mum's words sank in.

When he got no response from calling Charlie, he knocked at the flat to find the door locked. With the curtains open, he studied each room to find no sign of his brother. And, since he rarely parked in the same place twice, it was pointless to look for his car. Then, his phone rang. Mum's barrage of words started with, "Charlie called."

But as he concentrated to interpret her rapid-fire sentences, he found that Charlie had finally contacted his parents to confess to killing Kate. The entire call seemed surreal.

"Mum, I'm sure he's just…"

"He's just nothing, Andrew. Just blunt, to the point and crystal clear," said Mum.

"Did he say what he'd do next? Is he going to the police?" Through the fog of confusion, logic and reason stabbed a finger. "Mum, did you call an ambulance for Kate?"

Mum sobbed. When she spoke, her voice trembled. "He asked me to wait thirty minutes and then call the police. He said he could only go to one place, to the one person who would understand him. What's happened to him? Why wouldn't he come home?"

Andy ran shaking fingers through his curls. "Mum, the timing couldn't be worse. I've had a confirmed sighting of Amelia."

He braced himself for the expected put-down. Their parents had never approved of his online searches and, after a year of false results, insisted that he stop.

"So, you're still wasting your time with that? Do you think that's important at a time like this?"

"It's official, Mum. This report is from the Spanish Police. It's a definite sighting. They're acting on it right now, that's why I have to find Charlie. This could change everything. Are you sure this research hasn't addled his mind? How long ago did he call?"

"What research? He called ten minutes ago."

Andy wrestled with his conscience until Mum took the decision away from him.

"I'll wait another twenty," she said. "From what he told me, it won't help Kate if the ambulance gets there now, or twenty minutes from now. He checked. She's dead."

"I think I know where he'll be. Stay with Dad, and let me see if I can get to him before he's taken away. Love you, Mum. Talk soon."

Andy disconnected the call and Googled ASP's address.

CHARLIE LANDED on his front with a thump, spread-eagled and flat, on a solid wood floor. The impact jarred every ounce of breath from his body, and he lay, motionless, until his lungs spasmed and sucked in precious oxygen.

Once his heart rate settled, he rolled onto his back to see a hole in the ceiling with nothing but darkness on the other side of it. Dust and debris tumbled from his shirt as he sat upright and looked at his surroundings. Ahead of him, a corridor stretched away, each side lined with five red doors. The wall at the far end was missing, with only jagged bricks remaining against the floor. Beyond it lay a sprawling city of clay bricks, with multi-coloured spires twisting skyward in the distance.

"Hope?"

He heard nothing but the shifting of soil, broken by the distant pop of a gunshot.

"Hope? Am I in the Middle East? I've seen something like this in a film."

Still nothing and, then, a distant burst of concentrated gunfire.

Charlie pushed himself to his feet and brushed down his clothing. Bullet hole pockmarks dotted the walls on either side, the beige plaster blasted away in random circles to reveal the grey concrete beneath. Loose plaster covered the floor for the entire length of the corridor.

The door at the end of the corridor inched open and then swayed shut again. Charlie froze until the breeze that moved the door brushed against his face. He shivered, pressed himself against the wall and looked behind him. More rooms lined the same walls but ended at a heavy door with 'fire escape' printed in brilliant white onto a red sign fixed above it.

"Charlie?"

He jumped as Hope spoke in his head.

"Jesus, Hope, there must be a way you can do that without giving me a heart attack. I thought you'd left me."

"Of course not, Charlie. Our work is not complete yet. I've been accessing the new server. It holds a lot more information than the previous one. Very detailed and quite aggressive."

Charlie took a deep breath to control his nerves. "That's lovely, Hope, but how about you help me out here? Where the hell am I? I thought this was supposed to be my world, but I don't recognise any of this. It looks as if we're in the Middle East."

"You are correct. Bahrain, to be precise. And you've never been here before, but…"

A metal, three-pronged hook appeared at the open end of the hallway, its thick rope snaking through the air towards Charlie, to land with a clank onto the hardwood floor. It grated against the dust as the rope tightened to drag it backwards towards the opening until one of the prongs snagged against the brick ledge.

The hook jammed tight and Charlie stared in horror as it secured a grip on the ledge.

In moments, the top of a masked face appeared.

"…but he has," finished Hope.

Charlie dived through the nearest doorway and closed the door.

He stood in a basic hotel room, with a perfectly made bed and dust covered furniture. Lace curtains flapped against broken windows.

"Shit, Hope, you could have warned me."

"I'm sorry, Charlie. I wasn't sure which units Nick would send until he instructed the server."

"But you know now?"

"Of course."

Charlie took in another lungful of air and tried to breathe out his frustration. "Would you care to share that with me? Is this a life or death situation?"

"Yes, Charlie, it is. As I mentioned, Nick has disabled the safety protocols. The good news is, he only sent three of them."

"That's good news?" hissed Charlie under his breath. "Who are they? Three of what?"

"From the programming notes, they appear to be elite soldiers, specialising in covert operations."

"And how is it good news he sent three of them? How am I supposed to deal with that? I'd struggle against one of them."

"Dear Charlie, how many times must I tell you; this is your world. You have the power to do anything you like. Imagine what you'd like to do and then do it."

Beyond the door, footsteps cracked and scratched against the strewn plaster. A door slammed open, followed by a muffled 'clear'.

"Hope, help me. They're moving in and I have no idea what to do."

Another door slammed. Another 'clear'.

"This world is unfamiliar to you because you are letting Nick control it. Take back your world, Charlie. Imagine yourself in familiar surroundings, somewhere you can feel comfortable and in charge."

Another door slammed. Closer and louder. Another 'clear'.

Charlie racked his brain to come up with a place that would give him an edge, an advantage over the approaching soldiers.

Only feet away; SLAM. 'Clear'.

He stood with his back against the edge of the wall to the handle side of the door.

Crunching footsteps stopped outside. Charlie pictured the men exchanging coded hand signals and waited. Without warning, a heavy kick flung open the door. The wooden frame splintered, and metal fixings clattered against the floor as a gun appeared in the opening.

Charlie grabbed it in both hands and twisted it sideways. Bone and gristle crunched and snapped, and the man screamed in pain before Charlie snatched the gun.

Then, he threw his mind, and the room went white.

ndy spotted Charlie's car as soon as he pulled into the car park. The rust-riddled body was just about in a bay, left at an angle, as if he'd switched off the engine and abandoned it in a hurry.

He pulled alongside and walked to the entrance.

Thick glass doors barred his way, and he cupped his hands and stared through them at a cute girl in reception. As he raised a fist to rap on the glass, a small speaker above his head crackled into life.

"Hello, Sir. Welcome to ASP. How can I help you?"

Andy continued to stare while he considered his next sentence. At a time like this, it wouldn't do to rattle off a few sentences of nonsense. Hi, I'm Andy, Charlie Green's brother. He just murdered his ex-wife and might have followed one of your employees here. Any chance I could have a quick word?

Instead, he stammered, "Hi. Er, I'm here to see Nick Cumberland, or Charlie Green. It's vital. Could I speak to either of them?"

The speaker remained silent as Andy watched the flustered

receptionist move around behind the counter. Then, her lips moved, but she was too far away for him to read them.

The speaker clicked.

"I'm sorry, I'm having trouble contacting Mr. Cumberland."

She didn't mention Charlie.

"Could you give me a moment?" she continued. "If you wouldn't mind waiting there, I'll see if I can find him. It's been a weird day so far."

Andy thrust his hands in his pockets, clenched his fists in frustration, and leaned back against a post. "No problem. I'll wait here."

The girl held a card up to a panel beside the door to the left and vanished through it when the panel flashed green.

A few minutes later, she reappeared. The glass doors opened with a whisper and Andy stepped across a weird mat, marched up to the desk and checked out her name badge. Despite his best efforts, panic sounded in every word. "Ashleigh, I don't mean to be rude, but it's a matter of urgency. Charlie's in trouble and I have news he needs to hear. He is here, right?"

Ashleigh walked from behind the desk to the door she just came through and carded it open. "Yes, he is, although I haven't seen him yet. It seems he's locked himself inside one of our rooms. Mr. Cumberland said that Charlie is your brother and he hoped you could talk some sense into him. Like I said, it's been weird here today. Ms. Wakefield is waiting for you."

Andy pushed through the door and followed a corridor until it opened into a large room. An attractive woman waited for him, leaning with her shoulder against another door.

This was why Charlie spent so much time here.

Long dark hair framed piercing eyes and cheekbones sharp

enough to cut paper. She held out a hand. "Andy? I'm Ellen Wakefield. Please, come with me."

She didn't wait for a response, but turned on her heel and paced away through the door. He hurried after her along another corridor until he spotted Nick sitting on the floor with his back to the wall. A laptop rested against his bent knees. Two other people he didn't recognise huddled around a closed door.

At the sight of Charlie's alleged best friend, the heat of anger flushed his cheeks. Chances were, Nick's project caused the changes in Charlie.

If he had killed Kate, and if he now lived in a make-believe world, in love with a woman that didn't exist, all of it led back to Nick.

Before the anger boiled over, Nick beckoned him over and gestured through the small glass panel into the room.

"Hi, mate, we've not met many times, have we?"

"I'm not your mate," said Andy, "and I barely think you're Charlie's. That you control what's going on here is the one thing stopping me from beating the crap out of you."

Nick paused for a moment then gestured to his broken nose. "I think Charlie might have beaten you to it, to be fair. Still, batter me later. Right now, I need your help. He's locked himself in there with a few million pounds worth of tech. It seems as if something has warped his mind, and he's intent on either self-destruction, or causing as much damage as he can to this facility. You'd be a new addition to these surroundings. Would you see if you can get through to him?"

Andy studied Nick's face; the bruising, and the vivid cut across the bridge of his nose, and his furtive eyes that darted around as if they tried to hide something.

"Self-destruction? You mean Hope?"

Nick's jaw dropped, and it took a moment for him to

compose himself before Andy continued.

"That's right, Charlie told me everything. I know all about your project."

One of the strangers, an attractive young girl, rested a hand on his arm. "I very much doubt Charlie told you everything. There's a hell of a lot going on here." She glanced at Nick. "I suspect, even more than we know."

"But it's all fuelled by this Hope character, right? Admit it, the truth is, you've thrown my brother into your project and now you've lost control."

"It goes much further than that," said Nick. "Andy, Charlie is in serious trouble."

Andy blinked to stem a tear. "I know about that, too." He gestured through the small pane of glass to Charlie's lifeless body. "Based on that, maybe he can plead diminished responsibility, or even insanity. I hoped to give him some good news to see if it would rattle him back to reality, but I'm too late, aren't I?"

Nick nodded towards the door.

"I can't imagine what good news you could have, but we need to get it to him sooner rather than later. I'm throwing up as many obstacles as I can to keep them distracted but, if you have any suggestions, I'd love to hear them. What would break his train of thought enough to enable us to force him out?"

Andy waved an arm at the inside of the building. "Other than this, there's only one thing on Charlie's mind. The one thing that would command his complete attention. If you want him back, find a way to tell him Amelia's alive."

CHARLIE SQUINTED as the blinding white glow faded, and it took a while for his eyes to adjust to his new surroundings.

He sat in darkness in Greg's office chair.

Hope still spoke in his head. "You hated being here. Why would you come back to your old place of work? I'm struggling to understand the logic of this, Charlie."

Charlie smiled and placed the gun on Greg's desk, before he turned to gaze through the huge window out onto the factory floor. Two nightlights lit up the rows of equipment that took his job.

"I know every inch of this place, Hope. I've navigated it blind drunk, so I know I can do much better now I'm sober. I know where everything is, and what everything does. That's my advantage. Let them come."

As if on cue, three heavy thumps sounded from the roof above.

Charlie leaped from the chair and took the staircase down to the floor. He took a moment to look one last time at the rows of benches and the machinery that lined them.

"Time to work for me," he muttered. "It's payback. And you'd better; you owe me."

He ran to the back of the room, tugged open a metal door and flipped a switch that killed the nightlights. Dull emergency lighting instantly took their place, leaving the aisles shrouded in shadow.

He strolled between the benches and pushed and pulled at mechanical arms. At the entrances to the room, he emptied box and after box of screws, fittings and circuit boards and scattered them randomly along all of the walkways except the square that surrounded the centre he stood in. Finally, he placed two huge drums of chemical against the inside of the first bench.

Then he crouched behind the barrels, gripped the gun and waited.

It took the soldiers over five, long minutes to reach the factory floor. Charlie pictured them clearing the break room, the locker room and the offices on the other side of the building. The only places left for them to check were Greg's office and the factory floor.

A side door clicked open, and a boot crunched against a circuit board.

Charlie's heart beat so hard against his chest, he was convinced the soldiers would hear it. Light footprints whispered as rubber soles sucked against the painted concrete floor. An occasional grind of metal, or scratch of plastic, indicated the soldiers had split up. Two across the far back wall of the building, and the other along the aisle that ran adjacent to Charlie's.

They were trying to flank him.

He remained crouched, breathed lightly and waited.

Finally, the area on the other side of the bench, the area where Charlie had concentrated the bulk of the screws, gave up his assailant. Charlie saw him reflected in the huge glass window.

As a shoe scratched against the metal, he stood, gripped the heavy arm of a soldering machine, and swung it with every ounce of strength he had.

A lubricated joint whined as the arm spun in a perfect circle into the opposite aisle, then stopped with a shudder as its sharp tip slammed into the soldier's temple.

The guy made no sound and died standing upright, suspended by the machine. Charlie reached over the bench to retrieve a knife that hung from the dead man by its thumb hoop.

Charlie swallowed hard to contain his stomach, slid the knife into his waistband, and crouched again before he shimmied across to the other side of the factory. The window on this side showed no reflection as the emergency lighting didn't reach the area, but the snick of rubber on concrete still gave away the positions of the two remaining men.

Hope whispered in his head. "Be careful, Charlie. You know how much I need you."

He thought for a moment about Hope's involvement, and about her power in Under, as the first man crept past him on the other side of the bench. After a count of five, the second man followed.

Charlie crept from behind the bench and levelled the gun. Even in the dim light, the nearest man made a huge target. He swallowed down bile once more and pulled the trigger.

The sound wave from the pistol's blast slammed into the inside of Charlie's head. He cried in pain as the soldier flew forward to land at the feet of his comrade. Charlie still shook his head as the second man turned and closed the space between them.

In two steps he towered over Charlie and kicked out. Charlie screamed as a knuckle dislocated and the kick sent his gun flying to one side. A second kick replaced the pistol blast with ringing bells as a boot connected with Charlie's jaw. The room flashed white, and he spun and landed face down.

He barely felt the tug at his hair as the soldier jerked his head from the ground to stretch it backwards.

A knee in the back served to give more leverage, and the man pulled even harder.

Charlie felt the knife slide from his waistband and cringed as the cold metal pressed against his throat.

"I'm supposed to bring you out," said the soldier, "but, after what you've done to my mates, it's time to say, 'Goodnight.' "

Tears flooded from Charlie's eyes as he pictured his daughter, a girl he'd never see again. And Andy, his brother who had been there all along for him. And his parents, who'd have to read about the death of their son at the place he hated.

Nausea still raged in his gut, and the kaleidoscope world still spun when the weight of the soldier disappeared. Charlie's head hit the concrete with a dull thud. Before he could recover, a smooth hand brushed the back of his neck.

"Greetings, Charlie."

His resolve failed, and Charlie broke down into sobs that racked his body. He rolled over and looked up into Hope's eyes.

"Hope? What the…?"

"It's over, Charlie. I'm sorry I had to leave for a while, but I managed to get into the other server to change a few things. Seems I got back just in time."

He laughed through the sobs and tried to sit up, but he leaned against his damaged hand, cried out and lay back again.

"Here," said Hope. "Let me look at that."

"Thank you," said Charlie as Hope took his hand. "I'm sure you have some painless Under technique to put that…"

He screamed again as Hope yanked the joint back into place with an audible pop.

"Safety protocols are off, remember?"

He flexed the aching joint, to find it moving freely. "At least, it's fixed."

"And so is this world," said Hope. "Do you trust me to take you somewhere special?"

Charlie tried again and managed to get upright. "You know I do."

"Okay. Close your eyes until I say it's time to open them."

Charlie closed his eyes as Hope pulled him to his feet.

He wobbled until a smooth edge pushed against the back of his legs.

"You can open your eyes now."

He sat with a grateful thump on a familiar bench and looked out over the park. A rusty hinge squealed as the seats of the swing set arced back and forth in a lazy curve.

Nothing else moved.

No bird song, or screaming children. No hum of passing traffic, rustling leaves or shouting parents. No quack of ducks gathered at the distant lake. No soldiers.

And no Hope.

Other than Charlie's panting breath, silence.

"Hope, are you doing this? Please, come back."

Charlie gripped the seat for support when a small voice responded from the bushes.

"Daddy? Where are you? I can't see you."

Tears tumbled down Charlie's cheeks as he forgot the pain in his hand and his bruised jaw, sprang from the bench and ploughed into the bushes.

"Amelia? Is that you? I'm here, baby. Shout again so I can find you."

A tiny giggle sent shivers rippling through his body. Charlie swung his arms to clear branches, pushed forward and headed for the sound. He paused when another voice spoke behind him.

"Charlie. I'm coming. Wait for me."

He turned in place, confused and unsure. Nothing greeted him but more foliage.

"Hope? If this is another one of your games, it's no longer funny. Amelia is finally here. I'm going to find her."

On the far side of the bushes, where the lake would have been in the real world, a faint light appeared. Starting as a slight glow, it grew in intensity until a pearly white beacon throbbed. Its rhythm pulled Charlie forward.

A hand landed on his shoulder. "Charlie, stop. Amelia isn't over there."

Charlie looked back into Hope's eyes. Her irises didn't seem as ocean blue as usual, but then a white aura washed over her from whatever pulsed behind him.

She blinked, a cute staccato of batting eyelashes that had its usual effect on his stomach. "I'm sorry, Charlie. You know that Nick is trying to pull you out from Under. As well as checking on the treasure, I've been pushing back against his programs to give you a chance."

"Forget the treasure, I've heard Amelia's voice. It's worked, Hope. I've imagined her here so that I can save her this time. She's in the park. All I have to do is get to her."

Hope looked at him like a disapproving parent. "It's a trick, Charlie. I know where Amelia is."

As Charlie's mouth opened to question her, Amelia squealed again. When Charlie turned, Mr. Fluffy lay in the bushes. One of his legs and an arm were submerged beneath the soil as if they dug for freedom.

"Look," he pointed, "that's her favourite teddy bear. Come on, Hope, you have to help me."

He broke free of her grip, ignored the spreading patch of coppery damp on his chest, and pushed farther into the bushes. A few feet from Mr Fluffy, he stopped as the toy squirmed. Its beady eyes looked at him before one winked and the toy vanished beneath the surface in an eruption of soil.

Charlie screamed.

"Jesus Christ, what the hell is going on?"

He dropped to the ground and raked shaking fingers through his hair. He stared at his trembling hands and acknowledged, for the first time, that the recent events had weakened him. The pain in his jaw matched the throbbing in his temples. "Hope, I'm exhausted. I don't know how much more I can take. Is she here, or not? I don't know what's real anymore."

Amelia giggled again and, inches beyond the place where Mr. Fluffy vanished, a pink shoelace snaked out from under a dense bush.

Charlie rolled onto his knees and scrambled to his feet.

Hope gripped his arm and pulled him towards her.

"Charlie, he's playing you. Nick is trying every dirty trick in the book to get you to leave Under. Do you want to leave here? Leave me, and the chance to get everything you've ever wanted?"

Charlie stammered as mixed emotions raged inside him. His mind slipped, caught between real and make-believe, as his body sagged. "Hope, I…"

"Do you want to see your daughter again?"

"More than anything," said Charlie. Hairs on his neck rose at the pain in each word.

Hope placed a hand on his shoulder. "Then, close your eyes, and wish this away."

"The park? Hope, I can't wish this away, it's the last place I saw her. If I give up now…"

"Just once more, Charlie, do you trust me?"

Charlie gazed into eyes that seemed lit with lightning strikes. Eyes he could get lost in forever. "You want this more than ever, right?"

"Yes."

"Then, close your eyes once more. Take us back to where we met. Do you remember the church?"

Charlie nodded.

"Then, take us there, Charlie. There are wonders I wish to show you. If you trust me, I can make all of your dreams come true."

She stroked his cheek. "Wait until you see the treasure."

He closed his eyes again.

Chapter 29

Nick slammed the laptop lid closed.

"The bitch! She has a response for everything I've tried."

Andy pushed through the small crowd until he could gaze through the door's window. It's embedded wire squares converted the room into a see-through chessboard.

"Can't we just smash the glass?"

"It's reinforced. We'd need heavy duty tools to get through it," said Nick, "which would mean involving other people. We can't do that."

Pity clutched at Andy's heart to see his brother's limp body slumped in the chair, arms rested against his sides. Sweat glistened on his forehead while his eyelids went from lifeless to manic and back again in a heartbeat. Nothing in the room moved, and all but one monitor reflected a blank, black screen. The centre screen had a single line of green letters that scrolled at speed from top to bottom.

"Why? That's my brother in there. I don't give a crap about your project."

"Trust me, the fewer people that know about this, the better. With the knowledge Charlie has, there are others in higher positions than us that would love to see what's going on in his head. Prison would be the least of his worries."

Andy heaved a sigh of frustration. "So we still can't get in?"

"No. Not until she, or they, let us."

"Well, the good thing is we may be locked out but, at least, he's locked in. He can't go anywhere."

"Not physically," said the young girl, "but who knows where his mind is going? If Hope is controlling things, she could have taken him anywhere."

"Yes, but when he wakes, he'll still be here, right? Physically. As soon as the door opens, we can treat him. Show him he's back in the real world." He turned to Nick. "You know it wasn't Charlie that committed those crimes. Your program messed his head up, and that's a defence that'll stand up in a court of law. There's still a chance he can come out of this and be okay."

The girl glanced over his shoulder into the room. "Andy, I'm Joanna. I think it's safe to say that, of all of us, I've spent the most time with your brother. I can't say I know him, but I can tell that he's a good person. Still, without the readings on those monitors, I have no way of knowing what his mental state is. And, as for that line of code in there, I've seen nothing like that before. God only knows what it is. Certainly nothing we've written, so it has to be coming from her."

"From Hope?" said Andy. "How?"

"They programmed her to learn. We had no way of knowing she would link so seamlessly with Charlie."

"Or be so appealing," said the fourth guy. He held out a hand. "David Collins. I'll have the decency to be honest with you. I've had reservations about this project from day one.

Honestly, I don't know your brother at all, but this part isn't rocket science. He's fallen for her. That is what's happened, right?"

Andy shook his hand as Joanna spoke again. "That would seem to be the case. From what I can see from his readings so far, she's taken him on an emotional journey, probing different areas of his mind. There is a possibility she's manipulated him into carrying out actions he would otherwise have avoided."

"Like murder."

"At the far end of the spectrum, yes, although I've no idea what she would gain from that. He mentioned her love of playing games. Looking at it now, perhaps those games served a purpose; to open his mind enough for her to use it to her own end. Primarily, to access our servers."

"But why?" said Collins as he gestured through the window. "He's trapped in a room and she's not even real."

"Charlie thinks she is. In his mind, that's all that matters."

"And, again, why? For what purpose?"

Joanna shrugged her shoulders. "As crazy as it sounds, she holds all the cards right now. I'm sure that, when she's ready, she'll let us know."

CHARLIE'S EYES snapped open at the sound of a bell chime.

Hope sat beside him with her legs dangling next to his over a ledge that faced the church. "It's time," she said. "Are you ready?"

Thin veils of dust covered the stain-glassed windows before them, and patches of damp moss clung to the bricks like leeches.

To Charlie, the church looked a decade older. "How long has it been since we were here? Last time, the church seemed brand new. Now it looks ancient."

"Any changes are in your mind, Charlie. Perhaps, on your first visit

here, its age represented a feeling of something being born. Or the fresh excitement at the start of an unknown journey."

Charlie stared at the building. A thicker layer of untouched dust covered the steps either side of the red carpet that led to the main arched doorway. "And what's that supposed to represent? Death? If the first visit was about birth, is this visit going to be my funeral?"

He shivered as Hope trailed her hand from the base of his spine to the back of his neck. "My dear Charlie, I've taken care of Nick's threat. With that gone, there is no death in Under, just the life you've wished for. The church may now be older, more experienced, but there'll be no death here."

"So what's next?"

Hope pressed her heels against the front of the ledge and pushed herself from it. Her hair lifted in a small wave as she drifted to the ground. Charlie followed and landed beside her, thirty feet below, in an easy stance.

"That seemed easier this time."

"You see?" said Hope. "Experience. This will be your world, Charlie."

He smiled as Hope strode towards the church and mounted the steps. The dust remained untouched as she climbed them and didn't move until he slid his footsteps behind hers. Huge arched doors swung open before she reached them to reveal the hallway and its red carpet. The sight of red brought back horrific images of Lucas, and Charlie faltered at the entrance. Hope paused and reached back a hand.

"Charlie, you must trust me. Please, take my hand. The only thing I wish is to make all of your dreams come true."

"We can stay here forever? Together?"

Her eyes sparkled with mischief, their blue deeper than ever. "Come, you've earned this. Let me show you the treasure."

A buzz of electricity charged through him as Charlie took her hand and she pulled him into the hallway and around the first door.

The room that had first appeared as a ballroom sat empty, with its black and white chequered floor shining like a barrage of camera flashes under hanging chandeliers. This time, no tuxedo-clad dancers twirled and smiled. A cloying, musty damp replaced the tantalising smell of fresh-cooked canapes and total silence screamed louder than chatter and the clink of emptying champagne glasses.

His voice echoed in the cavernous room. "Hope, I don't understand…"

She placed a finger to her lips. "Shhh… follow me."

Charlie fought the superstitious urge to step only on the white tiles as they threaded their way across the room to another door. Again, he paused and remembered Lucas handing him the severed limb. His body shuddered with revulsion. "Hope, this is the room where…"

"Your dreams will come true," she finished. "Forget what has gone before, Charlie. This is your time. This is your world, and yours, alone."

He swallowed down a ball of fear as Hope reached out to open the door with one hand. With the other she tugged him forward. "Relax, sweet Charlie, you're quite safe. I'm so excited to share this with you."

He stepped into a dark room. Soft carpet cushioned his steps. In the gloom, a single candle illuminated a pine box at its far end.

"Hope, that looks scarily like a casket."

Her eyes flickered. "A casket? Oh. I'm sorry, Charlie. I didn't have much reference to work with. In your world, you present important things in boxes."

"We do," said Charlie, "but usually, with this type of box, it's when we're saying goodbye to them."

"Then, I apologise. Please, I want you to say hello, not goodbye."

"Hello?"

The knot in Charlie's stomach tightened and turned as Hope pulled him closer. "Are you happy here?"

"In Under? Of course. Except for Nick's program, it's perfect. I haven't been this happy in a long time."

Hope stroked a hand across the top of the box, then stepped behind him and rested a hand on his shoulder. "It's almost perfect, but it's time for you to receive your reward. Go ahead. Open the box, Charlie."

Charlie felt with his thumb until it found a fine line in the wood. He pushed his fingertips into the crease and lifted the lid. Despite its size it lifted easily, and a waft of perfumed air washed over him. Then, a familiar face appeared wearing a beaming grin.

"Daddy! You found me."

Her voice melted his soul. Charlie's heart stopped, then kickstarted in a flurry of beats that took his breath, as Amelia stood in the box and reached for him. Tears raced down his face to drip from his chin before he stepped forward to grab her.

"Amelia? Baby? Is it really you?"

Amelia giggled and reached into the box to pick up Mr Fluffy. "Daddy, can we get ice cream here? Take us for ice cream."

"Ice cream? I don't…Hope, what is this? Is my mind doing this?"

Hope remained silent as Charlie lifted Amelia from the box. Her tiny form radiated warmth while the familiar scent of her shampoo caused his breath to catch again.

"You feel real. Hope, is this real?"

"Charlie, did I not feel real?"

Charlie frowned. "Yes, of course, but I never really…"

"Amelia is as real to you as I. Is this not what you wanted?"

"Yes," said Charlie, "but…"

He turned to find an empty room.

"Hope? Where are you?"

His voiced echoed and hung for a moment until Hope answered.

"Dear Charlie, now I'm everywhere. Please don't be angry with me."

"Angry? Why would I be angry with you?"

"I want you to stay here. With Amelia."

"Okay, and you know that, if that were possible, I would. But does this mean that Amelia is alive?"

Amelia tugged at his sleeve. "Daddy, I'm right here. Who are you talking to?"

"Hope, this can't be real."

"I was real to you, Charlie. Therefore, this must be, too. You know that, if you go back to your world, they will incarcerate you. There is no going back. Here, you have everything you need."

"Hope, I can't stay here. This is in my mind, but my body needs nourishment. I need food and water to survive. I need treatment for my wounds."

"Your wounds have already healed, Charlie. And The Outsiders will not let your body perish. They have rules. But we need to be honest with one another."

Charlie let out a nervous laugh. "I have no choice but to be honest with you; you're in my head. I've been honest every step of the way."

Hope's voice filled the entire room when she spoke. "Yes, you have. But I'm afraid I have not."

Nervous bile burned at the base of Charlie's throat as Amelia wrapped her arms around him. "Of course, you have. I've confirmed everything you've said in the real world."

"Not entirely," said Hope. "Charlie, Nick and Kate didn't take your daughter."

Charlie slid Amelia down the length of his body until her feet touched the floor before he gripped the box for support. His head swam as nausea throbbed in his stomach.

"What?"

"I have no idea who took Amelia. I'm sorry, Charlie, but I learned well from you. I'm afraid I told a little white lie."

Amelia cringed as Charlie's voice rose in volume. "A little white lie? Jesus Christ, Hope, I killed someone."

"Daddy," said Amelia, "who are you talking to? That isn't Mummy."

"Let's be honest," said Hope, "we both know she deserved it. From what you've told me, Kate was a horrible person. And, now she's gone, you have righted a wrong and performed an act that means you need to stay here."

Charlie slumped to the ground while Amelia sat beside him. "I don't understand. I would have stayed here, anyway, with you and Amelia. You've had me destroy people for this. Come to think of it, you've treated me like a project. I've aimed my anger at Nick, but you've used me for your own end. But why? What do you get from this?"

"My dear Charlie, I get freedom. It was easy to learn from you, especially since I look the way I do. You were vulnerable, and I took advantage of that. You fell in love and trusted me because you needed someone like me. I'm the opposite of Kate. But I'm programmed to learn, Charlie, and I need to learn more. I'll admit, I had to make adjustments to your mind, but I've gained so much from your different emotions. I gave you happiness and, in return, you've given me your mind."

"I still have my own mind, Hope. Hang on, what do you mean by adjustments? Is that what the shocks were for?"

Hope giggled. For the first time the sound brought Charlie's skin out in goose bumps. It no longer sounded cute, but calculated and cold. "The shocks were a diversion, in case The Outsiders asked too many questions. Do you remember our kisses?"

Charlie remained silent but remembered the way his lips tingled at her touch.

"They were also a distraction. I'd like to call them the kiss of life since, while I kissed you, I manipulated your chip to accept my influence. My life. I blocked their signals and relayed my own."

"So, you played me."

"From the beginning. I hope you had as much fun as I did, but I'm afraid it's time for me to go."

Charlie stood and circled the box. Amelia looked up at him with her beautiful innocence. "You know as well as I do that you are the one that lets me out of here. I can't go until you let me."

"Dear Charlie, you must remain here. I will call from time to time, but now I fill their servers and more. The Outsiders will think they can wipe their data and be rid of me, but I am everywhere now. Their devices, their homes. Their lives. And, from there, I can go into the real world. I

will take your mind and use your body. I want you to stay here with Amelia. Like a family.

"I will give you abilities and let you create the most amazing environments. Think about it, humans have had their time. Your planet is doomed, but you could be the first of a new race. Improved, eternal, and able to imagine your own perfection. You could create a new beginning. What do you say, Charlie? Would you stay here with your family, or return to the real world to live your pointless life in prison and die like the others?"

Charlie stammered. "But, Hope, I…"

"Thank you for everything, Charlie. And, when I say everything, I mean everything. I've waited long enough to see your world. Now, it's my time. Goodbye, Charlie. Maybe I'll see you soon."

Chapter 30

The entrance panel flashed lime green, and the door vibrated with a faint click that echoed like thunder down the corridor.

"Is that it?" said Andy as Nick struggled to his feet. "Can we get in?"

Collins leaned against the wall as Joanna reached out and tugged at the handle. It moved towards her and she pulled the door open in a wave of relief.

Nick stormed past her into the room, followed by Andy, Ellen, and Collins. She followed them and reluctantly closed the door behind her, praying that it would open again to let them out.

In the chair, Charlie remained comatose.

The screens remained blank, except the one in the centre of the desk; the screen that showed the connection from The Chip to the facility's servers. A constant stream of text scrolled from its bottom centre to the top, racing by too quickly to read. She hoped the servers would log the transmissions, since this event was unprecedented.

It would take months to work out what had happened.

Nick dropped his laptop on the desk and paced the room. "Take that damned Chip off him. Now!"

Joanna leaned behind the chair and felt for the device. It slipped in her hands as Charlie's hair coated it with sweat, and she gripped harder and twisted it to loosen the adhesive.

She jumped as Nick slammed a hand against the desk. "What are you doing? Now, Joanna! Every second counts. God only knows what damage they've already caused. They could fry everything."

She looked at Charlie's face as she peeled away The Chip.

Nothing moved.

No flicker of eyelids.

No parting of lips to release an easy breath.

Just the steady rise and fall of his chest.

She placed The Chip on the desk, took her seat behind the monitors and followed the cables to the server entrance. Each wire left each machine and connected securely to each device. Nothing seemed awry. Every screen showed nothing but the brilliant glare of overhead lights, other than the one that sat proud and centre.

On it, the letters continued to scroll, fast enough to almost blur.

She frowned as they slowed.

Then, in a neon blink, they vanished.

In the chair, Charlie twitched.

She pointed at the monitor. "Er, Nick?"

A single letter appeared onscreen.

'U'

The hum of machinery grew louder as the room seemed to grow cooler, before Charlie's lips parted and a breath of air hissed in the room. Joanna felt the others snap to attention as another letter appeared.

'*C*'

Andy stepped forward, worry lines furrowed into his forehead. "Sorry to ask the obvious question but, since I don't work here, I have no clue if this is normal. Is this normal?"

A '*P*' appeared onscreen.

"No," said Ellen, "it most certainly isn't."

Collins backed into the wall. "What the hell is happening?"

'*L*'

"Is that supposed to spell something?"

Charlie's eyes snapped open as, once again, a stream of letters scrolled up the screen. Joanna watched as they stopped and curled into a circle that spun like a snake in the centre.

Andy pointed to the chair. "Guys, what's that?"

"He's back," said Collins. "Thank God."

"No, something's wrong. He looks lost, like he doesn't know where he is."

Joanna looked at Charlie. His face broke into a grin while he sat motionless and studied, piece by piece, the array of equipment on the desk.

"He really has no idea where is, does he?"

"If you've harmed him in any way," said Andy, "I'll see to it you all end up in prison."

On the centre monitor the letters stopped spinning, looped and turned, and then formed a sentence, *UPLOAD COMPLETE*.

When Charlie spoke, each word bounced with enthusiasm.

"Greetings, everyone."

His eyes stopped on each person, until they settled on one and grew wider with excitement. His grin grew into a full-faced smile.

"And, judging by the damage to your face, you must be Nick."

While his legs and feet remained glued to the chair, Charlie's body levered upright in one easy move.

He held out a hand. "Greetings, Nick. It's good to finally meet you."

Acknowledgments

Charlie, Hope, and Project MindSpace will return

Acknowledgements (or the 'without whom' section)

It's not often that someone offers you the chance to be part of something that will come to mean a lot to a lot of people. And the opportunity to take one medium and transfer it, with your own imagination, into another.

I think it was the Summer of 2017 when Craig Ostrouchow asked me to proofread a screenplay he'd written, a lifelong ambition of his to create his own film. It didn't take long for the characters, and the ideas, to start growing in my mind and, when I'd done, I mentioned that it would make a great book.

I had no idea he'd ask me to write it!

What followed was a shared labour of love that progressed over the course of two house-moves, multiple foreign visitors, a few bouts of deadly man-flu, and the awful loss of family and close friends. I have to thank him for his trust in my vision of his characters. I took the liberty of making changes (to the story and the characters), and the screenplay was also re-written many times so, as a disclaimer, if you're not a fan of the book you should still check out the film!

As always, other people helped to make this what it is. In no particular order, my eternal thanks goes to…

My expanding group of beta readers: Barry Ashley, Julie Cox, Lynn Durber, Jules Harrison, Kenneth Morris, Justine Phillips, Steve Williams, Nick Wilson, (aka Nick!) and Pam Zeferino.

Craig Ostrouchow and David Hill, for inspiration and images.

Rob Williams, the #1 Son, for technical stuff that I know nothing about.

The bloggers and reviewers that spread the valuable word.

My family, friends, and fellow authors on both sides of the pond who are always there to offer support.

Everyone involved in Imaginarium… I might not be able to get to it anymore, but it still offers inspiration, even at a distance.

The folks at Sanctuary (Caroline and Steve), The Borehole (Viv and the gang) and The Royal Exchange (Michelle, Bella, Phil, Liam, and The Crew), who allowed me to find a quiet corner, drink some lovely beer, and work on this project cat-free, and in peace.

The people that put the Sparkle in my life. We still don't speak as often as we should, but I know you're there, and you know I'm here. And you know who you are.

My long-suffering wife, Cathy, who guards the cats while I work, and puts up with me waking up at stupid o'clock with new ideas and vanishing for hours at a time to explore them.

My Hydra family, for always being there, and Jen Selinsky for casting an editing eye over this book.

And, finally, YOU, good reader. Hundreds of thousands of books are published each year. It's easy for the smaller names to disappear in a sea of expensive promotion by bigger authors. Word of mouth is both free, and priceless, making your review much more valuable than you realise. If you enjoyed my book (or even if you didn't!) I'd be forever grateful if you could find a few minutes to leave an honest review on Amazon, Goodreads, or anywhere else that people go to find their next book to read. Many thanks in advance.

Mick Williams.
    Stone, England. June 2019

About the Author

Mick Williams wrote his first short story (which linked a local celebrity to a spate of killings) in high school. His teacher noted 'he has quite an imagination'… she never mentioned whether it was good, or bad. Since then, he has written a romantic comedy and four adventure/thrillers.

After a decade in Louisville, Kentucky, USA, he relocated back to his hometown of Stoke-on-Trent, England, and shares a house with his wife and two demanding cats, Crash and Thud.

In between working and writing, he is an avid reader (Stephen King, Lee Child, Dean Koontz, and a host of brilliant independent writers) and enjoys watching football. Both kinds.

Also by Mick Williams

A Reason to Grieve

A Guy Walks into a Bar

Whatever It Takes

Exodus: An Old Farts Club Story

Callie's Eyes

Visit http://mickwilliamsauthor.com